The Fisherman's Gift

A NOVEL

JULIA R. KELLY

Simon & Schuster

NEW YORK   AMSTERDAM/ANTWERP   LONDON
TORONTO   SYDNEY/MELBOURNE   NEW DELHI

Simon & Schuster
1230 Avenue of the Americas
New York, NY 10020

First Simon & Schuster hardcover edition March 2025

SIMON & SCHUSTER and colophon are registered trademarks of Simon & Schuster, LLC

Simon & Schuster strongly believes in freedom of expression and stands against censorship in all its forms. For more information, visit BooksBelong.com.

For information about special discounts for bulk purchases, please contact Simon & Schuster Special Sales at 1-866-506-1949 or business@simonandschuster.com.

The Simon & Schuster Speakers Bureau can bring authors to your live event. For more information or to book an event, contact the Simon & Schuster Speakers Bureau at 1-866-248-3049 or visit our website at www.simonspeakers.com.

Manufactured in the United States of America

1   3   5   7   9   10   8   6   4   2

Library of Congress Cataloging-in-Publication Data has been applied for.

ISBN 978-1-6680-6868-7
ISBN 978-1-6680-6870-0 (ebook)

For Oliver, Calum, and Emily

Come away, O human child!
To the waters and the wild
With a faery, hand in hand,
For the world's more full of weeping than you can understand.

William Butler Yeats

Prologue

Scotland, 1900

Joseph knows the storm is coming. He sees the yellow glow of the halo around the moon and the ice-glitter of the winter sky when he comes up from the beach, pausing every now and then to give his knees rest from their groan and creak.

Later, the wind shifts, swinging from west to east and, waking in the night, he feels the beast of it crouched far out to sea, its arctic breath, its changed salt smell. He could have warned the villagers who'd forgotten how to read the signs—the low flight of the gulls, the night sky, the wind—but why should he? Let the storm take their chimneys, frighten their dogs, send shirts and sheets flying like winged banshees over rooftops. After all, what had anyone done, all those years before, when the storm had taken so much more from him?

A squall has picked up now over the Tops where cattle huddle in the barn and sheep lean together in the field. It rushes between the houses and the shops of Copse Cross Street and past the open window above the grocer's where Mrs. Brown, still awake, peers down the narrow street and beyond to the black sheet of the starlit sea. She smells change on the wind and, securing the shutters, returns to her stove, scoops the dog, Rab, into her lap, and waits.

Farther down the hill, in a cottage near the Steps leading down to Skerry Sands, Dorothy lights a lamp and places it

I

on the ledge of an upstairs window, a light in the darkness to guide home those lost in the heave and surge of the sea.

When the storm lands, there are things it steals from the little fishing village clinging to the cliffs. It takes roof tiles and sheep; it fells trees and splinters two boats against the Rocks. But it brings something too, something which Joseph will find when he goes back to check on his own boat in the watery light of the next day's dawn.

A gift.

Now

Dorothy

Eager to get home to fires and cooking pots, the women hurry round Mrs. Brown's shop, dirty slush seeping under the door with the wind still bitter from the storm. As usual, Dorothy pays no heed to the rise and murmur of voices by the counter. It is the silence she notices. Basket almost empty—a few potatoes, some onions—she sees the way they are gathered at the window, and the strangest sensation comes over her. The skin on her arms tightens, a chill moves up to the back of her neck, and she puts her basket down and goes to the window too. She wipes the mist from it and peers out. The sleet is settling between the cobbles and the skies are leaden. She looks up the hill and sees the villagers toiling up the narrow street, huddled into themselves, heads down, eyes squeezed shut, and then she looks down toward the Sands, and that's when she sees him.

Joseph.

He is walking in the middle of the road. When she realizes what he is carrying, a cry is torn straight from her chest, an animal's sharp keen. Joseph's face is as shocked as hers must be—white, wide-eyed. The hair of the child he is carrying is dark silver from the sea, the body limp, the skin of his face gray. His body is still slick with water, beads of it in his hair, clothes dark and sodden. And then she hears the gasp of the other women, feels their faces turn to her. Mrs. Brown places a red, weathered hand on her arm, and Dorothy turns, understands that the shopkeeper is saying her name, though her ears are ringing now, because she has already seen it—

The way one small foot dangles in its brown boot, and the other hangs blue and cold and naked.

She steps outside, dreamlike. All the women do, and some are watching her, and some are watching the man with the child. Dorothy is a piece of knitting, unraveling, for surely she's seen a ghost. She moves toward them and stretches out her hand, but he walks on, up the cobbled street, and the women from the shop follow, like mourners at a funeral. At the corner he turns and shakes his head to stop them, and then they see it, all of them—the naked foot twitching, the limp arm stiffening, and suddenly the child gives a choking cough, and Joseph starts running now, as well as he can in the freezing rain, round the corner to the Minister's house and out of sight.

Dorothy hasn't moved. She tries to separate then from now, but it's too hard. She nearly goes with them, almost believes it's him, but instead stumbles home and drags herself up the stairs, not even closing the front door, her body too heavy or too light, she's not sure which. She hardly recognizes her bedroom as she passes the cupboard she never opens and drifts toward the chest of drawers.

The sleet, blowing in sideways from the sea, thuds and rattles at the windowpanes, and the wind cries through the front door and up the stairs and finds her on her knees on the floorboards, opening the lowest drawer. She feels her way through woolen vests and undergarments, till her fingertips touch it. For a moment she is shocked it is not still wet. She feels the familiar creases of the leather and she pulls it out and places it in the cradle of her apron, hands cupping it gently. She closes her eyes and leans her forehead against the chest of drawers and breathes in the smell of the small brown boot, still with its whisper of salt water, even after all these years.

Back in the shop, Mrs. Brown picks up Dorothy's basket, puts back the onions and potatoes and, despite the early hour, turns the closed sign out to the street.

That night Dorothy dreams of Moses for the first time in years. He is playing in the water, in the shallow waves. She leans against the rock, feels its warmth through the thin cotton of her dress, lets it seep into the skin of her shoulder blades. She watches him, silver hair lit by the sun, by the spangled light from the sea, by all the differences memory lends. In her dream she drifts into sleep, and when she wakes, it is winter, the sky low and dark, the storm wild. The waves are huge and she runs along the shoreline, up and down, calling for him, but the wind catches her voice and throws it at the sky. And just when she thinks he is lost, she finds him again, pulled along the beach by the tide, standing just as before, waves crashing over him, over and again. He turns and makes his small, quiet smile, eyes green and shifting like the sea.

"Mamma?"

When she wakes up, really wakes up, the wind is wailing outside the window, and the pillow clutched in her cold fist is wet.

Opening Time

All the village wants to talk about it the next morning, though they pretend they don't out of common decency. The women try to hurry over the icy cobbles to Mrs. Brown's shop to buy a few things they don't need before the roads in and out of the village freeze over and cut them off, as they do every winter.

They place this and that in their baskets and gather to pay, waiting for Mrs. Brown to take the lead as she usually does, leaning one hand on the counter and using a pencil to pin loose gray hairs behind her ear with the other. But she is uncommonly quiet today and her eyes unreadable as she busies herself adding up the cost.

"Oh, for the Lord's sake, is nobody going to say it?" It's Norah, as thin and sharp as Mrs. Brown is not, and the others relax and put down their baskets, glad someone is daring to say what they are all thinking. "Lord bless us—I thought I'd seen a ghost!" She closes her eyes, opening them again quickly to make sure everyone is looking. "That child was the very image—I mean—I thought it was—till I realized the age was the same. How many years ago was it now? Fifteen? Twenty?"

"Where did he find him?"

"Washed up on the beach in the storm, the Minister said—"

"But alive, can you believe it!"

"I heard he told them—"

"Oh, shush, I was up there this morning. He's not said a word!"

"Did you see him, then?"

"Well, no, but Martha said—"

The others share knowing glances, showing what they think of that information.

Norah's voice is low and secretive. "It means something, I'm sure of it. Even the boot . . . "

They all fall silent at this; it's too uncanny, too similar. Even Mrs. Brown has paused in her adding up, onion in one hand, pencil in the other, caught in the strangeness of it all.

Norah tests the water further. "Well, I always said that child—"

At last, Mrs. Brown breaks her silence. "That's enough of that talk. Have you no pity? I don't know about you, but I can't be chatting all the day. There's snow coming, and I want to get home before sundown, thank you."

Coins clatter resentfully on the counter as the women pay, pick up their baskets, and leave, affronted and somewhat surprised. For if there is someone in the village who's not had much pity for Dorothy Gray over the years, surely it has been Mrs. Brown herself.

Joseph

"How's the lad?" Joseph stands on the doorstep, twisting his hat in his hands.

The Minister's wife, Jenny, steps back from the icy chill he's brought with him, eyes flicking over his face and looking up and down the street. She sighs. "You better come in, out the cold at least."

He steps over the threshold for the second time that week, but the last time the shock of the child had robbed him of any powers of observation. This time, he notices how close Jenny must be to her time, her belly low and swollen; he notices the pram made ready in the hall and how Jenny brings him through with only the smallest sign of her reluctance. The maid, Martha, looks up from kneading dough and nods.

Jenny excuses herself. "Wait here, Joseph, and I'll fetch my husband."

The heat from the range makes his hands prickle with pain, but he moves closer, grateful for its warmth. As soon as Jenny shuts the door and her footsteps die away, Martha brushes her floury hands on her apron.

"You'll be wanting something hot to drink, Joseph? You look half frozen." She smiles more naturally now.

"No, I'll be back by my own fire in a minute." He glances

at the shut door, listens to the silence in the corridor. "The lad, then, how is he?"

Martha looks nervously at the door too, then speaks in a rush. "He's not said a word. He's been asleep mostly. I made a beef broth, and I've been helping him with that and keeping the fire going."

"He'll live, then? He's not going to die from the cold or the—" He swallows hard.

Footsteps sound in the corridor, and Martha takes up her kneading again. Joseph holds out his hands to the range, and Jenny looks pleased to find them both in the same positions, Joseph with his coat still on, not sitting down or making himself comfortable.

"The Minister is busy at present." Her tone is clipped, and she looks pointedly at the ice now dripping on her kitchen floor. "The boy will live, Joseph—you did a good thing in bringing him to us. As soon as he's well enough and the weather allows, he'll be taken inland to a hospital and then, God willing, his home." She turns toward the kitchen door. "As you can see, we're quite busy, so . . ."

He briefly nods his thanks and goes back out into the snow. He was sure they used to talk about him, as though what happened that night long ago had somehow been something to do with him. And now they would again. You'd have thought he'd be hardened to it by now, but he isn't, and he kicks the stone step of the Manse as he leaves.

Down on the Sands, he throws himself into the work needed on his boat, tearing at the rotten wood of the deck, jaw clenched, hands only just warm enough in the small heat of the brazier.

And then he sees her. Dorothy. She's standing at the bottom of the Steps, looking out to sea. She hasn't seen him yet, and he seizes the moment to stare.

She is no longer the cool young woman she'd been when she first arrived at the village so long ago, whose glance could cut and whose every expression was a challenge. He remembers the quickening of his heart, the breath caught in his throat when he'd seen her first, standing just where she is now, hand to her hair. Always so different to the Skerry girls, their flirting around him, their giggling and lightness.

When had she started to look old?

He's watched her in the Kirk over the years, always there before anyone arrives, staying on after they leave, doing her duty, taking food parcels to the almshouses, to Jeanie in the cottage on the cliff, and he knows she teaches at the school still and knits for the fishermen, though he doesn't know who wears her jerseys. Her husband had never returned and, with Moses lost, he wonders, as he has so often before, why she's stayed in Skerry at all.

He brings his thoughts back to the moment.

There is something else different about her. He kneels back on his haunches and squints. That's it. She doesn't have outdoor boots on, and her coat—he frowns and peers again to be sure—her coat is buttoned up wrong, one side hanging lower than the other. And she isn't walking briskly like she usually does. She doesn't seem sure of where she's going, in fact, and keeps stopping and looking out to sea. She's white, pinched around the mouth, not quite so straight in the back anymore, that slim waist he had once imagined circling with his hands thickened, her red hair dulled and shot through with silver.

He turns away and pulls at more of the soft wood, ripping it up from the deck. Because of her, love has escaped him. The breakfast made in the morning, the fire laid on homecoming, the supper on the table, the warm body held in sleeping—all the homely kindnesses a man might expect, all have escaped him.

She doesn't look in his direction, she never has since Moses went, and that has been fine with him, but the time is coming to make her look him in the eye once more.

Because he hasn't forgotten the argument and the wrong done to him. And he knows she hasn't either.

Dorothy

She can't help herself; she has to see. She knows in her heart it isn't him. She's a teacher for goodness' sake. A logical woman. A child can't—her heart turns away from the brutal words needed—can't *be lost*, and then come back years later the same age. She knows that. Yes, she knows that, she thinks, breathing out in relief and leaning her hand on the wooden table, its solidity giving weight to her thoughts. But the face of the child as he was carried up Copse Cross Street comes to her, and just for a moment, she can't breathe.

Before she can change her mind, she grabs her coat, puts on her boots, and opens her front door. The cottages that line the street, and the street itself, are almost lost in a heavy veil of snow, the sky still sullen with it, but Dorothy hurries up the hill. She doesn't look in Mrs. Brown's shop as she passes it, doesn't want to see all of them at the counter and that woman staring out, though for a moment she feels her hand on her arm again, and with it a sort of angry confusion. *Bit late for kindness now*, she thinks. In her mind, she shakes the hand off.

When she gets to the Minister's house, she is shaking as she tries to knock on the door. Martha is singing tunelessly in the kitchen. Dorothy can't hear the words but, accompanied by the clashing of pans, the song creates an air of simple domestic life, and she knocks loudly this time, as though they were keeping her waiting.

Martha answers, flustered. "Mrs. Gray. Why, you're the second visitor today. Joseph was here just now."

Dorothy's heart clenches.

When Jenny comes in and sees Dorothy standing in her kitchen, her hands instinctively go to her rounded belly, as though to protect the child inside her from the long shadow of Dorothy's loss, the inconceivable thing. "Mrs. Gray. Can I help you?"

"I would be grateful if—could you let me see the child?" She can't bring herself to plead and holds herself stiffly in that kitchen where a pregnant woman is cradling her unborn child and a maid is stirring a pot on the range and the good warm smells of stew fill the room.

The door opens and the Minister comes in. He stops short when he sees Dorothy.

"She wants to see the boy," his wife says, glancing meaningfully at him.

For a moment he looks like he doesn't know what to do, but then a fleeting expression of understanding crosses his face and he nods. "Come with me, then, Dorothy."

Hearing her first name makes her eyes suddenly sting, and she blinks quickly and follows him, along the flagstoned corridor and up the stairs, till they are standing outside a door and she knows the child is inside. It is for a moment as though the door might open onto her own box room, with the small wooden bed along the wall under the window, and she can step inside and into the past.

But of course, she can't. In this room the flame of an oil lamp blooms and shrinks on the bedstand, and a fire crackles in the hearth. The curtains are drawn so it's warm and cozy, yellow light flickering on the walls.

It takes a moment for Dorothy's eyes to adjust, and when they do, she sees the boy is asleep. Again she feels the shock of his silver hair against the pillow. She takes in his cheeks, the light catching the soft childish fuzz of them. He is drawn and thin, with shadowy bruises on his skin. He opens his eyes. They are green. Her breath catches.

He makes his small, quiet smile, eyes green and shifting like the sea.

"Mamma?"

He stares at her blankly, while her breath comes quicker.

"It's not him, Dorothy. You can see." The Minister's hand is gentle on her arm, and she is suddenly ashamed. She, a grown woman, thinking such nonsense, but she feels the emptiness of her belly as she nods.

"Of course. I knew that."

His hand is still on her arm and squeezes it. "It was a terrible thing, Dorothy." She can feel him looking at her, but she keeps her eyes ahead. "Never to know, not to be able to—"

"Yes, well, I thank you, Minister. I do. The lad looks well looked after. I don't know why I came, really," and she gives a brittle laugh and turns. As she hurries back down the stairs and across the hall to the front door, she turns to say goodbye and sees the Minister's expression, confused and slightly shaken. And behind him, by the pram, on the floor, the discarded brown boot. She rushes outside where the snow is freezing over now and ice glitters on her breath.

The cold air is such a shock, she thinks she'll be sick.

As she gets nearer to her home, she starts to run and, once inside, slams the front door shut and leans her back against it, her hand to her beating heart, gasping for breath.

She feels the past at the door, trying to get in, and squeezes her eyes tight shut against it.

She'd known as soon as she'd woken up that night, the way you know when you knock at a door that no one is home— Moses wasn't there. The storm was howling, the house a ship torn loose of its mooring, the wind buffeting every window, every door. She doesn't know how she'd known, but her frantic glance into his room had confirmed it.

Not tonight, not tonight. Not in this.

And she'd run through the two rooms downstairs, eyes widening in horror.

But she can't go farther than this; she never has been able to. She breathes deeply, slowly, waiting for her heart to return to its steady beat. She waits a while, till she knows she is herself again, then stokes up the stove, puts the broth on to warm. No, the past may be at the door, but too much time has passed to be letting it in. She may not be able to ignore the awful similarities, but there is no need, no need at all, to be dragging all that up again.

Joseph

Joseph could have a nip at home, but tonight he is drawn to the alehouse in the village, to the ebb and flow of human voices. The snow has turned to sleet. It's thick and wet as he pulls his jacket tight around himself. *More snow's coming*, he thinks.

The door creaks as it opens, and then the wind slams it shut behind him. The flames in the hearth flicker over the faces of the fishermen as they turn to look at him. Joseph steps into a fug of stale ale, tobacco smoke, and fire warmth.

After a moment's surprise that lasts just a little too long, someone calls out, "Hey, Joseph, lad, it's been a while!" and Agnes pauses her wipe-down of the counter, stops still, and stares at him, before seeming to remember herself. "And what'll be your tipple?"

Joseph approaches a table, where some of his crew sit with a few others. There's room, but Scott, Agnes's husband, squares his shoulders, fills out the space.

"Bit of a squeeze here," he says.

A look from the others silences him, and a stool is fetched. Joseph sits down, the men shuffling to make space. For a moment they look down at their drinks and then sideways at each other.

Someone clears their throat. "So, how are things with you?"

16

"Good. It's cold out. More snow's on the way," he says.

"Bad storm," someone else says, and everyone mutters their agreement and leans in, now it's been mentioned.

"So, he was just there, on the Sands?"

Joseph sucks in the head of the ale, nodding.

"Where, though?"

"Was it over by the Rocks?"

The savagery of the other storm all those years ago comes in a roar of noise and, briefly, Joseph closes his eyes.

"It's strange that you should be—"

"Now, now, could have been any of us."

"Yes, but it wasn't any—"

"I heard he's doing all right. Have you seen him yet, Joseph?"

Joseph gives them only part of what they want to hear. "I went to the Manse. He was sleeping. Jenny says he'll live."

A quiet voice says, "Watch out, lad," and Joseph steadies his hand around his drink as Scott pushes back his stool, knocks into him as he passes on his way back to the counter. One of the reasons Joseph avoids the alehouse.

Joseph drinks his ale, making himself as uninteresting as possible, and the chat drifts to other things, to the damage that's been done, the roofs to be mended, the strange way the storm ripped the sand from the beach, exposing the ancient landscape beneath, with boulders of fossilized forest breaking through, disrupting the shape of the shore.

When the door creaks again and Joseph leaves, the past has crept closer for him too.

"It was a strange business, wasn't it?" The question is ambiguous enough that the man could be talking about the boy then or the boy now.

"He was never the same after."

"Joseph is a good man; a quiet one, and there's no harm in that. A fisherman you can rely on."

"You would say that, though—you work with him."

"Yes, and proud to do so." The man nods as though that is the end of the matter.

But of course, it isn't. It never is, not with Scott around.

He won't leave it alone. "Tell me this, then—how did he know where it was? The lad's boot, I mean?"

Agnes sighs and leans her forearms on the counter. "Really? Can we please talk about something else tonight?"

There is a surly silence. A few attempts at chat fall away. Scott goes to the counter, thuds his pint down more heavily than needed, and wipes the foam from his lip. "Well, thing is, we still don't know what happened, do we? And that's as true now as it was then. Everyone knows what Joseph thought of Dorothy, and jealousy will make a man do desperate things. Good fisherman he may be, but there's those of us still want to know."

There are grunts of agreement, though there are more of exasperation as Agnes reaches for the bell.

"It's time," she says, though it isn't, and coats are shuffled on and hats pulled tight on heads, for sure enough the sleet has turned to snow again, the flakes bright against the black sky, and the men file out into the swirling night.

Alone at last, Agnes sags against the counter. Not this again, not after all this time. There may be those who still want to know what happened, but hasn't she suffered enough?

And it's the knowing that's been the torment.

Then

Dorothy

The Minister meets Dorothy at the station and carries her case as they walk the last mile to Skerry, the road descending gently, the sea just a sun-glitter in the distance. The scent of gorse is in the air, and as the road bends right and downward, the village comes into view. So here she is at last, her first home away from home. The lonely funeral of her mother back in Edinburgh drifts into her mind, the dutiful mourners, the cold Kirk, but that life is done with now.

Dorothy takes a deep breath. They pass the Manse and a row of almshouses, then the Kirk itself, set back from the road, and next to that again, the Schoolhouse where the Minister is both principal and teacher. First, the Minister wants to show her the cottage that comes with the post, and everything is as she'd hoped, clean and tidy, freshly painted, even some of the essentials already in the kitchen, and she is excited but tired too after her long journey, weariness making her bones ache. After lots of polite goodbyes and an insistence that she take supper at the Manse that evening with the Minister and his new bride, Jenny, the Minister leaves, and Dorothy sits on a chair at the small table in the kitchen and lets out a long sigh.

And so it is that by the time she goes to bed in the unfamiliar room, the chill and quiet of the night settling around the house, she can listen to the sound of the sea, washing in and out on the shore she's not yet seen. She imagines it, black under the night sky, the waves catching the stars, till at last she falls into a deep sleep.

That first Saturday morning, she starts to organize her classroom in the way she wants for the Monday, remembering the watchwords she was taught in college—*order and discipline, to be held true for the teacher, the classroom and the children*—ideas her own mother had drummed into her as a child. She positions books according to height, cleans slates, straightens desks, smooths her dress, excitement and nerves making her stop every now and then to glance over the pattern the desks make, the view of the village through the clean windows, the smell of paint on the newly washed walls. She spins the globe and checks the bell is gleaming, ready to summon the pupils on the first day, and breathes in the fresh, clean air of her own life, though her mother's voice is never far away. *Skerry? Where's Skerry? No wonder I've never heard of it—so small! Surely more minding children than teaching them, though perhaps that's the best way for you*, until suddenly she is desperate to get outside.

When she leaves for lunch, Dorothy has time to do the one thing she's wanted to do since she's arrived. She's been able to smell it, to see it in the distance, even hear it from her cottage—her cottage!—at the top of the village, but she's not yet set foot on the beach. Skerry Sands.

As she ventures down the hill, she is aware of people staring at her, some of the men touching their caps, the women looking then leaning to say something to friends and husbands. They must all know who she is; they are bound to be interested, so she composes her face into the expression of distant politeness suited to her profession and carries on walking, feeling their eyes still on her back. On the right there is Brown's Grocers and Confectioners, the paned windows clean and stacked high with familiar products—Lipton's tea, Colman's mustard, Quaker Oats—and on a whim, Dorothy goes in to see what else they have. Perhaps there is something she can have for lunch. She pictures herself sitting on Skerry Sands, eating a pie, watching the boats, before pushing the thought aside. Eat outside? On her own? What an idea, and she pushes open the door, the little bell jangling, waiting for her eyes to adjust to the gloom.

A group of young women are gathered round a counter to the right, a shaft of sunlight picking out their faces, turned toward her. Dorothy smiles and nods, feels their eyes on her new dress, its wide lace collar, her polished shoes, and sees a look pass between them.

"You the new schoolmistress, then?" The woman is all planes and angles, and Dorothy can't detect any friendliness in her voice.

"Yes, Miss Aitken—Dorothy Aitken." She steps forward, hand outstretched.

Someone snorts, then coughs and there is that shared look again. *So here they are,* Dorothy thinks, *just as Mother said—keep your distance from the gossips, you have a position to uphold*—and, her smile stiffening on her lips, she raises her eyebrows just high enough.

The woman behind the counter reels off everyone's names, "Miss Bell—Ailsa Bell; Miss Barclay—Norah Barclay," and it takes Dorothy a moment to see she is being gently mocked. Well, it is only what she expects, so she greets each in turn and then wanders round the shop slowly, lifting packets and turning them to read, to show she isn't unsettled. In the end she chooses something she doesn't even need, Cadbury's cocoa, pausing before the counter till the women let her through, placing her coins on the wooden surface, the stiff smile never leaving her face. She is relieved to have won this small battle, learned first in the playground, amongst sly words and shared looks, where the trick is to hold your smile and eyebrows just so, letting their judgment glance off you as though you don't care. But as she leaves and the door is closing behind her, the words "Well, aren't we lucky to be visited by Lady High and Mighty" and a burst of laughter follow her. She steps out into the sunlight and, after a moment, walks briskly away.

At the bottom of the hill, the road curves left along the cliff until suddenly Dorothy is standing at the top of a steep rocky staircase down to the beach and all in front of her is the sparkling, light-spangled sea, the fresh wind carrying the smell of salt and fish, the boats in the distance, the shriek of gulls, wheeling and diving.

Her shoes are all wrong, and she hopes no one will see her as she scrambles down the stones, basket in one hand, till she is finally standing on the sand. She gazes at this huge, breathing, heaving thing, its surge and swell, and she doesn't know what to do with the strange thrill she feels. A man on one of the boats stands up and shields his eyes from the sun to stare. She finds herself staring back at him, and they stand like that, each taking in the detail of the other. He raises his hand and suddenly Dorothy remembers herself. What would her mother say? Looking down, she notices the scuffed leather of her boots and the sandy damp of her hem. Without looking back, she turns and hurries up the cliff steps.

The Kirk

Dorothy looks forward to her visit to the Kirk the next day.
St. Peter's, patron saint of fishermen, and maybe the one
place where she knows exactly who she is and where she
belongs. The Kirkyard is tidy, she notes with approval, the
work of many hands; the Kirk itself simple with a battle-
mented tower without decoration or ornament, other than
pretty, arched windows flashing in the sunlight. People are
arriving and Dorothy tries to pick out the children she'll be
teaching, imagining herself greeting them at the door of her
classroom where they will all line up in order and each find
their place, with its grammar and slate and chalk.

The Minister is at the door of the Kirk welcoming the
congregation. When he sees Dorothy he raises his hand.

"Miss Aitken—perfect! Do come and meet some of the
villagers."

Dorothy's heart races, but she smooths her dress over her
waist in that way she has of preparing herself and joins him,
arranging a polite smile on her face. Once she is next to him,
the Minister reels off names as people file into the Kirk, following each one up with a personal detail.

"This is Norah and Ailsa," then as an aside, "Norah is one
of our best knitters, you know, and Ailsa's baking—well, just
you wait." Dorothy recognizes them from the shop the day

before, and her stomach clenches a little. Behind them comes the shopkeeper on her own. "This is Mrs. Brown." Dorothy notices the formal address, and Mrs. Brown's look of cool appraisal as she passes by. The oddity of her clothing takes Dorothy by surprise. The loose dress with twine for a belt, and—surely those aren't men's boots, are they? But the Minister is talking again. "Mrs. Brown knows everything and everyone, so anything you need, she's the one to ask. I've learned that quickly. Ah, this is Jane and William coming here. Sad story there, I'll tell you another time."

The woman is older than the man, who still has something of the boy about him, despite his height. They stop and shake her hand. The woman, Jane, stands very close to her companion, and Dorothy can't tell if they are brother and sister or man and wife. William smiles and squints against the sunlight. "Good morning, Miss Aitken. It's nice to see a new face in the village," but Jane pulls him away with a pinched face and a "Yes, indeed."

Wife, then.

She meets carpenters and net-makers, farmers and crofters, coopers and fishermen. The women spin and weave and gut and cure fish; one is a seamstress—Dorothy makes a mental note of this—and so many have children too, hanging on to their skirts or holding their hands. Dorothy soon loses track of names, there are so many, wanting to escape their scrutiny and the Minister's running commentary in the cool dark of the Kirk.

Everyone is inside by the time Dorothy enters, and she sits on a pew at the back with an old man, grateful for the settling quiet as the Minister starts to read the notices: knitting evenings, the rota for work on the Kirk, alms for the poor. His voice fades as Dorothy casts her eye over the villagers, the shuffling, nudging children, the families and couples, all

24

the people she will have to learn to live with, telling herself that she isn't seeking out one person in particular, the fisherman whose hand had shielded his eyes, the other raised in greeting, for a moment just the two of them on the Sands and nothing else.

He isn't there.

Agnes

The thing about Joseph, Agnes thinks as she puts the water on to warm and unwraps the soap in readiness, *is he's different*. Different from her father, different from the other boys. Oh, she can have a laugh like the rest of them, and the flirting is nice with the lads and their bawdy jokes, their sly hints, but Agnes knows what it is and where it all leads. Just that very morning a bruise was blooming on her mam's cheekbone, the flesh puffing up and squeezing the eye half shut.

A hasty marriage with the wrong man.

Joseph will be here later, always on a Friday for his supper, sometimes bringing a choice crab or lobster from the creels. The water is nearly ready now, and with the little ones at school and the older ones working away and Jeanie still at the fish house, Agnes strips and gets the flannel and drying cloth ready. The thing is, how does she get him to see that she's growing up now, that she's not so much like a little sister anymore? She may be five years younger than him, but there are other girls already married with little ones at eighteen. She sighs. A friend told her that lavender is good to bathe in, so she crumbles the heads she has in the bowl and pours the water over them. The earthy smell blooms into the room. She scrubs her face and under her arms and breasts; she digs the dirt out of her nails, then scrubs them too with

26

the laundry brush. She washes between her legs and then, finally, puts the bowl on the floor and bathes her feet. A vigorous rub with the drying cloth and she puts her stockings on and her other dress, her workaday one ready to be washed in the morning with everyone else's. She brushes her hair, counting—the same friend told her to brush it for a hundred strokes to make it shine. Agnes gets to twenty-three with the comb before the end-of-school bell rings faintly up the hill.

She hurries with the bowl into the garden, where she tips the murky contents in a corner near the pigsty, and rushes back in to chop the onions for supper as though she's done nothing special to prepare for Joseph's visit.

As the afternoon light catches the gleam of her nails on the knife, she relishes the feeling of her young body, clean and fresh in her newly mended dress. One day, she will be making this supper for a husband, with a baby on the way, maybe a youngster at her skirts, a sturdy boy, and she'll make a family, a good one, where no one's scared and the children don't hide under the covers telling stories or singing rhymes to drown out the sound of their father bashing their mother round the kitchen.

And maybe, she thinks, as the onions start sizzling and she adds the scraps of meat from the butcher's, just maybe, tonight will be the night Joseph finally notices her.

Dorothy

She hadn't heard anyone knock, but there the note is, just the edge of it visible where it's been pushed under the door, part of her name showing in neat script. *Miss Aitken.*

Her heart skips as she picks it up and for one ridiculous moment she thinks of the fisherman again.

Miss Aitken,
    You are invited to join the ladies for knitting at Brown's Grocers and Confectioners on Thursday evenings.
    Mrs. Brown

She sighs.
Miss Aitken, not Dorothy.
Mrs. Brown.
Dorothy swallows hard. The pointed echo of her formal greeting, and the sidelong response of the women in the shop, makes her cheeks flame.

She sits in the kitchen and rereads the note. Maybe she's mistaken.
Ladies.
Lady High and Mighty.
Huddles of girls in the playground drift into her mind, her own stiff separateness. Just like her mother, standing

away from the families at the school gate at the end of the day; how Dorothy would walk toward her under her cool eye, while others ran. Mamma hadn't liked running. Or playing. Or voices raised. A pinch to the soft flesh of her arm had been an effective teacher when she forgot.

She'd always felt ashamed of her easy tears as a child, her clinging need to be shown love, to run toward it. It had taken a long time to recognize her mother's satisfaction when she did, her easy manipulation of Dorothy's feelings, the power it gave her.

There had always been the same pattern. The swelling silence that slowly filled the home, the way it would become harder for Dorothy to breathe or move, the worrying about what she'd done to warrant the closed face, the air of disappointment, the mouth pulled tight like a purse.

Her attempts to appease with small gestures—the tea made and drunk in aloof, righteous judgment—would make Dorothy weak, faint with growing nervousness.

Whenever her mother finally decided to forgive her, she would open her arms to signal the punishment was at an end; it would also be the signal for Dorothy to cry in gratitude and remorse for the sin she hadn't even known till then she'd committed. In return for this her mother would hug her. Dorothy would hate herself for obliging, for giving her mother the power.

The day she refused to cry had changed everything.

It had been the day she stole the candy cane. Her eyes had always been drawn to the sweets in the grocer's at the corner of their road in Edinburgh. On the way to school, she would loiter at the window, eyes lingering on their glow in the jars, humbugs with glistening white and black stripes, brightly colored gobstoppers, candy canes, gaudy sticks of rock, even the names delightful in her mouth. At playtime the girls would bring out their rustling paper bags and peer into each other's, one cheek swollen with a sweet treat, lips fishlike with sucking, swapping one for another, and she longed to have some to share or swap—she didn't even care about the sugar or the taste, but how she wished she could stand with them, be a part of their chat, compete in the games to put three in your mouth, one in each cheek, and the other, where? Instead, she would stand apart and play cat's cradle by herself, pretending to be absorbed, casting sidelong glances.

And then came the day she'd gone into the grocer's to fetch some tea and on the counter had been a new delivery of candy canes. They'd not been put in the jar yet, which had been standing on the counter too, sugar dust in the bottom, and there'd been no one else there, at least no one at the counter, not a customer or the shopkeeper. She'd never done anything like it in her life, Dorothy who knew her Bible verses, did duties at the Kirk and always went to Sunday school, but she'd taken one and shoved it in the pocket of her coat and run out of the shop and home where she'd hidden it when her mother wasn't looking. All night she'd lain awake, worrying about the sin she'd committed and wondering how she would be punished, but it had all been jumbled up with imagining playtime, when she'd be able to bring out her sweet treat too.

In morning lessons, her hand had slid again and again into the pocket of her smock, fingering the sweet that had flecks of lint stuck to it now. The first playtime had come and gone, and she'd stood in the yard, the candy cane huge in her pocket.

She'd stood in the same place next playtime too, hands out of her pockets, so she didn't draw attention to it.

"Are you quite well, Dorothy?" The schoolmistress had frowned at her and Dorothy had nodded, terrified.

At the end of the school day, some of the girls had run home as usual in a lovely, laughing, chattering gang, and for others their mothers had been waiting, smiling. Her own mother had stood apart, and Dorothy had seen straight away that she knew. Her breath had locked in her throat. The shopkeeper must have seen her and told, and now it was too late, there wasn't even time to get rid of it. The path to her mother had narrowed, and Dorothy had experienced the strangest sensation of shrinking with every step so that by the time she'd been standing in front of her mother's stern face, she was tiny.

The pinch had been vicious. Her mother had sharp nails that left crescent moons of split skin.

The walk home had been silent, the candy cane banging heavy and hard against her thigh, Dorothy weak with fear. By the time the door had closed behind them she'd thought she might faint, but her mother had walked away from her, saying nothing.

And so the pattern had begun again—the swelling silence, the air of disappointment. And for herself, the searching of her mother's face for a sign of softening, the making of a pot of tea, asking her mother about her day, the strangled desire to confess and the desperate need for the final act of forgiveness almost choking her, because this time, she really had done something wrong.

At last her mother had come into her room. She'd stood in the doorway, her head on one side, a half smile of beatific patience on her face. "Now, we are going to remember to make our bed next time, aren't we, Dorothy? You're not too high and mighty for that, are you?"

Dorothy's blood had pounded in her ears and she'd stood stock-still. Her bed. Her hand had drifted to the sore skin of her arm. Pictures of the other girls at school, running to their mothers at the end of the day, their smiling mothers, and her own mother's unlovingness.

And so she'd broken the pattern.

"Dorothy?"

Her mother had stepped into the room, arms opening, but there had been puzzlement in the stitch of her eyebrows.

It had been a moment before she could speak, but she'd held her mother's gaze and used all her will not to cry, to stay dry-eyed. "Yes, Mamma?" she'd said, pinching the sore spot herself to stop the tears. She'd raised her eyebrows as though wondering why on earth her mother was saying her name and, curving her mouth into a small, cold smile, she'd picked up the broom and continued to sweep, not looking at her again.

This time, her mother was the one to shrink as she'd stood uncertainly in the room, before turning away and leaving Dorothy alone.

Dorothy had sunk down onto the bed, shaking.

On her way to school the next day, she'd ground the candy cane under her heel into dust, and every playtime after that she would stand on her own, fingers locked in the cat's cradle, never casting a glance in the direction of the girls and their chatter, their rustling paper bags, their sweets which made her feel sick.

Lady High and Mighty.

Sitting in her kitchen all these years later, she blinks quickly. How stupid to think things would be different here, and without reading the note again, she scrunches it in her hand and throws it on the cold grate.

Agnes

That Friday he brings flowers—bell heather, cranesbill, and broom—which she puts in a jug and sets on the table. Her mother has tried to hide the bruise with a bit of powder, and Agnes listens anxiously for her father's step on the path, hoping there won't be a scene.

She puts the pot of Scotch broth on the table, leaning past Joseph, hoping he notices the lavender she bathed in.

"What's that stink?" Her brother pinches his nose as Agnes ladles the broth into his bowl. He makes a retching sound, and the others laugh. Agnes's heart skips a beat. Did she put too much in the water? She sits on her stool and ducks her head to eat.

"How was the catch this week, Joe?" Jeanie's the only one who shortens Joseph's name, claiming familiarity through his mother, her best friend before she died of cancer.

"Good enough, Jeanie." He smiles in that easy way he has. "And good broth, Agnes." He toasts her with his spoon. "You'll make someone a happy husband one day."

Later, Agnes barely waits for the door to close behind Joseph before she swings round to her mother. "Did you hear what he said?"

Her sisters' eyes widen. "What? What did he say?" and "I didn't hear anything!"

Agnes shushes them out of the kitchen. "Wash your faces and hands, then bed." She knows they'll go straight out to the garden to play and use the privy, putting off bedtime till the last second, and maybe she'll finally get a few minutes alone with her mam.

"You heard him, didn't you? What he said?" Agnes desperately searches her mother's face.

"I did. I told you, Agnes—Joe is already a part of this family. Like a son to me, he is. Only one step more for him to be one in God's eyes too," and Jeanie smiles, though wearily, and winces as she passes a bowl for Agnes to dry.

They quietly clean and tidy up, get the laundry ready for the morning, put the oatmeal on to soak, all the tasks that make up their long, busy day.

"You better get the kids upstairs now, that'll be your father," and Agnes pauses in her work, notes the widening of her mother's eyes, her held breath as they listen to her father's heavy step. Outside, the day is fading in bruises of dusky blue and yellow. The children haven't washed, but it's too late now.

"Quick—to bed. Daddy's back," and she wets her apron in the water butt, wiping their faces and hands as they stop their play and file past her and up the stairs. "I'll be with you in a moment—quiet now."

Agnes goes into the kitchen to greet her father, and her mother frowns her warning just too late. He pushes her out of the way before sitting, swaying silently on his stool while Jeanie eases his boots off. Agnes picks up the jug of flowers. It can go in the room she shares with her sisters and brother tonight, and on the way up the stairs she buries her face in the gentle fragrance of the wildflowers and hopes Joseph picked them just for her.

The Fisherman

At the end of the first week, a week in which so many children arrived at the school at different times that she had to restart lessons over and over, when she was bruised on the arm by a hurled slate, had to reprimand a class heaving with laughter at a rude picture passed hand to hand, and all the other humiliating failures she has endured, Dorothy is exhausted. It's all so different from the schools where she'd done her practice, tidy Edinburgh schools, not like this raggle-taggle of children, some unwashed, some unbrushed, many entirely unprepared, all sitting in the wrong places, chatting and giggling, the Minister popping his head round the door to see what the noise is about, his kindly smile almost worse than the humiliation of the children knowing she's scared of them. She wants to go home and cry, but instead she heads down to Skerry Sands where the wind can whip her cheeks and sting her eyes.

She loves the Sands. There is a wonderful sense of freedom that she never found in Edinburgh with its narrow streets and tall houses. It smells different, of salt and fish and seaweed. She likes watching the work on the boats, the gulls dipping and diving for fish farther out, the water breaking on jutting reefs and crags. Children are down there too; they touch their caps and say "Morning, Miss," then run off laughing or whispering to each other, throwing glances back. The adults call her "Miss" too, the men nodding in the same gesture of respect as their children, the women more stiff-lipped. "Miss" quickly becomes a symbol of her unassimi-lated position in the village, unnamed, unmarried, outside.

Her eye always wanders to the boats when they're in. She pretends to herself that she isn't looking out for the fish-erman she saw that first day, but she can still picture his face, his raised hand, recapture the strange feeling she'd had that he was somehow more real than anything else.

Today there is almost no one down there, and she walks into the wind, toward the tumble of granite that the villagers call the Rocks, scattered at the bottom of the cliff and sub-merged at high tide. She sits down on the nearest boulder to watch the surge and swell of the gray sea. Most of the villag-ers will be with their families now, eating their suppers, and she thinks of her supper for one that she might or might not eat when she goes—where? Home? Home conjures up child-hood dreams of warmth and company, not the cold house with the cold mother where she grew up, where she'd never invited back the few friends she'd struggled to make. And here she is again—a schoolmistress—one step distanced from people who might have been friends, men who might have become . . . But she doesn't let herself finish the thought. Instead, she tightens her lips and stands up. This is how she likes it, she tells herself.

When it starts to rain she wraps her scarf around her head, but as she turns to go back to the Steps, she stays too long on one foot, twists and slips, cracking her ankle against the rock. Her cry of pain sounds like it comes from somewhere else; she grips her leg and waits for her breathing to subside, then tries to move. The pain is sharp and uncompromising. The damp from the sand has seeped through her skirts and the rain is getting heavier. In the fading light she tries to judge the distance to the Steps, then pulls herself up using the rock until, with gritted teeth, she hops into a standing position. There is nothing for it. Staying close, first to the rocks then to the cliff face at the back of the beach, she hops, leans, winces, stops; it takes a long time, and when she gets to the bottom, daylight is dying and she realizes the impossibility of getting to the top.

"Miss? Can I help you?"

Dorothy is holding on to the uneven rock and turns her head. Her heart jumps. It is the fisherman. Beads of rain cling to his jersey and hair. In the fading light and drizzle, she has the impression of warm brown eyes that show concern and something more that makes her look away. She wants to say no but knows the ridiculousness of a refusal.

"Yes, if you wouldn't mind. A—a stick, or something like that." But he is already crouching before her "May I?" and she is in too much discomfort to protest. He holds her ankle and she winces. "You need to get the boot off before the ankle gets too swollen." He quickly unties the knot, loosens the laces, and eases her foot out. When he gently lets her go, Dorothy's breath is caught in her throat.

"I don't have a stick on the boat, but there's one in the cottage—it's not far once we're up at the top."

She has no choice, and together they limp and stagger up the slippery steps to the path above. His arm is around her waist and hers around his, and she suddenly thinks of the three-legged races she had to endure at school, and a part of her wants to laugh at the absurdity of it. At the top, she hops, leaning on him, to his cottage, which is a little farther along the cliff, separate from the huddle of thatched homes along the path to the Steps.

He pulls out a chair for her, but Dorothy doesn't sit down

and, instead, leans on the wooden back. He lights a lamp and in the glow that blooms in the darkness, she notices the tidy order of the kitchen. There seems to be no wife or family, but she supposes a fisherman must keep his boat organized and get into good habits. There is a plain wooden table and shelves lined with foodstuffs, and the hob with a blackened kettle on top, an open fire with both wood and peat neatly stacked to the side of it.

He moves from the woodpile to the stove, where he checks the weight of water in the kettle before hanging it on the hook over the embers of the fire. He is at ease with himself; it's there in the way he carries himself, the line of his shoulders, his stance. And he's handsome. The thought comes unbidden. *If you like that sort of thing*, Dorothy thinks quickly. She tells herself she doesn't know what she likes but feels suddenly uncomfortable, as though the room is too small for the both of them, too warm.

"I'll just be a minute," he says, and goes through the door to the place where he must sleep.

Dorothy's ankle is throbbing. She feels cold again now and wet, her skirts heavy with rain, and she wants to be home, where nothing is troubling. He returns with a walking stick. It looks like it's been hewn straight from a tree, unfashioned.

"Plum," he says, "and sturdy. It's served me well anyway. But will you not sit down and get yourself dry?" He goes to the stove again, stirs the catching wood; a small spark flies. He adds another log and the reawoken flames lick around it. "Let me make you something hot to drink. You look half frozen."

She rushes out her words, inching toward the door. "No, though I thank you. It's better I try to get home." There is an

38

awkward moment. "My boot," she says. It is still slung over his arm.

He urges her to sit down and then takes the lace out completely so it is as loose as it can be. He eases her heel into the shoe. In the warmth and quiet of his home, with the spit and crack of a fire and its golden glow, it feels suddenly too intimate again. And then she is as quick as she can be out the door, limping and hopping with the rough-hewn stick. She doesn't turn back, but she knows he is watching her because of the way the shifting light of the lamp and the fire ease the darkness.

Much later, warm and dry beneath her blanket, Dorothy lies awake. She shuts her eyes, wills sleep to come, but feels the warmth of his body at her side on the Steps. She turns over, listening to the thud of the rain on the roof, but instead hears his voice offering to help. She turns the other way and breathes in his smell of spice. She sits up. This is ridiculous. But her mind keeps returning to one moment in particular—his hand through her stocking, before the fire in his kitchen, the way he held her ankle, tender and firm.

Agnes

He hasn't come. Not yet anyway.

"Just a few more minutes," she says to Jeanie. The children are already sitting down, pushing each other with elbows and kicking each other under the table.

"We can't wait any longer, Agnes." Jeanie's mouth tightens. "I'll be having words with him, though. Messing us around. His mother would have had something to say about that."

Agnes sighs when she hears her father outside. A little squall of cold wind comes in with him. Agnes glances at his face and her shoulders relax. He's sober for once. He sits heavily on his stool. "My boots, Jeanie. I'm done in," and Jeanie leaves her soup to help him.

He looks around the table. "No lover boy tonight?"

Jeanie ladles some broth into a bowl and sets it on the table. He pulls it toward him. "Don't know why you're so set on him." Agnes opens her mouth to protest. "Oh, don't tell me you're not. I see the way you look at him. And the way he comes here every Friday, eating our food like he's the head of the household." He tears his bread and soaks it in the broth. "Now that Scott's a good lad. Always asking after you he is, at the alehouse."

Agnes and Jeanie share a quick look.

"I saw that," her father says. "But he's a good boy, I tell

you. No airs and graces," and Agnes knows what that means. "Good soup this." He scrapes the last of it, pushing his bread around the bowl. Afterward, he pats his pockets.

"Now, what have I got here?" and the children, seeing tonight will be a good night, jump off their stools and crowd around him.

He pulls out a bag of sweets. "Who's for a game of pitch and toss before bed?" and they jump up and down, shouting, "Me! Me!"

Agnes gathers the scraps, the peelings, the ends of the onions in a bowl to take out to the pig. At the back door, she glances up at the rain-dark sky and, pulling her apron over her head, hurries to the sty. She scratches the pig's head, who's nosing through his gate, snuffling and snorting. *Don't worry*, her mam had said, but it's not like Joseph. Where is he? He's hardly missed a Friday in years. And she tries to ignore that faint touch of fear that comes so easily these days.

When Joseph knocks the next day, Agnes breathes a sigh of relief, pats her hair, and makes herself wait before she opens the door. He has a wheelbarrow with bundles of hay, reeding pins, a mallet, and all the tools needed to replace the rotten thatch. Agnes waves aside his apologies for not coming the night before and invites him in. His jaw is newly shaven, and he brings with him a smell of soap and woodsmoke. She pushes the basket of laundry along the table to make room and turns to fill the kettle.

He stays standing. "I'll not sit down. Can't trust the weather today, and I want to get this done."

"I saved you some lamb broth. I got some hogget from the butcher's, specially."

"No, I—I have a pot of something cooking myself today, actually. I'll get back to it when I've done this."

41

Agnes tries not to show her surprise or the disappointment that follows it. She keeps her voice light. "Not like you to miss a Friday-night supper."

Joseph lowers his eyes and runs his thumb over the blade of his knife before looking up again. "Sounds like I missed a good one. Bread and cheese doesn't really compare." He clears his throat. "I'm sorry for not letting you know."

Agnes tries to smile as though it doesn't matter, as though her insides aren't churning. "I'm sure you had something important to do."

Joseph is quiet then; he's looking at Agnes, but Agnes gets a strange feeling that it's not her he sees. "Right, well, I better get up that ladder. You need a hand with the basket before I start?" He gestures at the table.

Agnes wants to say yes. She wants him to see her, to notice the new way she has done her hair, to look at her the way she looks at him. She wants him to tell her where he was. "No, thank you," she says instead.

Outside, as he prepares his tools and leans the ladder against the thatch, the children are getting in his way, putting together string, pails, and nets for crabbing down on the Rocks, and if she squints slightly so their faces blur, they could be any children. They could be her children, and Joseph her man. She shuts her eyes to conjure the picture, to hold on to it.

When she opens them again, the children have gone, and she can just see Joseph's boots through the window, on the ladder.

She lifts the basket of laundry and shifts position so it rests comfortably on her hip and starts down the path, not looking back, so he can't see how hard she is trying not to cry.

On the drying green on the cliff, she pegs up the lines of washing, the brisk wind blowing sheets out like sails, whipping stockings back in her face. She stops for a moment and looks out over the sea without really seeing it. It's only the one night he's missed but—her heart leaps with fear and hope at the very thought of it—it's time to make him see she is a woman now.

Dorothy

Dorothy's ankle is blue and swollen. She can put only the merest weight on it before the pain is impossible. She uses the fisherman's stick to hobble downstairs in her nightgown. She builds a fire, dragging a chair close to it to stay warm. She is glad that the delivery boy will be bringing her shopping, and plans to make stovies because she won't have to stand over them; she can stay in a chair with her shawl wrapped around her for as long as she needs.

She sleeps fitfully, waking in discomfort to change position. The light in the room changes as clouds scud across the sky, sometimes gray, sometimes bright with the washed-clean light between showers. A knock wakes her fully. She reaches for the stick, then calls out instead to the delivery boy, "Come on in, it's not bolted," and hears the now-familiar creak of the door.

But it's the fisherman who walks in.

Dorothy is flustered, stumbling to her feet and pulling her shawl tight around her. He waits in the doorway, holding a parcel and a pot. She leans on the stick and hopes he blames the warmth in her face on the fire. She doesn't know what the correct thing is to do. Should she invite him in? She doesn't even know his name.

"It's Joseph," he says, as if reading her thoughts. "I brought you something to eat in case you were still struggling." He smiles—a wide, natural smile—and there it is again, that sense of something more, a question he is asking her that she doesn't know how to answer.

"You shouldn't have gone to the trouble," she says, hating the cold formality of her voice.

"It's only what I was making for myself, some Cullen skink; it was no bother," and she feels stupid then for imagining—what? That he has a special interest in her? Dorothy feels wrong-footed, so she stiffens and nods her head.

"Of course. Well, thank you anyway, I'm sure there's no need."

"Where would you like me to put it?" He comes fully into the room, spies a pan hanging from a hook. "In here?" and she nods as he pours from one to the other. She should offer him tea but she can't. He places the paper parcel on the side. "Some haddock I had left over—it's filleted. How is your ankle?"

"It's better, much better," Dorothy lies. She has an absurd fear that he will ask to look at it or urge her to sit and then kneel before her again, supporting it in his hands.

But he simply nods. "Well, keep the stick while you need it." He looks around the room. "These windows won't keep the wind out—I'll have a word with the Minister," and then he is at the door again. "Try to keep it up off the ground, Miss Aitken." He pauses. "Dorothy," he says after, softly, as if no one has ever said her name before, and then he leaves before she has time to say thank you.

Joseph is as good as his word. Dorothy hasn't minded the fresh sea air and the sweet scent of gorse blowing in through the windows that won't quite shut, but the Minister tells her that as the cottage belongs to the school and the school belongs to the Kirk, he will send a man to mend them. And that is how it happens that she opens the door the next Saturday morning when the rain is falling soft and gray from a pale sky, to Joseph.

Dorothy pulls her cardigan close around her and invites him in, trying to remember what a fool she felt last time and concealing her leap of agitation. She puts the kettle on the hob while he looks at the window and tries to make conversation.

"Where have you come from, then?"

She wraps a cloth around her hand to lift the kettle and pour the steaming water over the leaves to steep.

Take no notice of the attention of men, her mother used to say, and goodness knows, if those clean, white-faced men at Kirk weren't good enough for her, this man with the brown weathered face and the warm eyes most definitely isn't.

"Edinburgh," she says, setting out one cup.

"You'll be finding us very backward, then, I expect?"

She makes a noise that is neither a yes nor a no, but probably a yes, checking the tea to see if it is ready.

His eyes flick to the single cup. "Will you not be joining me?"

Her cheeks warm at the unexpected intimacy so, keeping her back to him, she says, "No. No, thank you," and pours the milk into a jug and sets it out on the table. Though brought up to be scrupulously polite, she feels a pinch of pleasure in being almost, but not quite, rude.

The window frame needs replacing; neglect has left it swollen and rotting on the inside. It is more than a ten-minute fix, he says before he leaves, setting his cup on the side; he needs to go to another job but will be back the next Saturday, and she nods, feeling a twinge of something, and is irritated when she realizes it's because she's glad he's coming back.

46

She is even more irritated with herself the following Saturday when she realizes she is waiting for his knock. She is wearing her blue dress, the one that tapers in slightly at the waist. She smooths it over her hips, thinks she likes the effect, but it is her mother's voice she hears. *What makes you think you're so special?* This, when she'd been caught admiring herself after sewing a lace collar, a gift from an aunt, onto one of her dresses for the school dance. The next time she'd gone to wear it, the collar had gone, the tear to the neck testament to the violence with which it had been ripped off.

The sin of vanity.

Dorothy makes herself change out of the blue dress and ties her hair into a bun, though she leaves the swing of a lock over her cheek, pretending to herself it is because she's in a hurry.

When the knock comes, slow and steady, she jumps a little, then composes her face and waits a moment at the door before opening it. The Minister has said he must check all the windows, Joseph says, and replace any that are rotting. This time she knows straightaway that the flash of feeling she has is one of pleasure, but she purses her mouth over it and puts one cup out again, but this time with some shortbread, just warm from the oven.

And so a pattern is set. He arrives on a Saturday morning, his steady knock always the same, toolbox in hand, his smile easy, and Dorothy tries to respond to his increasingly comfortable manner with an impassive face, or a short answer to his many questions. But it gets harder the more he tries, and she likes catching his smile as she turns away from him to butter bread for his sandwich.

When he's not there, she imagines engaging him in conversation, being light, making him laugh, but when she's with him, her heart beats too fast and the words fail on her lips.

47

But she knows in her heart that they both like this dance, his warmth and her coolness, her there in her navy dress now, pinched in at the waist, hair falling loose over her shoulders.

Now

Dorothy

Dorothy's sleep is disrupted by dreams. She is up earlier than usual, awake and lighting the lamp before dawn. She picks up her knitting from the night before but can't quite settle to it, so instead sits at the kitchen table and chops onions and potatoes, even going into the garden for some winter cabbage while the new day glimmers on the horizon. A few times she has knocked on the door of the Manse after the school day has ended, asking after the child who she has heard is getting stronger; she hasn't seen him again after that first silly episode of hers but wants to offer help and support where she can.

Later, when the stew is ready, she secures the pot with a lid, wraps it all in a cloth, and sets out up the hill. The village is white now, the sky so snow-heavy that it appears dark even after sunrise. She's taking the food to the almshouses, but as she's passing, she might as well knock at the Manse. While she waits, she looks up at the small window of the child's room.

When Jenny opens the door, there is a fraction of a second before she lifts her mouth into a semblance of a smile. Dorothy tries to ignore it.

"I've brought some stew. I was taking some to—"

"Really, Mrs. Gray." Jenny takes a deep breath and briefly closes her eyes. "It is very kind of you, but Martha and myself can manage." Her hands go to her belly, which is

49

straining against her dress, and she winces. "The boy is very tired. No, he hasn't said anything; no, he doesn't seem to understand anything, but yes, he is getting stronger. Between you and Joseph . . . " She sighs.

"Well, if you're sure you don't need this, I'll take it on up the hill," and she steps back from the door. Almost immediately she steps forward again. "I could always sit with him sometimes. Only if it would help, of course. If Martha is busy, I mean."

"I'm sorry, I know you want to help. I know it must be very hard for you—the circumstances. After what happened to Moses."

Dorothy's breath catches. "I'll be on my way, then," she says, and Jenny winces again as she closes the door, but Dorothy doesn't ask. She doesn't even look at her ripe, pregnant belly, the baby come so late in life. She's sure Jenny would rather be private about the aches and pains that women feel when they are in that condition, and besides, she's stung. She's shocked that Jenny would say his name, just like that, straight to her face. Long years have taught her it is better to stay silent, even to oneself, about some things, and she walks away, trying not to think of the curtained window and the silver-haired child asleep inside.

Joseph

Jenny's pains come suddenly, embarrassingly, in a rush of water on the kitchen floor and a pulling, dragging at her thighs, and Martha is dithering—what to do first—to clear up the mess or help Jenny to a chair?

But Jenny says, in a voice made weak with the shock of pain as her body clenches and tightens, clenches and releases, "Go fetch your mam, Martha, for pity's sake," because Martha's mam knows all about birthing and comes to all the laboring women of the village, so Martha rushes out the door, still with her apron on, not even a coat, the cold taking her breath away. On the way she sees Norah, patterned scarf covering her hair, who asks her what the hurry is, wondering—hoping, actually—if it might be the boy so she can talk about it in the shop. And after that she is stopped by the seamstress, who wants to know why Martha is coatless and breathless in the snow. And so it isn't long before Norah is holding forth with the women in the shop about the suddenness of Jenny's pains, the way she'd shrieked and almost collapsed with the horror of them, her waters everywhere—"All over the kitchen, and it only just scrubbed!"—and the seamstress tells her husband so that soon even Joseph finds out, shoveling snow on the front path of his cottage on the cliff, where he straightens up, one hand at his back, and wonders out loud:

"What about the child? Who will take care of the child now?"

"What do you think? Mrs. Brown is set against the idea."

"I think she would do her duty by the Kirk," Joseph says to the Minister, though later he wonders why he spoke up for Dorothy at all and even whether he made the suggestion in kindness, or in some other way, more bitter than he would like to admit. He does know he's grateful the Minister at least respects him enough to ask his opinion. "She's been alone with no one to look after all these years."

"Would it not be better, then, for him to go to a house where there are children already, or where at least there is—" He stops, clearly not sure that what he's going to say next is fair, or right.

"She's taught generations of the children here, Minister, and was a mother herself for six years, and this child, this boy—"

"Is the very age, I suspect, that Moses was when he drowned, Joseph. I saw her not two days ago, and it was clear a part of her wondered if it could be him."

"Whatever she is, she's not stupid." Joseph feels his anger rising, whether at the Minister's ignorance or his own defense of her, he's not sure. "He is very alike, you must see it."

"But that's my worry. He's too alike—in age, in his looks. Maybe Mrs. Brown is right. It could confuse the mind, do harm—?"

"Or good. I don't know she ever faced any of it—I saw no sign of it myself. Did you?"

The Minister is quiet then, and Joseph wonders if he is remembering the memorial service, the pulled-too-tight stitch of Dorothy's figure in the Kirk, her white face and dry eyes, the way she nodded politely as the people of the village

52

came to pay their respects and sing their psalms and say their prayers for the boy whose body was never found, never washed up anywhere and whose small bones are probably even now tangled in the seaweed not far from home. He stops his thoughts. They all, all of them, took out their boats and their nets, even as the water was still heaving and breaking against the rocks, hoping at least to bring back a body to bury. But in haul after haul they found nothing, and afterward, she asked to work at the school again, as though none of it had ever happened, and never visited the plain wooden cross in the Kirkyard, because he wasn't there.

"He isn't anywhere," she said after the funeral, and then never spoke of him again.

What was Forgotten, Returns, When the Sea is Ready

When the rumor had rippled through the village, carrying into houses and shops the news that a child had come, maybe even the child returned, she'd put her hands against the window and gazed toward the Manse as though she could see through stone into the very room where he was sleeping.

Who is he?

She had hoped the years would set down layers of silence, of forgetting.

But she knows the world doesn't work like that. Bodies wash in on the tide years later. Wrecks disgorge their treasure. What was forgotten, returns, when the sea is ready.

And no one, no one at all, knows what this means for her, and her breath had come more quickly, misting the glass.

Then

Agnes

Agnes's chance never seems to come. He's back to eating his supper with them on a Friday night, but the kids are always there, or her father, and he never stays long after. And the thatch isn't finished, not yet, because he's doing some work at the Schoolhouse now for the new schoolmistress, but at least things have been better at home. Agnes's father has been coming home after the day's work and not giving in to the temptation of the alehouse. The children are starting to relax too, waiting for the sweets after supper.

It's just those times you think you might be in for a spell of settled weather that the storms come.

When her father isn't back for supper that Thursday, Agnes's muscles tighten. No one says anything, but the children are quieter than usual and rush their food.

"Get those kids to bed, Agnes," Jeanie says, and they both know why.

Agnes helps them get a wash and hurries them up the stairs. "You be quiet up here, now, none of your silliness. I'll be up to bed myself soon enough."

She goes back down to finish off the clearing up with Jeanie. Through the window it's a black night. "Keep the pot on a simmer, Mam. If he comes in and it's cold—"

"It'll boil away if I leave it on for too long." But she does what Agnes says and puts it back. "The potatoes are ruined."

Agnes moves quickly round the kitchen. "I'll make an apple crumble. That'll keep him sweet," and they look at each other and nearly laugh at the impossibility, only it's too serious, of course.

"You get on up to bed now, Agnes."

"You're all right. I fancy a cup of tea anyway," and she puts the leaves on to steep.

They drink in silence, one or other of them getting up to stir the pan of stewing fruit, the silence thickening around them.

Outside there are muffled voices and guffaws of laughter. The bang at the door makes them both jump even though they're expecting it. Agnes hurries up and opens the door. Two of the village men are holding him up between them. One of them is Scott.

"There you go, Agnes. He's in a bit of a bad way." He staggers himself, either under the weight of her father or because he's drunk too; Agnes can't tell which.

They get her father to a chair where he slumps, head wobbling.

Scott takes a deep breath in. "Smells good in here."

Agnes's voice is brisk. "Yes, well, time we got him to bed."

Scott reaches for her, his breath yeasty with drink, and misses. He tries again and Agnes slaps his hand away, trying to keep it light-hearted. He makes another clumsy grab for her waist, and she shoots an anxious look at her father.

"Leave it, Scott."

His lopsided smile fades as he wobbles toward the door, turning once. "You think you're better than me, Agnes, that I'm not good enough for you, but you'll see. I'll show you. You and me are the same."

She shuts the door quickly behind them. She turns back into the room, hoping her father is already asleep, but he's sitting up and peering at them, the vicious light of drink in his eye.

"You flirting with him under my own roof?"

"Your own roof? The roof you left for another man to fix?" Jeanie's voice is full of contempt.

Agnes looks at her mother in horror.

He's on his feet in a moment, rage clearing his senses, sturdy now on wide-apart legs. "You dare to speak to me like that? You think I don't see what goes on?" and then he swings round to Agnes, knocking over the chair. "You sniffing round Scott now?"

Jeanie scoffs. "It was your drunken self brought that lout round here. He's no better than you are."

Agnes realizes what her mam's doing, trying to draw his attention back to her, but he leers toward Agnes again. She backs away, comes up against the edge of the table, and his fist is already swinging. The blow hits her hard on the side of the head, on her ear and jaw. She doesn't feel the pain, not yet, and she can't hear what Jeanie is screaming at him or understand why they're the wrong way up until she realizes she's on the floor. Sound rushes back and the kids are on the stairs, screaming at their dad to stop. Agnes manages to scramble upright and go to them, hurrying them up and into bed, under the covers, where they don't tell stories or sing rhymes but cling to each other, while Agnes shuts her eyes against the pain and the noise downstairs and the warm blood blooming on the sheet, arms gathering the children to her, her heart shrinking with the shame of it all.

On Friday, she's in the garden picking kale when Joseph next comes. She doesn't stand up straightaway, and when she does, she pulls her hair across her face and keeps her head turned away.

57

He steps toward her. "Agnes—" He moves her hair where she knows her jaw is swollen and the side of her mouth split. He nods as though finding what he expected. "We need to get you out of this house as soon as possible. All the children, in fact," and Agnes wants to cry, because this is what she's always dreamed of—safety for herself and her siblings.

She turns to him and, after a moment, touches his hand. "I know I can give them a better life than this." She ventures further. "When I have a home of my own." He gives her a kind smile and ruffles her hair, and she follows him inside.

The children are regaling Jeanie with tales of the new schoolmistress, Miss Aitken, her precise Edinburgh accent, how she can't keep control, the kids always using language and throwing things at her.

Her brother says, "You should have seen how red she was when she ran out. Everyone said she was crying!"

They are all laughing, and as Agnes passes round bread, her eyes drift to Joseph. He isn't laughing. "It's a good story, isn't it, Joseph? Bet you were a terror yourself at school. I heard this one's a bit of a dragon."

"Actually, she's a nice woman. I've spent a bit of time with her. You know, fixing the windows." He clears his throat and looks at her brother. "You should be kinder, she's new," and Agnes's smile fades at the tone of his voice. It's not lost on Jeanie either, Agnes can see.

Agnes turns back to the stove so he can't see her expression. Who is this woman who thinks she can come to the village and disturb its steady rhythms? She feels a tremor of fear and the old feeling rises, that she's not good enough, not for someone like Joseph.

Later, Jeanie tries to soothe her. "You're reading it all wrong. He's a generous lad, inclined to think the best of people. What's he going to be wanting with a woman like that? Cold, she looks to me. Like she's got a rod up her arse. You've seen her yourself."

Agnes tries to picture Miss Aitken from the Kirk, but it's hard because she's always managing her brother and sisters, no time to be giving her attention to the new schoolmistress; they come and go so often. Her head throbs and she puts her hand to her face and sighs. It isn't the first time Joseph has tried to tell the children to behave, and she likes that about him. He'll make a good father one day—patient but firm. Her heart lifts a little. No incomer is going to spoil her chances, not now. Maybe her mother's right, after all, maybe she's not the sort of woman he'd look at twice.

But she'll still have a good look on Sunday nevertheless, just to be certain.

As it turns out, she doesn't have to wait that long.

The Shop

"He's turned her head, that's for sure."

"Do you think? Well, good luck to her. She's not the first young woman to notice our Joseph." Norah laughs her brittle laugh, but Mrs. Brown rolls her eyes at the choice of words. *Our Joseph.*

"You'd think Agnes and Joseph were betrothed, the way Jeanie goes on." Ailsa tucks an unruly red curl back under her headscarf. "What do you think, Jane?"

Jane Gray, still in mourning black so many years after losing her brothers, is dawdling by the flour, listening, but comes forward now and places the biscuits she has chosen for William on the counter. She sniffs. "You know me, Ailsa, not one to gossip. I'm sure people's likes and wants are their own business."

Ailsa hides a smile and folds back the cloth on her basket. "I made more scones than I need this morning, ladies," and the newly made buns breathe out the scent of warm barley.

Jane declines but the others each reach for one without halting the chat.

"For all her faults, Jeanie was very good to Joseph when his mam died, and you can see why she'd want him for her Agnes."

"Maybe you can. Doesn't make it true, though. You're

60

always too easy on people. He doesn't want to be setting his cap at an incomer, mind you. Better someone who understands the life. Lorna's back a lot, now her grandad's so frail. She'd suit him more than some schoolmistress." Norah closes her eyes with the first bite. "Perfect, Ailsa."

Ailsa nods her thanks. "Don't know how you can eat so much and never get a pick on your bones. Talk of the devil."

Mrs. Brown looks up as the door swings open, and Dorothy enters. Mrs. Brown waits for the way her eyes always glance at the counter with that nervous sideways movement of hers, the way her cheeks flush, but this morning she makes her way straight to the Lipton's tea and puts a box in her basket. *Second time in a fortnight she's bought that*, Mrs. Brown thinks. She watches her as she walks round the shop. Is her hair different? Dorothy is frowning as she runs her finger along the shelf. She pauses, and a small, quick smile curves her lips. When she comes to the counter, she lifts out the Lipton's tea and a Lyons treacle tart, not something Mrs. Brown can get hold of very often out here, and not cheap.

"I hear there's work going on up at the teacher's cottage?" It sounds almost like an accusation, though Norah looks innocent enough.

Mrs. Brown notices Dorothy's deepening color.

"Why, yes, there is. It's very kind of him. The Minister," she adds quickly, fumbling in her basket. "I . . . I seem to have forgotten my purse."

There is an awkward silence.

"Not to worry—I'll put it on account." Mrs. Brown pointedly ignores the knowing looks from Norah and Ailsa. "So easy to forget," she says, thinking that Dorothy never forgets anything and watching how she hurries more than usual to leave the shop.

Agnes's mam won't be pleased at all, she thinks as she bites into her scone, *not at all*, but it's Agnes who catches her heart. If she is setting her sights on Joseph, it'll end in tears anyway. And now this woman coming to Skerry with her airs and graces, stirring up the pot.

And she tries to resist the urge, but it's just too tempting not to wonder what will happen next.

Dorothy

Dorothy tries to slow her pace back home. She glances at the tart in her basket and can't suppress a flutter of nerves. He's only someone mending the windows because the Minister asked him to. Is it too much? She is so preoccupied with this she doesn't see till the last moment that Joseph is already at her door, waiting.

He shuffles from foot to foot, and it is then she notices that instead of his wooden toolbox, he has a basket. His smile is hesitant.

"I thought maybe you'd like to see the boat while the tide's out? Seems too fine a day to waste inside." As if he's just remembered, he holds up the basket, and she thinks a flush might be deepening his color. "I brought a bite to eat, if you want? Some bannocks and cheese."

The flutter Dorothy felt before is in her throat now, and she tries to swallow it down. "I—what about the windows?" which is not quite what she means to say.

"Well, of course, if you'd rather—"

"No!" Now it's her turn to be flustered. "No, I'd be very . . . interested . . . to see the boat. Actually"—she lifts her basket now—"they happened to have a treacle tart at the shop and I—it reminded me of home." She promises to atone for the lie later.

"We'll have quite the feast, then."

Joseph looks more relaxed, and his smile is easy now, natural. They stand for a moment in silence, then both speak at the same time.

"Do you want to put your things in my basket?" and "I'll just put the tea away." They both laugh nervously, then Joseph steps aside and Dorothy rushes inside, forgetting to invite him in. She puts the tea and tart on the table. Does this mean what she thinks it means? She tries to shut out her mother's voice. *Why would someone look at a sourpuss like you?* She's seen some of the Skerry girls, hardworking fisher-girls, quick to laughter and easy chat. She smooths her dress over her waist. Is it too formal? Never wearing quite the right thing, never quite fitting in. Her heart sinks a little. When she goes back to the door, she is more in control of herself. Joseph's eyes search her face. They're warm and kind and she'd like to respond in the same way, but her smile is stiff.

They walk together down the hill, not Copse Cross Street, but the one behind her house with a hedgerow on one side, crowded with the soft white flowers of traveler's joy, ripening bramble berries, glossy and purple, and pink mallow. The wind comes straight from the sea, salty and fresh, and high above them in a clear blue sky a kestrel hovers. Gulls shriek and circle over the boats on the shoreline.

At the top of the Steps, Joseph moves ahead of her, and as she puts her foot carefully on the uneven rock, he turns. When he takes her hand, the calluses of his palm are rough on her schoolteacher's skin. She accepts the courtesy, and soon they are standing on the Sands. The beach is busy, and Joseph explains that the fishermen use the weekend to mend nets, wash out creels, scrub decks. There are children everywhere, helping on the boats, kicking balls, paddling in the shallows, climbing on the Rocks where she turned her ankle. Dorothy is surprised there are so few mothers.

Joseph seems to catch her thought. "Everyone looks out for the children," he says. "The women are busy. It's a good washing day." He points up to a drying green on the cliff top, just visible from the shore, sheets and shirts flapping in the wind, women with clothes baskets on their hips.

Dorothy nods. When the children she teaches see her with Joseph, some stop what they're doing and gather, talking behind their hands, laughing, while others simply stare.

Dorothy is grateful that the boats are farther down the beach and that soon they have left the children behind them. They walk in the shadows of the barnacled sterns that loom much higher than she'd expected, rearing up out of the sand, with names like *Bonnie Lass* and *Kittiwake* and *The Maid of Skerry*. When the other fishermen see them, they raise their caps or hands; some call out to Joseph, give a nod to her with knowing grins.

"She'll know how to keep you in line, Joe!"

"No misbehaving with a schoolteacher about!"

Joseph smiles back at them. "Sorry," he says to her, "it's only their way of being friendly."

Dorothy wishes she could do more than just nod in reply, but it's all so new, all so different from her life before. His boat is the last one, barnacled like the rest, with seaweed catching and waving in the breeze, but the wood is clean and its name—*North Star*—looks freshly painted. There is a ladder resting against its side and he goes first, leaning over when he reaches the top, stretching out his hand. She gathers her skirts, feels for her balance on the rungs, then hauls herself up until he can pull her up and over, and then she's on the deck, breathless, hair loosened, exhilarated by the wind, by the smell, by the way he is still holding her hand.

When he releases her, he shows her round, pointing out the creels and the coils of rope, the nets and sails, the two towering masts, answering her questions about storms and how the boat is built to withstand choppy seas and wild winds.

They sit on the warm wood of the deck after, up at the bow, looking out at the wind catching the waves farther out, blowing the white foam into frothy peaks, watching the birds. His bannocks are good, if a little dense, and each time he passes her something, it feels almost domestic, as though they are familiar with each other, intimate even, as when he held her ankle before the fire.

"Why *North Star*?" she asks.

He points at the sky. "Look for it tonight, its position is always the same. A fisherman can always find his way home by the North Star if he needs to. Some call her Star of the Sea because of that." He smiles. "And anyway, it was what my father called the boat, and it's bad luck to change a boat's name."

"Are you superstitious, then?"

"You won't meet a fisherman who isn't. Strictly speaking, I shouldn't be letting you on board."

"Is that so? And why is that?"

"Women are bad luck on a boat," he says, and Dorothy finds herself laughing with him.

"That's quite a risk, then."

He smiles again, his slow, natural smile, his eyes holding hers. "Well, I'll trust my own judgment on that score," and Dorothy feels her cheeks flame. "As is whistling, because you'll be whistling up a wind. Painting the boat green—"

"Green!"

"Don't want to attract the faery folk." He notices her raised eyebrows. "It's true. You won't find many round here that don't believe in the faery folk or don't have stories of their

66

dealings with them. Stealing babies, swapping them, spoiling crops, curdling milk. Best not disturb them if you can."

Dorothy can't tell if he's joking or not but finds herself relaxing.

And he, in turn, asks her about her life in Edinburgh, and teaching, and she asks him about his family. Both his parents are dead and his brothers moved away, like so many now, to work in the busy ports, and his sister married a naval man. He talks about his father, a fisherman himself, and Dorothy likes the warmth in his voice when he does.

"And your mother?" she ventures.

"My mother . . . " He hesitates. "My mother wasn't always an easy woman. My father was a patient man, for sure," and she recognizes something in the guardedness of his tone. *Not an easy woman* is a phrase familiar to Dorothy from conversations overheard in the Kirk about her own mother, the truth much harder, crueler.

She smiles at him. "I understand," she says simply.

Sometimes they are awkward and shy with each other, at other times Dorothy is surprised at how easily the time passes.

When it is time to leave, they pack up the basket, and Joseph stands first and helps her up. She feels more comfortable than she would ever have thought, but as she turns toward him, on the cabin behind, a huge black seabird lands, wings outstretched. It is monstrous, reptilian with its long neck and powerful wingspan. She gasps as it opens its hooked beak wide and emits a loud guttural sound, and with it the stench of rotten fish, before rising noisily into the air again and flying out to sea. Dorothy's hand covers her mouth.

Joseph sees her face. "Have you not seen a cormorant before? Great fishers, they are, though quite a sight close up. The spirits of those lost at sea, some say."

Dorothy tries to laugh. She's not superstitious, of course, but as she watches it fly away, black and low over the water, she feels suddenly cold.

Up on the drying green, Agnes is unpegging the washing. When she sees them, her heart misses a beat. She stops what she's doing and shields her eyes. Is that a basket he's carrying? Where have they been? Her gaze moves to Dorothy and she takes everything in—her well-fitted dress, the way it swings above her ankles, her wide collar. She looks down at her own skirts, the fade of the fabric, the darning and restitching of it, and her body sags.

So this is what the bad feeling was. All this time, while he's been mending her windows, the new schoolmistress has been making eyes at him. She blinks quickly and watches as they walk toward the Steps, then pulls the rest of the linen down from the lines with shaking hands. She picks her basket up and tells herself it's not fear she feels, it's anger. But when she gets home, she slumps at the kitchen table. She needs to think. What can she do? How—and she pictures again the schoolmistress's dress, her walk—how can she possibly compete with someone like that? If there's one thing she knows for sure, it's that she can't just stand by and let this woman ruin everything she's ever hoped for. She wipes her face with her apron and steadies herself.

Jeanie will know what to do.

Joseph

It's a chance meeting a few weeks later. Joseph has walked the few miles back from the neighboring village and passes behind the school, drops of rain spitting tinnily on the corrugated folds of the roof. From the front of the school, the bell for the end of the day rings out, and Joseph can just see the Minister in the playground as the children stream out of the gate, but he's not looking at them. He's searching for someone, the bell now hanging silent from his hand. Some instinct tells Joseph who he's looking for, and then he spots her. Dorothy is leaning against the back wall round the corner. She is pushing her fists into her eyes, the skin white and stretched over her knuckles.

She doesn't hear his approach, and he reaches out to touch her arm, saying softly, "Dorothy?"

When she sees him, she moves away.

"Are you all right? I think the Minister is looking for you," just as the Minister's voice carries on the breeze, "Miss Aitken? Let's talk about what happened. I'm sure Jamie didn't mean to throw it at you."

Dorothy's eyes widen, and she takes hold of Joseph's hand and pulls, and then they are out the back of the school and onto the lane and half walking, half running up the hill, the rain heavier now, through the gate to the lower field and up to the Tops.

At last, under cover of the trees, they stop and stare at each other in surprise, breathless, till Joseph suddenly laughs at the ridiculousness of two grown adults running away from the Minister, and after a moment, Dorothy does too.

When she straightens up, her face is worried again. "Do you think he saw us?"

"No one did, not that I could see," Joseph says. Fat drops patter from the leaves of the branches that intertwine above them. Joseph glances up. "Come on, there is a place we'll be drier," and he takes her hand again and they walk through the copse of pine and silver birch, the woodland breathing out its scent of rich, wet soil, of leaf mold and sharp sap. He leads her to a great sheltering oak on the edge of the copse. The light is green and soft with rain. Veils of it sweep in from the sea. They are at the summit of the hill, and Skerry is spread out below them. She pulls her hand from his and turns away, gesturing toward the misty view. He realizes he is staring at her profile and turns too.

"It's quite the view," she says.

He likes her soft, precise way of talking. "Were there views like this in Edinburgh?"

"Not quite. The fog comes in from the sea, like here, and can stay for days, but on a clear day, from the high points, the city has its own beauty, looking out over the roofs and spires—" She stops abruptly as though she's got carried away. "Have you never been?"

"Me? No." He doesn't want to appear unworldly. "I'm a man more for the sea than the city . . . " He pauses before continuing. "And Skerry? Here? Do you like it?"

She casts him a sideways glance, then gazes back out over the little town and the bay where the rain is becoming less heavy—coming in fine and gauzy and sunlit now as the breeze hurries the clouds along.

"I'm glad to be here." Her face remains unreadable, but it is the most personal thing she has said to him. "I don't miss my life—living in Edinburgh. I am content here with my job and my cottage."

He seizes the moment. "Do you not miss your family?"

"I have aunts and uncles, but no, I have to confess I don't miss any of them," and she turns to face him for the first time. "Is that bad?" She is smiling.

"Not if they're not worth missing," he says seriously, and she laughs.

He is uncertain of his next question. "Being the schoolmistress here—is it very hard?"

Her face closes up again, and there's a pause before she speaks. "Are people saying things, then?"

"No, not really. It's the same with every new teacher. Agnes's little brother mentioned some mischief, that's all."

Her face falls. "What did he say?"

Joseph sees her alarm. "It was nothing, really—you know, children will just be mischievous. Weren't you?"

He sees the way she has to think about this, how she lifts her chin before answering. "No, I wasn't, actually." She seems embarrassed by her answer. She faces him. "Were you, then?"

"I was. A terror at times. I drew very good pictures of the teacher on the blackboard, if not very flattering." He smiles at her shock. "And once I put a stag beetle in the desk drawer—it went straight for the teacher's finger when he opened it." He searches her face. "They are only children—doing what children do, you know. It isn't personal."

She shuts her eyes and doesn't speak for a minute. After a breath, she says, "A stag beetle, you say?" and starts to smile, and then they are laughing again and they're looking directly at each other, and he notices every detail of her eyelashes, the glint of rain in her hair, the chip in her tooth, until suddenly she turns and points.

"Look," she exclaims, and he looks and, up above, the light is such that a flock of birds flying out to sea glitters like stars in a constellation of flashing wings and rippling light. "It's like the sun on the sea," and they look out then at the sun sparkling on the waves in just the same way, and he doesn't want the moment to end but realizes it's stopped raining and that they have no more excuse to be standing close together under the leaves of the sheltering oak.

She seems to realize it too because she gives him a brief smile. "Well, I must be going. I think I have some explaining to do at the school," and he says, "I'll walk with you," not even asking her because he doesn't want her to say no.

Instead of going back through the trees to the road, they walk down across the rough heather and thistle of the field to the back lane, and he opens the gate at the bottom, and too soon they are behind the Kirk and the almshouses when it starts to rain again, and without noticing how, he has reached for her hand and swung her round and, hands clasped, he kisses her. It is the most natural and the most astonishing thing he has ever done.

Her lips soften and she moves in closer to him and he wraps his free arm around her. When they step away from each other, they hold each other's gaze in surprise, and then she's hurrying away to the school and Joseph stays standing in the middle of the lane, in the shimmering light of the rain, of the moment, of this feeling.

Later, when he sits at his table to mend the fastening on a creel, he finds he can't settle to the task. Instead, he is thinking of the way the sunlight caught the dark red of her hair as it came loose from its bun, her gray eyes and quick smile.

Her manner is cool, prim even, but he likes that. He senses her mistrust, and beneath that her uncertainty—it's there in the way she smooths her dress, the way her eyes flick away from his, but he remembers too how they ran up the lane, hand in hand, the unexpected freedom of her laughter. He went to the West Highlands once, and in woodland there came across a hind, away from its herd. It raised its head when it saw him and became completely still, alert. He had felt strangely moved by its wariness. He knew that any sudden step or noise and it would bolt, so he too kept himself still, hoping to reassure it with his lack of threat, thinking what a rare thing it would be, even for a moment, to gain its trust. Dorothy reminds him of this, and Joseph knows he mustn't scare her because if he does, he'll lose her.

Please, God, if you grant me one thing, let it be her.

Now

The Shop

Everyone says they've never seen a winter like it. The snow just won't stop. On some days the air is thick with soft swirling flakes, on others the villagers huddle around their hearths as blizzards rattle windows and whine down chimneys. The crofters on the hill have to dig their sheep out of drifts; some families bring their hens inside, like the old days, letting them roost in the cottage, fluffing up their feathers to catch the warmth of the stove. There are days too when the flakes float down silently, gently, and then the men gather to clear Copse Cross Street while the children fight and play in the ancient way of children, feudally, pitching Carnegies against Mackintoshes, boys against girls, older against younger.

The shop is busy. It's warm in there with the stove blazing, and Mrs. Brown has brought down her big black kettle to heat on the hob and keep the tea coming.

Ailsa rests her knitting on her knee and stretches her fingers. "They'll be talking about this winter for a long time to come."

Norah turns from her place at the window, knitting sheath at her waist, needles never still in her hands. "They'll be talking about a lot of things for a long time to come." She waits for a response, then carries on anyway. "I've not seen Joseph so out of sorts since—well, you know, the other storm."

Ailsa holds the jersey up and tilts her head. "You still need to show me the trick with your anchor pattern, Norah.

Joseph, you say? There's been talk at the alehouse about him again. It's not right, it isn't."

Mrs. Brown pauses in her restocking of the shelves. "Oh, yes, Scott stirring trouble again, is he?"

"Not just Scott, my Bert said. People should know better, they shouldn't talk about things they know nothing of."

"It *was* strange, though, wasn't it?" Norah casts a meaningful look at Mrs. Brown. "How much it changed him, I mean. He was never the same after."

Mrs. Brown's answer is swift. "Wouldn't it change you, finding the boot of a child swept out to sea in a storm? Then everyone wondering but never asking what you knew about it?"

Ailsa puts down her knitting. Her voice is uncertain, and she fiddles with a stray curl, as she always does when she feels uncomfortable. "Well, there was what Jeanie saw from her window. You know, Dorothy and Joseph the day of the storm. You can't deny that, whatever you think."

"I don't deny what she said she saw, but that woman loves to tittle-tattle. How much could she really see? And she certainly heard nothing. And"—she turns back—"we all know why she doesn't like Dorothy."

Ailsa and Norah share a glance.

"Anyway." Norah sticks to her point. "I'm only saying. The talk at the alehouse is the old talk. That he knew just where to go to find Moses's boot—he went straight to it. No smoke without fire, as they say."

The set of Mrs. Brown's shoulders makes her feelings quite clear. "You can't tell me Joseph would hurt a child. I mean that's what these hints and sly comments amount to, isn't it? Let's not beat about the bush. It's a wicked thing to say."

Norah's face flushes. "Well, of course that's not what I think—"

"Then best say nothing at all," Mrs. Brown says as she goes to the shelves at the back of the shop, as though that's the end of the matter. Once out of sight, her shoulders sag.

If only they'd leave the subject alone.

Ailsa and Norah don't know the half of it.

And not for the last time, she wishes she didn't either.

Dorothy

On the days Dorothy teaches, just two a week now, she is grateful for the routine that is second nature to her after so many years, the letters and sums formed, unthinking, on the board, the lessons she knows like the back of her hand. And on the days she's not teaching, she goes to the Sands. Today when she goes down the Steps, bent sideways on the climb to lean and support herself, ungloved hand gripping rock, it's as though the land itself is melting away, from the thick blanket of white at the top of the cliff to the patchwork of snow on the sand that thins at the shoreline where the sea washes in and washes out. On the Rocks, a cormorant lands and balances, wings outstretched, eye spun toward her.

Dorothy quickly turns away and, unbidden, a memory comes, of the way the wind would froth Moses's curls, and she'd hold his hand tight, him pulling like a dog on a leash, but the sea was treacherous just there, not one for swimming in with its unexpected depths and sly currents, but pull he would, and lead her to the frill of waves, before the sea sucked them back in. They did what you are meant to do, crouching down to pick up small crabs—*carefully, carefully, don't let the claws get you*—and the claws waved impotently as they were sloshed into the bucket, and shells went in there too, razor clams—*be careful of the edges, no, not that one, there's something in it, I think it's dead.* They'd thread their way between the hulking sterns of the fishing boats, nod to the fishermen working on their boats, and the boy would want to get closer to watch, but best not disturb them at their labor. Later, they'd pour Moses's treasure into a rock pool, or the bottom of the spring that bounced over the rocks on to the beach, and clamber up the Steps, and Dorothy would tell Moses to take his boots off, put his empty bucket down, and change his trousers, and ignore his complaints, because you couldn't get your own way at that age, not at any age, not really.

Dorothy searches her memory for his smile.

She doesn't hear the Minister clambering down the stony steps and crossing the beach; she's at the very line between land and sea, its foaming edge thinning to a dark shadow in the sand just where the toes of her boots are.

"Dorothy?"

Dorothy startles and turns. She has always been Miss Aitken or Mrs. Gray to the villagers, a nod to her coming to the village as a teacher, and all the mothers and fathers calling her that, and then all their children, even when grown up. She likes the distance it has made between them, all of them always at arm's length. And she knows the women don't really like her; her so stiff, with some learning, not knowing how to be a part of their womanly talk, their sly jokes about their sex lives, their eye-rolling about their husbands.

She grips her jumper tight in her fist, just at the place between her breasts where there is nothing, no bone, no muscle. What can the Minister want with her now that's so urgent he's followed her down to the Sands? Dorothy's mind skips over the possibilities. Not the boy, not the boy. The Kirk? The knitting. She's not been doing her knitting.

"Is it the knitting?"

"The—what?" The Minister looks Dorothy up and down,

and it's only now she realizes she has forgotten her coat and her gloves, notices the way her hand is balled in the middle of her chest, hair blowing this way and that in the icy gusts that blow in from the sea. Briefly, she looks back. The cormorant has gone.

"Dorothy—are you—?" He stops. His voice softens. "I wondered if I could talk to you? The Kirk—I—need your help. It's Jenny—the baby has come early. Why don't we . . . ?" He puts out his hand tentatively, as you might to a wild animal, trying not to scare it, pausing to judge, then letting it rest gently on Dorothy's arm, to hold her there. "Why don't we go back up to your house to talk about it?"

Dorothy follows him. Her hands are numb, and she can't think how she forgot everything when usually she is so particular. When they get inside, it is the Minister who makes the fire come alive again, who puts the kettle on to boil. He even fetches a blanket to put around her shoulders as she shivers in her chair.

He places the cup in her hand and explains. "Jenny's pains came very suddenly. We thought there were still a few weeks at least to go. I had wondered about asking before and have left it a bit late, I'm afraid. I thought maybe Jenny would feel able to—anyway, the boy needs somewhere quiet, somewhere safe. We'd manage at school for a short while without you. Margaret won't mind doing a few more days till the Christmas holidays. And even after, if it comes to it." It would just be till the snow thaws, he tells her, and they find out where he has come from.

Dorothy can't quite understand what it is he is saying at first. He isn't asking whether the child can come to live with her, is he? Then the thought arrives. *Surely he can't think that in the place of one lost child, another can come?* She frowns and tries to think, pulling the blanket tighter around her

80

shoulders. Her own minister back home used to tell them that in the face of a difficult duty, you must be strong and courageous, and here was her minister now asking her Christian duty of her in this request to look after one of the flock, a lost sheep. Her mother would have expected no less. She shuts her eyes, and for a moment it is as though she is in the room. *We are unworthy servants; we have only done what was our duty*, she would say if the Minister praised Dorothy for anything, for a reading, or her studies, or her work in the Kirk.

But this? This is beyond all call of duty. She knows this has nothing to do with—all that—but to be faced every day with . . . No, for once, she is going to say no.

"I'm sorry, Minister, I would like to help in your time of need, but I think, maybe, there is probably someone else who could do this for you," and after he's gone, she sinks farther into her chair, tightening her hands around her cup of tea, steadying fingers which are trembling because the past is at the door again, banging against the timber, louder and more insistent, trying to get in.

She sleeps, which is unusual for Dorothy during the day, always keeping busy with the Kirk, the alms for the poor, the knitting, when she's not at the school. The cottage is quiet and still when she wakes, and it is like a fever has broken, her troubles of the last few weeks just a dream.

The fact is it was all a very long time ago. She can barely remember any of it now and, in truth, why would she try? She's sure the other villagers think she was cold, that she didn't grieve, but we are all different, and she wasn't brought up to make a public show of herself. You just got on with it all and made the best of it. And, as she keeps telling herself, this poor child is really nothing to do with it.

She sits up, shaking off the blanket. The Kirk needs her and so does the Minister; he trusts her to take on this responsibility, he has asked her. She stands up, her resolve growing. No, she will show herself that she can do this, do her duty by the Kirk and look after the boy until his home is found. And so it is that a short time later she finds herself standing outside the Manse, hearing the bell ring through the house and waiting for Martha to open the door. It is the Minister who answers, as luck would have it, and Dorothy takes a deep breath.

"Minister, I wasn't quite myself earlier. First of all, I didn't congratulate you and Jenny on the birth of your baby, you must forgive me. But also I've had a think about what you asked and, on reflection, the child can come to me, as soon as you need."

He looks uncertain. "Are you sure?"

"I am, completely. I don't know what came over me."

His face sags with relief. "Thank you so much, Dorothy. I am grateful I can rely on you. Jenny is keen to—anyway, she'll be very glad. I'll be down to see you soon to discuss arrangements."

Dorothy takes her cue and steps back from the door. But before she leaves, she glances up at the window of the bedroom the child is staying in, and her heart beats just a little bit faster before she turns for home.

Mrs. Brown

Mrs. Brown is later than she should be getting up. What would her husband have said? But he's gone now, along with one of her brothers, so close together she'd barely reeled from the loss of her husband before the storm came that took the *Fulmar* down, and her brother with it. And then, before all that, there'd been the babies that never opened their eyes or drew breath. She can feel their tiny weight in her bloodied hands even now, feel those first tugs of pain that had her gripping her belly, the flood of warmth on her thighs, the cruel pantomime of woman's labor. So many times. Until at last there was Fergus, the child that clung to life, the one she held while he drew his first gasping breaths, the one who stayed just long enough for her to believe. Mrs. Brown closes her eyes against the memory of his still form in the crib, white and cold.

When she opens them again after a long breath out, she goes to the window and looks down at the cobbled street below, then up the hill. The snow is falling fast and silent again, and she watches the lamplighter climb his ladder to quench the street lamp on Copse Cross Street, snowflakes like sparks of fire in its golden glow. Lights are appearing in windows now, but it's still too early for anyone to have ventured forth. Mrs. Brown thinks of the morning Joseph carried the boy up the hill to the Manse and remembers his shocked expression.

And Dorothy's.

Have some pity, she had said that morning . . .

. . . and remembers the day of the candy cane.

She hadn't often stocked sweets in those days—not like now, with her glass jars all in a row on the shelves behind the counter, stuffed full of them—but the seller had had a box of candy canes left over that a shopkeeper in one of the seaside towns didn't want. You know the places—women strolling on the beach with their sun umbrellas or straw hats, boys with their trousers rolled up for paddling, rowing boats for hire, and goodness knows what else people do these days for the fun of it. Not like Skerry Sands, where the boats are for going out to the fishing grounds and the children sit on the Rocks to dangle for crabs with cracked black mussel shells.

Anyway, they had been a sight to see, these candy canes, bright white and red stripes, and she'd bought them on a whim and put them in a jar on the counter, and you'd have thought that the whole village had been waiting for them, because hadn't they just flocked in all day with their sticky hands and coins?

Well, that day there had been a blue sky, and the sun had been bright and warm. Everyone had been out and about, or that's what it had seemed like, the bell jangling nonstop, till she'd wedged the door open to let in a bit of air. In a quieter moment, she'd stood outside and seen Dorothy and Moses coming up the hill, him pulling like a puppy on a lead, and her in her summer frock, all buttoned at the neck and wrists, one of those people who looks like their clothes have been pressed while they're wearing them, and the lad the same, shorts stiff like cardboard, socks pulled up to the knee, no sagging around his ankles like the other kids, and there he'd been, straining at the end of her arm. When she'd seen where they were headed, she'd gone inside and taken up her position behind the counter.

It had been cool and dark, and the candy canes had gleamed white and gaudy in the gloom. His eyes got big at the very sight of them. He didn't speak much, so people said, but she'd heard him, all around the shop, whispering, "Mamma, mamma, mamma," but you'd think Dorothy was deaf, for she'd never said a word, nor looked at the lad nor showed any sign at all he was there.

When she'd got to the counter, she'd laid out her usual purchases, asked for sugar and cheese, but the boy's eyes had never left the candy canes, and while Mrs. Brown had been weighing and slicing, he had been pulling at Dorothy's arm, yanking it, but Mrs. Brown had seen nothing in her, and she'd thought, *If you'd only get off your high horse, maybe I could like you, maybe we all could, because we all know children will drive you to madness with their begging and nagging, and sure, they'd all have understood, if only she'd said something, or asked for help, even once.*

What she'd done, she'd done on an impulse, maybe to please the child or get something, anything, out of the mother, she hadn't been sure, but she'd finished her wrapping and taken one of those glowing canes out of the jar and leaned over the counter till she was eye to eye with the child.

"There you go, lad, you can have that, as a wee gift from me," and then she'd straightened up, rolled her shoulders back, and pulled the pencil from behind her ear, and added up the cost of everything else as though nothing had happened at all.

"That'll be two shillings and sixpence, please," and she'd looked at Dorothy and willed her to say something, but Dorothy's face hadn't moved at all, though she'd held Mrs.

Brown's gaze as she'd put the coins on the counter and taken the parcel. Moses, meanwhile, hadn't been able to stop staring from his candy cane to his mother's face, and back again. They'd left the shop, and Mrs. Brown remembers looking at Dorothy's hand holding his free one and noticing how her knuckles had been pure white.

Later, when the afternoon had cooled, and all the candy canes had been sold, she'd swept and tidied the shop, then gone outside to sweep and tidy her patch there too because the boats would be coming in soon, and there had been supper to make.

Suddenly something white had caught her eye and there, in the shadows of the alley by the shop, had been a neatly folded handkerchief.

Mrs. Brown hadn't needed to unwrap it to know what was inside.

She sighs now. She was only given one small child herself, just the one chance, yet here is Dorothy, about to be given another when Mrs. Brown isn't sure she'd even deserved the first. She shakes her head free of the thought. *There's always a plan, even when we can't see it ourselves*, she reminds herself. It all means something, of that she is sure. The sea gives and the sea takes away, you learn that, here in the towns and villages that cling to the cliffs. What it has given this time she doesn't understand, but she knows it is for Dorothy, and maybe— and she couldn't have said how she knows it—not just Dorothy, and she goes downstairs, slowing her pace so Rab can keep up, his old legs struggling these days but his tail still wagging, and starts to make the shop ready for the day.

Dorothy

Dorothy stands outside Moses's room, blood pounding in her ears. She takes a deep breath and puts her hand on the door handle for a second time. It's been years since she's been inside. Her arm drops to her side again. She's been trying for five minutes to go in, but now she's wondering if it would be the wrong thing for the child to be in there anyway. She will need to look after him during the day. Maybe better to be by the hearth downstairs, close to the kitchen, rather than her running up and down the stairs to check. Yes, much better as well not to be in the room of a child who is lost.

She makes up a bed in the room downstairs that looks out to the sea and brings in a bowl for washing and a jug. The Minister assured her they would bring clothes that the villagers had given for the child, and a stew that Martha had made, but she'll go to the shop to get a few things herself.

"The child is coming to you, then?" Mrs. Brown's eyebrows are raised as she calculates the cost of oats, carbolic soap, flour, cheese. For a moment she holds on to a box of tea. "Are you ready for him?"

Dorothy is surprised at the blunt question, though less so these days at how Mrs. Brown always knows everything. "Nearly, thank you. A few more things to organize." She places the goods in her basket, hands over a list for another day. "I'd be grateful if the delivery boy brought these, as I may not be leaving home for a while."

Mrs. Brown nods and glances at the piece of paper. "Good to be prepared," is all she says.

On the way back down the hill, Dorothy ticks off the things she has needed to do or get: breakfast oats, bed made, bread made, peat and wood brought in to keep the fire going, eggs in the egg basket. Yes, she is prepared.

It doesn't occur to her that this is not what Mrs. Brown means at all.

Then

Dorothy

In the Kirk, Dorothy sits in her usual place at the back. She tries to listen to the sermon, but her eyes keep drifting to Joseph. The few times she's seen him he has always been in the same place, on the other side of the aisle, between Jeanie and Agnes. She wonders whether this is custom or choice, and if it's choice, whose?

After the sermon there is the rustling and low murmur of people rising to leave, but Joseph stays seated, his head bowed. Dorothy looks at him for just a little too long to be able to avoid, as she usually does, some of the polite chat outside.

"How are you, Miss Aitken?"

Dorothy stops and turns. It is Jeanie, alone, Agnes standing farther away with her friends. She feels their sidelong glances, hears their brittle laughter. Jeanie has never spoken to her before. She has a lined and careworn face close up and pale eyes, like someone who has been rubbed out slightly, faded. Dorothy isn't sure if it's the way the light is falling or whether there is a suggestion of a bruise on her cheekbone. But she has a strong feeling she is not simply inquiring after her well-being. Jeanie doesn't wait for Dorothy to answer. Instead, she leans in and her eyes narrow. "Let me give you a word of advice," and she taps the side of her nose, "the reputation of the schoolmistress is very important—there's no place for gentleman friends."

Dorothy is stunned. "I beg your pardon?"

"You don't want to be starting tongues wagging."

Agnes and her friends are making no secret of the fact they are listening now. They stare with folded arms. Dorothy is taken aback by the judgment in their faces.

"He's only mending windows. Being polite. That's our Joe all over. I've known him since he was a wee lad. His mother was my best friend, and he and my Agnes—well, I'm sure you can work it out. No point you getting the wrong end of the stick and embarrassing yourself."

Is this what people are saying? That she's making a fool of herself? She glances back at the door to the Kirk. In the dim shadows inside, she thinks she sees Joseph's shape in the aisle, his face turned toward her. Or is he looking at Agnes? And quickly, before she can find out, she turns on her heel, trying to contain the horror rising in her chest until she gets home.

The next Saturday in the shop, Mrs. Brown is cutting butter for Dorothy with the wire expertly balanced, paper ready at the side for wrapping it.

"Will you not be wanting the delivery boy to bring it over for you? Maybe with a little ham for Joseph? He's partial to a bit of ham."

Dorothy stares at her, but Mrs. Brown doesn't look up. Butter wrapped with deft fingers, she reaches for the cheese, holds the wire. Dorothy opens her mouth to say something, then shuts it again.

"Here?" Mrs. Brown brings the wire down, then moves it to indicate a larger block. "Or here?"

Dorothy points to show the smaller piece. She steadies herself. "And no ham, thank you." Her voice is quiet. She knows she is being mocked.

When Mrs. Brown finally looks up, her eyes are unreadable, her voice light as though commenting on something of no importance. "You should know—you're not the only woman with plans for Joseph."

Dorothy feels like somebody has winded her. Her hands shake a little as she puts the coins on the counter. She tries to raise her eyebrows as though she can't think why Mrs. Brown would imagine she is interested in this tittle-tattle.

She hates the breathiness of her voice when she speaks. "Have my shopping delivered for me today, please," and she leaves the shop, shutting the door briskly behind her, the little bell jangling.

She can only be thankful that, for once, the other women weren't there to hear.

When Dorothy leaves the shop, she feels so blinded by humiliation that she nearly walks into Agnes and her group of friends. They are talking in low voices, but when they see Dorothy they fall silent. Agnes gives Dorothy a sidelong look, one that seems to take in everything about her, but then she turns her back and starts to speak again to her friends, elbowing one of them in the ribs.

"It won't be long now, Mam says. He's as good as asked. He's always up at the cottage."

Dorothy can't help but hear because she is meant to hear.

"Mam says Joseph will make me a fine husband, and I think I know how to make him a fine wife." The others gasp, then look shamefaced as Agnes starts laughing.

Dorothy hurries up the hill with her basket but all she can see is Agnes's open laughing mouth, the way she stared at Dorothy, the discomfort of the others. They pity her, just like the girls at school used to; this is why Jeanie spoke to her, this is why Agnes was so full of hostility outside the Kirk.

She has managed to walk away with her back straight, but

91

inside she feels sick with her own stupidity. The only thing that matters to her in this moment is that Joseph never, ever finds out—not now, not later—what an utter fool she has been.

Once home, she can barely breathe with the shame of it. Upstairs, she changes out of her dress, and by the time Joseph knocks on the door she is ready, shawl pulled tight and hair scraped back. She returns his look, but not his smile, stands back to let him in, saying nothing, only checking he's felt the ice in her. Dorothy barely notices his stricken expression as she steps out into the brisk wind of the summer afternoon.

And so a new pattern is made. She leaves before he is due and walks down to Skerry Sands. She has a hard-wearing pair of boots now and has made a dress that hangs slightly shorter than her others for wet days, and down here with the wind blowing the white foam off the cresting waves, the fish-salt-seaweed smell blowing with it, she walks. She never speaks to the fishermen or goes near the boats but sits on the rocks at the back of the beach, watching the birds and waves, watching the fisher-girls coming in and out of the fish house halfway up the hill at the far end of the Sands, their chatter and laughter drifting, half heard, on the breeze.

What had she been thinking? *I didn't raise you to have your head turned by the first man who pays you an empty compliment.* A picture of herself in her navy dress, making sure she has good bread and cheese ready for him, her hair freed from its bun, haunts her. And the kiss. She shuts her eyes. How sorry he must have felt for her. Who was he, really, other than the man the Minister had asked to mend the windows? She knows the other women think she is prim, and so she is. How stupid to think she can be anything else.

She makes herself think of Agnes, of them together,

walking on the sand, or alone in the kitchen at Jeanie's house, the girl waiting for the leaves to steep, two cups on the table, maybe a cake, their easy chat, how she knows the way to make him laugh, comfortable with him in a familiarity born of long attachment. He'd even mentioned Agnes the day they'd stood on the Tops together in the rain. She twists the skin of her arm with thumb and forefinger. How foolish she has been.

And so a day comes soon when she returns to the windows tight and secure, the job done, the frames fitting snugly together, just in time for the cooler autumn breeze that can't get in now but sometimes picks up the dead leaves and throws them, brown and dry, against the cold glass.

Joseph

Joseph doesn't understand. What did he do wrong? That first time when she opened the door after going to the Tops, her icy politeness made him weak. The next Saturday, there was a note on the door to let himself in, so he did his work without her there, listening always for her step. Then he came early to catch her, hoping she would open the door to him wearing her blue dress, her hair soft and loose, but instead she'd already left and, in fact, he saw her hurrying down the hill toward the Sands.

Maybe he'd misjudged her. He looks at his hands, their roughness. On his boat, despite how hard they work to keep it clean, there is always the lingering smell of the daily catch, the barnacled hull, the mess the seabirds make. And then there was the cormorant and her horrified, frightened expression.

He starts to comb over every detail of their times together: how different she seemed after taking in the tea; had she said yes because she didn't know how to say no? Her first comment, *What about the windows?* comes back to him. Why hadn't he noticed that more at the time, instead of thinking she was nervous or shy? Did he imagine the way she stepped into the circle of his arm in the rain? As he tries to understand what went wrong, her smile and her questions, the kiss, the thrill he was sure he'd sensed in her on the boat start to fade, until all he can remember is her fear and her wariness and her reluctance to come at all. After all, who was he really, other than the man the Minister had asked to mend the windows?

He thinks of the hind in the woodland and knows it is already too late, so the last Saturday when he goes he stays longer, finishes the job, ensures the cottage is wind-tight for the winter. He completes everything so that he need never come back to the empty house and her absence, or—even worse to him now—her presence with its distant, cool politeness.

And as he leaves, closing the door for the last time, he sees, in amongst the pile of dead leaves and twigs swept to the side of the house for autumn burning, the hem of a dress, soft and blue.

Now

Dorothy

Dorothy has checked and checked again that she has everything she needs. There is a lively fire in the room that leads from the kitchen, a good soup bubbling on the hob, a teapot with the leaves steeping for when the Minister and Martha arrive with the child. She goes into the other room to check again that everything is ready, then upstairs to fetch a lamp for later, but as she passes her own child's bedroom, she stops. She puts her hand to the wooden door, pictures the bed, the toys that have lain so still in the box, unplayed with, for so long.

What is she doing?

She swallows hard and hesitates. It's not too late to change her mind—no, they'll have to understand. How could she possibly have thought . . . ? She turns and runs downstairs. If she leaves now, she can be at the Manse in time, and she rushes to the door and opens it—

To Joseph. Holding the boy.

Joseph's face reflects her own shock. It is a moment before she sees the Minister and Martha behind him.

The Minister smiles, a small frown puckering his brow. "Shall we come in? Dorothy?"

Dorothy steps aside, wordless, caught in the face of something that feels inevitable, that is too late to avert. Joseph is carrying the boy like he did that first day, and Dorothy turns her thought away from the memory of his white face, his wet clothes, his blue hanging foot. Now he is warm, swaddled in a blanket, and Joseph brings him inside with a squall of snow.

The Minister takes control. "Through here, Joseph. Martha, put the stew on the table. Dorothy, where do you want the clothes and toys?"

Dorothy feels dazed. She takes the bag and puts it on a chair. She glances through the doorway and sees Joseph gently tucking the child into the bed she has made up. For a moment, she is somewhere else, out of time, and she turns away, unable to watch anymore. Back in the kitchen, she hurries to fill the teapot.

She clears her throat, puts a hand to her bun, and wishes she'd worn a different dress. "Does everyone want . . . ?" She holds up the teapot.

Joseph comes through and shakes his head and addresses himself to the Minister instead, in a thinking aloud kind of way, so that she hears. "I imagine he'll need his food, Minister, maybe more often than at the usual times? And a fire will need to be kept burning too."

"Yes, Joseph. I think I know that, thank you," but Joseph doesn't look at her when she says it, and when he goes to leave, she follows him, holds open the door. They are standing close to each other, and suddenly she wants to say something, anything, but there is too much and nowhere to begin—and what would be the point after all this time anyway?

"Goodbye, Joseph," is all she says, but he is already closing the door, turning his back on her, and Martha and the Minister are telling her this and that, what the boy has and hasn't done, what he can and cannot do, about his clothes, and Dorothy tries to follow what they say, while her heart bangs in her chest, because of the child, because of Joseph. She can't think, offers more tea, anything to keep them there.

"So you know what to do?" Martha's smile is kind, but her doubt is not lost on Dorothy.

The Minister cuts in. "You don't need to worry about Dorothy, Martha. She's taught several generations of our children here, and of course was once . . . " He coughs, clearly unsure how to end the sentence. "I didn't mean that. I meant . . . Mrs. Gray, are you all right?"

But Dorothy is barely listening now. *Mother*, the Minister had been going to say. *Was once a mother*, and she's looking through the doorway at the boy, who is looking back at her with haunted eyes, uncertain.

"Mrs. Gray?"

She comes back to herself. "Yes, Martha, don't worry," and finally it is time for Martha and the Minister to go, and she is left with the silence, the snow-light, and the child.

She stays in the kitchen, twisting her apron in her hands. She can't seem to move from her place by the stove. She stirs the soup again, though it was made almost before daybreak. At last, taking a deep breath, she goes into the other room. The child is half propped up in the bed and looking straight at her. He is more awake, more alert than the last time she saw him, when he was staring blankly at her in the bedroom at the Manse. The bruising on his face is almost gone and he looks less drawn. This has only increased the uncomfortable similarities: his age, the color of his eyes—all meaningless, all coincidence, of course, but unfortunate. The silence stretches between them while she tries to think of something to say.

"Hello," she says in the end, helplessly. She puts her hand to her chest. "I'm Dorothy." Then she repeats it, more slowly. "You?" He stares back but shows no understanding. Then she says the most obvious thing, the thing a mother might say. "Are you hungry? Food?" She uses her hand to show what she means, lifting her fingers to her mouth. The boy tilts his head and carries on staring. She's relieved to go back into the kitchen. She'll save Martha's stew for the next day and ladles her soup into a bowl instead. There is only one tray, and she goes back in and he sits up when he sees what she is carrying.

"Here you are, then," and settles it on his lap. She goes to pick up the spoon, but he has already reached for it, so she fetches her own and balances the bowl on her knees by the fire.

The child is busy eating, and Dorothy sips hers till he's finished. He's eaten most but not all of it and nibbled some of the bread. She takes the tray away and her own, almost-full bowl, and when she goes back in, he is sitting up, heavy-eyed with sleepiness now. Dorothy stands uncertainly in the room, then picks up the box of toys the villagers have donated. She puts it on the little table next to his bed.

"Toys," she says encouragingly. "Shall we see what's in there?" and she rifles through, picks out different things. "Building bricks! Crayons! Oh, and what's this?" It's a little pull-along toy, a small dog on a piece of string, and she goes to put it on the floor, but the boy is showing no interest. "You look," she says, pushing the box toward him, and he leans over, gazes listlessly into the box, but then his eyes brighten and he smiles. He delves into the box and pulls his hand out holding a brightly colored ball.

Dorothy freezes. She looks from the ball to his face. "Give it to me," she says. "Choose another one," but the boy's fingers tighten around it. Dorothy stands up and stumbles into the kitchen. She leans on the table and tells herself she's being daft. It doesn't mean anything. Nothing. But still.

She goes to the doorway.

The boy is already asleep, the ball held loosely in his hand.

She's never been back into his room, though she could never have told anyone why—she has never been able to tell anyone anything—but now she goes upstairs. When she turns the handle, for a moment she sees nothing. Slowly, shadow shapes loom in the darkness: the wooden bed with its high headboard below the covered window; the chest of drawers where his clothes are, folded and mothballed; the blanket box that holds his toys in the space between the end of the bed and the wall.

She takes another step and sees somebody's head on the bolster. Her throat traps her breath as she tries to scream; she wants to turn and run, but she's transfixed by the glitter of eyes staring in the gloom. She starts to back out of the room before she sees it is just Arthur, Moses's teddy bear, and her knees nearly give way in relief and fear. She stumbles to the curtains and rips them open. Light and dust fill the room, clouds of dust, ancient universes of it, till Dorothy is coughing and gasping, her apron to her mouth, bent over.

She sinks to the bed, shaking, and it is a few minutes before she can raise her head. She picks up Arthur, looks into his black face, his snout, his glassy gaze. Moses had loved Arthur fiercely, protectively. She'd hear him talking to the bear at night, whispering, and she would wonder what he said when he said so little to her.

Arthur stares back at her, mute, unblinking, and she wonders what he knows that she doesn't, what he remembers; she wishes she could open his head, so full of the secrets Moses shared in the dark, but suddenly she can't bear his unflinching gaze and drops him back on the bed. And besides, she has come in for a different reason.

She kneels on the floor then and opens the toy box, the smell of must and age billowing out, but here, sealed away, the toys still look bright and ready to play with—the tin soldiers lying side by side, the spinning top with its gaudy elephants and clowns, tipped on its axis; she even touches it, flicks the cold metal, and it spins, much quicker than expected after all this time, the elephants and clowns merging together till she can't tell which is which.

But none of these is what she has come in for. Where is Moses's own ball? Jane had given it to him, a red India rubber ball, and Moses had been obsessed with it, insisting on taking it everywhere. It had driven Dorothy half mad, leaving marks on clean glass and whitewashed walls, rolling across the floor to be tripped over, even breaking a plate when it had bounced on the hard kitchen floor. In fact, it had caused so much bother that Dorothy wondered if that had been the point of it, after all—not a toy for Moses but a trial for her.

Where is it? Everything else is in the toy box where it should be, but not that. She starts searching more frantically, pulling clothes out of drawers, feeling under the bed, dragging the bed linen onto the floor. Afterward, she looks at the mess she's made. It's no good, it isn't anywhere, and she goes downstairs, makes another pot of tea, and sits at the table. She steadies her breathing, lets time pass till her behavior starts to seem faintly ridiculous now that shadows have been chased out of corners with the brightening afternoon. When she goes back upstairs, she puts everything back; she dusts and shakes and organizes and smooths and sweeps till the room is spick and span, till it looks like no one ever lived in it. She needs to pull herself together, her silly imaginings, her tiredness; the past cannot be revisited, nor can it revisit her.

Once downstairs, she stands again in the doorway, looking

at the sleeping child. Why the ball? Why that toy? And quietly she goes to him, lifts his fingers, and takes it away.

Later, what she will remember of those first few days of the child staying—when the past blew into the house with the wind, and with it the ghost of her child, Moses—are these moments; the child asleep, hand like a starfish under his cheek, silvery hair on the pillow, his gentle breath. He sleeps for hours at a time, and she watches him, wondering how far he has come, how he came to be in the sea, what journey he has taken. That first night she settles in a chair near him, an oil lamp burning in case he should wake.

A gale is battering against the panes, and she pulls the blankets up to her chin, and in the gap between sleep and wakefulness she feels some presence flying on the wind, over the tips of the waves toward her, as she dreams of the gift the sea has brought to her.

Joseph

Joseph kneels on the deck of his boat, hunkering down by the brazier, and opens his parcel of food—the bread he made, heavy and hard without a woman's touch, cheese from Mrs. Brown's—and gazes up the beach at the clumps of dead grass growing out of the cliff that shiver now and then in the icy breeze and thin snow squall.

Seeing Dorothy, speaking to her, has shaken him. Where he'd wanted to lean on his familiar resentment, he'd felt something unexpected—was it pity? Bringing a child to her door in his arms, when she'd lost so much, when it was something he'd been unable to do so many years before, seeing her flustered in her own home had made him want to reach out, to reassure her. What a fool he is, after everything. How much easier anger is to feel than this dreadful weakness.

He curses the tremble in his hands, clenches and unclenches them again, to get control of it. A movement catches his eye, and when he turns a child is running toward him erratically, as children do, chubby legs stumbling, and in the sun flare that catches the snow on the cliff, for a moment he falls back in time, and it's almost as though it's Moses, slipping loose of his mother all those years ago, scrambling down the stone steps toward the sea.

Joseph's heart had quickened back then, seeing a chance

not only to return the boy to safety but also to see Dorothy herself. When he'd held out his hand, the boy had reached up with his own, fingers outstretched like a starfish, squinting against the sun's glare, which haloed his hair. Joseph had felt sad for the boy with no daddy, and for Dorothy with no husband, or at least no husband who was there. No one quite bought the story that he'd only moved away for a job, because why did he never visit? And on a whim, instead of walking Moses back up the beach, Joseph had said, "Come on, lad," and had led him to the water, the edge of the great sea, where the waves were tiny, shushing on the pebbly sand, and he'd taken off the boy's little socks and the shoes with a buckle and placed them safely above the tide line. The boy had looked up at Joseph, eyes wide with surprise and then delight, and together they'd run at the waves as they were sucked out to sea, and away from them as they rushed back in, and then, on a whim, Joseph had swung the boy up in his arms and waded out a bit and dipped Moses's feet in the water with a great "*Woooooo*" before quickly pulling them out again, and soon Moses had made the same noise whenever he felt the cold water, but quieter, and Joseph's heart had opened at the sound.

After a bit, though, he'd known he must take him home, so he'd dried off his feet while Moses watched his face, head tilted, smiling each time he caught Joseph's eye, and they'd walked back across the warm sand, hand in hand and up the rocky steps, with the gulls' wild cries above them and along the path back to Dorothy's house.

"Why is he with you?" Her voice had faltered. "I didn't realize he'd gone out the door. I—" and she'd looked as though she was about to say something else, but her cheeks had flamed red and she'd snatched Moses's hand back. "Where was he?"

Joseph had seen her gaze drop just for a second to the boy's legs and the telltale dusting of sand. "Just down on the beach. He was doing no harm."

She hadn't quite raised her eyes to meet his. "Come in now, Moses. This must not happen again. Goodness knows what could have happened," the word *goodness* carrying the weight of her tone, and she'd closed the door while Moses had craned his neck back to look at Joseph through the narrowing gap and had smiled his small, quiet smile when he'd caught his eye.

But as he'd walked away, Joseph was puzzled at her surprise because he'd been sure he'd seen her at the upstairs window looking down on them as they'd climbed the Steps.

Back in the now, Joseph shakes his head to dislodge the memory. Gray clouds have hidden the sun, and a young woman has reached the running child with the chubby legs and caught his hand. "David, don't go on ahead like that!"

Joseph clenches and unclenches his hands, putting down the bread he can hardly hold anymore for the shaking.

Dorothy

In the morning, she comes downstairs with a lamp before the day has broken. She goes through the clothes from the villagers: hardy trousers, jerseys well used but well made, with a wave design on, like so many in Skerry. There are woolen socks and a warm hat, a pair of boots. She'll need to help him get stronger, encourage him to remember and to speak, find out where he's from. She must ask the Minister what efforts are being made to get him home.

When it is light, she goes through with the porridge and gently wakes him, trying to ignore the way her heart jumps each time she sees him. He opens his eyes, frowns, and pushes the tray away, then turns his back to her.

She tries to imagine what it must be like for him, tries to remember what to do with a child who doesn't want what you have to give. She seems to remember Martha saying they'd only given him broths and soups and stews so far, so she takes the porridge back through and warms the last of yesterday's soup and brings that through with a bannock.

"Here," she says, "try this." She touches his shoulder, but this time he pushes her away. She places the food on the little table and goes back into the kitchen. If there's anything she's learned, surely it's waiting and patience? But it's been so long, and frustration rises up. When she goes back in, he has turned his back on the untouched food.

She kneels down and, taking a deep breath, tries again. "Mmm, lovely soup. Might eat it myself." She clinks the spoon in the bowl. She can tell from his stillness that he's listening. "Lovely potatoes." *Clink, clink.* "And cabbage." *Clink.* "Might eat it all."

At last he turns. When he sees there's still soup in the bowl, she's sure he almost smiles. Dorothy sighs in relief and settles the tray on his lap again. She is glad to go back in the kitchen. She sinks into a chair, lifts her cup of tea, then puts it down again. She'd forgotten how trying it can be, how tiring, not knowing what a child wants.

When the doctor visits, Dorothy stays in the room with them. He listens to the boy's heart and lungs, asks him to cough and breathe in, then shows him what he means when he doesn't understand; he feels his arms and legs, flexes them and pronounces him to be recovering well.

"What about other damage?" Dorothy waits till they're out of the room to ask this, so the boy doesn't hear, while the doctor is packing his case at the kitchen table. "Damage you can't see, I mean?"

"You mean to his head? His brain?"

Dorothy nods, closing the door between the rooms.

"There are only superficial cuts and bruises to his head. How he survived at all is a miracle. I was worried at first about his lungs, but unbelievably, there's not even a bone broken. Just a very shocked child. And that"—he snaps his case shut—"is what we're seeing here, I think. Shock, confusion, maybe even temporary amnesia. But physically? With good food and exercise, there's no reason to think he won't make a full recovery. And in time for us to trace his family, hopefully, when the lines are up and the roads open again." He settles his pipe between his teeth and pushes down a plug of tobacco. "That's my recommendation, Mrs. Gray: rest, food, and exercise." He goes to the door, buttoning his coat. "Won't be long," he says, "and he'll be out of your hair."

Through the window, Dorothy watches him cradle the bowl of his pipe from the wind and whirling snow, sees the flare of the match in his cupped hand. *Won't be long.* She breathes a sigh of relief.

The doctor is right. The delivery boy brings food, Dorothy makes soups and stews, the boy eats them, and over the span of a week he gets stronger. She helps him to the privy and bathes him in a tub by the fire, and they've even begun tentative walks round the garden at the back, where he wobbles a little at first, gripping her arm, but every day is stronger, and the snow keeps falling, then falling some more, silent and thick, and still the boy has said nothing, nothing at all.

The Minister's Wife

"Did you take down the jersey I knitted?" Jenny picks the baby up again and tries settling him on her lap and patting his back in the endless round of feeding, winding, changing, comforting. "I'm not sure those donated by the villagers will have fitted." She sighs as the baby starts up his familiar wail and places him, belly down now, over her knee and rocks him from side to side. Colic, the doctor said. Every evening, the exact same time.

She feels a snag of guilt at her impatience with Dorothy, always at the door before the child went there to stay, with one excuse or another. "Alastair? Did you hear me?"

The Minister looks up, frowns, then answers. "Yes, of course I did. Sorry, I'm trying to sort out the rota for the Kirk." He smiles at the baby in her arms. "He's such a good boy."

Jenny rolls her eyes and tentatively places the baby, quiet at last, in the basket. She holds her breath, waits for a whimper that doesn't come. "How was she?"

"Oh, you know Dorothy, she never really changes. Hard to know what she's thinking at the best of times. Unless she disapproves of something—then you know. One thing I did notice though, going in, was that her own little lad's bedroom door was open. In all the years since, I've never seen it anything other than firmly shut."

"Really? That's odd."

"Yes, though she was probably getting something for the boy, I expect." He smiles and finishes his tea. "Definitely a good choice of home while we find his family. Always one to do her duty without fuss." He stands up.

"Are you going out again? I was hoping to heat the water for the tub."

The Minister clears his throat. "I have a bit of delicate business to address with Norah's husband; best if I don't say. I thought I might catch him at the alehouse. I'm sure the little lad won't disturb you. I won't be long."

If it's about Norah's husband and the postmaster's wife, Alastair must be the last one to know, she thinks. "I'll not wait up, then," she says, and sighs as the door closes.

She leans back, enjoying the peace. The tiny snuffle of the baby, the occasional sputter of the fire. Her thoughts drift back to Dorothy. Her story is part of the fabric of the village. The lost child. So hard to think of, especially now she is a mother herself. The baby is still asleep, but she bends down and picks him up anyway, holds him close to her chest and breathes him in, her cheek to his soft hair.

Jenny thinks about the door in Dorothy's house, the one to Moses's bedroom, the door that had always been shut. Wouldn't that have been just like Dorothy, so closed up herself. She finds she doesn't want to put the baby down, but instead carries him through to the kitchen, intending to fetch a pan to heat the water for the tub. The baby wriggles and wakes up, and now she's there she changes her mind. She cuts herself a slice of Martha's fruit loaf one-handed and, bobbing the baby up and down, eats it standing at the table.

Maybe they'll go straight to bed—she'll have him with her for the first part of the night.

But later, even when she's lying under the blanket, the baby warm on top of her, chubby hand entangled in her hair, she still can't settle.

Her mind turns back to the door again. She shivers and clutches the baby closer. She can't help it, but somehow it is not the door to a bedroom she sees at all, but one to a tomb that has just been opened instead.

Dorothy

Each morning, Dorothy is up before dawn to carry out her new routine: waking up the fires, filleting fish, knocking back dough to make loaves or bannocks in the solitude before it's time to rouse him. A silence has fallen around the house with the snow so that, these mornings, she can almost imagine her home is an island in a frozen sea of white.

Today there's a soft pad of feet, and when Dorothy turns, the child is standing in the doorway, rubbing his eyes. Dorothy rushes to the table and pulls out a chair before he can go back to the other room. The boy sits down, waiting for breakfast, and Dorothy sits opposite him while he eats.

She wonders if this would be a good time to try to get him to talk. "Home," she ventures, with a gesture that includes the kitchen and everything else. "This is my home." She emphasizes the word *home*. "Where is yours?" She pauses, then tries again. "Home? With your mammy and daddy?"

The boy looks up and frowns.

"Where is your home? Where is your mammy?" Dorothy repeats.

It's the wrong thing to have said. The boy's mouth turns down. His face whitens, his breath coming quick and fast, and the spoon slips from his fingers, clanging loudly on the table. His face crumples. Dorothy pushes her chair back and kneels on the floor next to his.

"I'm sorry," she says. She doesn't know what to do. His cheeks are wet with tears. "I'm sorry," she says again, but it's not enough because now his arms are on the table and his face is buried in them. "There, there," she says uncertainly. She reaches out to touch his shoulder, to pat his back or make one of those gestures people do to comfort each other, but rests only her fingertips there, in more of a tap than a pat. "There, there, I'm sorry," till at last his breathing settles and she quickly removes her hand. When she moves to the other side of the table again, his cheeks are still wet. Despite her difficulty touching him, she feels a pinch of pride; it's progress, however small, a sign that he's starting to remember.

Later, she bakes shortbread, a reward for the small breakthrough they've made, light and rich with a sprinkling of the sugar Mrs. Brown sent down when he came. He has stayed up longer today, dressed himself and come back to the kitchen where he is sitting, watching her bake. The fire is crackling and the white of sky and snow presses against the windowpanes, the room fragrant with the smell of warm butter.

She wipes her hands on her apron, remembering something. In the other room, from the box of things the villagers gave, she brings back wax crayons and paper. Once she's given them to him she carries on with her cooking, glancing over every now and then to look at the boy bent over the paper. His tongue is poking out of the corner of his mouth and he is frowning with concentration. She resists the urge to peer over his shoulder but instead busies herself with making a pot of tea and tidying his bed.

When the biscuits are cool enough to eat but still warm, she brings them to the table, sets the pot and cups down.

The boy doesn't look up. He is pushing down hard with the crayon clutched in his fist, his face close to the paper, scribbling. When he finishes, he looks almost surprised to find himself still in Dorothy's kitchen. His eyes are dark and scared.

She holds out her hand. "May I see?" She tries a smile. After a moment he passes the piece of paper. Dorothy thanks him, then looks down, curious to see what he's drawn.

It's a picture of a storm. Taking up much of the foreground are rocks, coal black and sharp. He has drawn the sea as children do, the up and down dipping of the waves, overlapping, interlocking, higher and higher, the scribble of a wild night sky. She peers closer; between the waves, tiny against the heaving water, is a stick figure, a child, arms raised, and there, in the corner, is a stick woman in a dress, her eyes and mouth horrified circles, arms waving, looking for him.

Dorothy's breath catches.

It's Skerry Sands. There are the Rocks, there the headland to the north of the beach. It was Joseph who found him, so who is the woman?

She stares at the boy, then back down at the picture. She swallows hard. Before she knows what she's doing, she's scraped back her chair. "Excuse me," she says, her heart banging in her chest. She goes out of the room to the door at the back of the house and into the garden. The pain of the icy air in her lungs brings her back to herself, to the stunted apple tree, to the henhouse and the sound of soft clucking, to the ruts of the winter vegetable garden frozen under the snow. Beyond, the sea is gray, white spume just visible as waves heave and break against the headland and the Rocks.

For goodness' sake, she tells herself, he was lost in a storm. What else would she expect a picture of it to show? It's her imagination tricking her. She knew it would be hard, though

115

not in this way. *These things are sent to try us.* She breathes the cold air in deeply. Grips her hands together. She arranges her face so it is expressionless and goes back inside to sit down and pour the tea. The boy has noticed nothing and is nibbling a biscuit he has helped himself to.

Dorothy pulls the drawing toward her again and peers at the woman. He hasn't colored in her dress. All around her are black rocks and seething waves, but the dress itself is the pure white of the paper.

Just like Dorothy's that long-ago night when she was searching for her own child in the storm.

Then

Dorothy

She avoids him. It is getting colder, so she stays indoors more. She knits and spins and sometimes she reads in the evening by the light of a lamp or goes to the Kirk to sweep the path clear of leaves before the light fades. She spends longer in the schoolroom tidying or planning what to do the next day with the children who are set against learning. But mostly she just sits in her chair and stares at nothing.

She won't cry.

Her name is on the work rota for Thursday evenings, when she sweeps the stone floors of the Kirk, then mops them. She dusts and polishes the pews, which never need dusting and polishing because there is always someone willing to show their devotion in this way. Dorothy likes how tired it makes her. The autumn evenings are colder than back home, and wetter. The roof is leaking at the east end in front of the altar and sometimes when she is working, Dorothy puts a bucket there to catch the rain.

One Thursday she goes and there is a ladder leaning against the side of the Kirk, its feet in the graveyard between two drunken headstones. She can't see who is at the top but heads in, ties on her apron, and begins her service. It is not long before she has to fetch the bucket. A fret had been drifting in all day, and now the drizzle has started and gathers into fat drops that make a tinny sound as they hit the metal.

The door opens behind her and there's the thud of boots on stone. When she straightens and turns, she recognizes William Gray, who is always with his wife, from Sundays in the Kirk—dark-haired, tall, with an awkward smile.

"Came at the right moment to fix a leaky roof, didn't I?" His hair is wet and he wipes his hands on his trousers before holding out a hand. "I'm William," he says.

"Dorothy," she replies and shakes his hand briefly before letting it go.

The rain is heavier now and splashing in the bucket.

"I'll wait to see if it eases." He sits on the edge of a pew while she carries on sweeping. He clears his throat. "You clean here every week, then?"

She barely stops to smile and nod before sweeping farther away from him.

"My sister, Jane, does too. You've probably seen her at the Kirk with me on Sundays," and Dorothy does stop then, concealing her surprise before he sees it. He stands up. "Let me help. I've got to wait anyway. It's just the two of us at home, so I do what I can. I'm quite handy."

"Thank you," she says, passing him the brush and fetching her cloth for the dusting. Maybe he'll make less conversation if he's busy, and so they sweep and clean in silence together. Dorothy is somehow moved by the fact that Jane is his sister, how protective she seemed when they were first introduced. More like a mother or a wife. Or was it possessive? She remembers the pull on his arm when he stopped to say hello, the drawn face and pursed lips. The Minister's words come back to her, *Sad story there, I'll tell you another time*, and she wonders what it is.

She thinks of her own mother, that uncertain edge between protection and control, and her father, a figure she hardly remembers, who might have been kind to her if he'd had the courage but instead had left them for another family. Not that she ever found out who, the taut nature of her mother even tenser after the disgrace, even less approachable.

When they are done, he helps to collect her things and offers to carry them home for her. She quickly refuses, though she appreciates his boyish eagerness to help, and he smiles as he says goodbye. He has asked nothing of her, he has expected nothing from her; she feels as silent inside as she did before he entered the Kirk.

He is there again the next Thursday, fixing the leaking roof. When he talks, he glances at her every now and then, and it occurs to her that it's approval he's looking for. Her mind turns to his sister again—her name is woven through his talk, and she wonders, in a village where everyone seems to know everyone else, where are his friends, where are his people?

"Is she not married?" she asks one Thursday as he is strengthening a pew. The Minister is in and out of the vestry, and Dorothy is dusting the cobwebs from the stone walls.

William looks up from his position kneeling between two rows of pews. "Jane? No. She has never felt the need. Kept home and hearth even when Mam was alive. She earns a bit of money mending nets, and there's me with the boat building and repairs. She looked after all of us boys—" He stops, and she has the feeling there is more to say.

"All?" she ventures, stopping what she's doing and turning. He's never mentioned brothers. His head is bent at his work again. "All?"

The Minister is standing at the vestry door. He comes into the Kirk and rests a hand on William's shoulder. "There were five Gray boys—including our William. The others went down with the *Fulmar* eight years ago now."

William nods his head, and when he looks up, Dorothy sees the loss etched on his face. "Jane never really got over it."

Dorothy has heard these stories many times since coming to Skerry. The sea's greed, the danger of storms, the women putting out stone lanterns to guide their men home. How thankful Jane must have been to keep even one of her brothers.

She thinks back to the day she first saw them at the Kirk and understands why Jane seemed so possessive of him, how he might be less like a brother and more like a son, to a woman who has lost so much.

And yet somehow, Dorothy wonders if that is the whole story.

A few days later, William knocks for her at home, shuffling from foot to foot. He has a paper parcel in one hand and a bunch of holly in the other. He holds one up, then the other. "Mackerel, a gift from a customer," he says, "and holly for the house with Christmas round the corner."

Dorothy's body tightens, remembering Jeanie's warning about schoolmistresses. Does he expect her to ask him in? "That's very kind. There was no need, really."

His face drops. "I could bring them in?"

"I—" She looks out onto the road.

William's face clears, as though suddenly understanding her worry. "The Minister knows I'm here. It was the Minister's idea, actually."

Dorothy smiles a little uncertainly.

"It's just I wondered if you'd like to come for supper. Jane will be there, of course."

Dorothy pauses. She likes his kindness, his lack of any threat, and thinks of her quiet cottage, of the coming winter, of the summer's broken promise. She hesitates. "Can I let you know?"

"Of course—I'll see you at the Kirk," and he gives her his gifts and smiles.

She watches him walk away and feels a sudden rush of gratitude at this offer of friendship, but when she shuts the door, the dull ache in her chest returns.

Joseph

They avoid each other now. If she is walking on one side of the street, he crosses to the other. If he is down on the Sands at the same time as her, she turns her back and leaves. He is glad when they are out at sea; he spends longer than he needs at the docks, bargaining over the cost of the catch. He's glad even when the weather is a challenge, enough to distract him from the ache in his chest, his bewilderment.

But a day comes at the shop when they meet each other unexpectedly. He stretches out his hand to open the door, and it jangles before he touches it and swings it open. Dorothy looks up from her basket and freezes. He doesn't have time to mask his response to her, the way something in him leans toward something in her, but her look of alarm shakes him, and he steps aside.

When he goes into the shop, he has forgotten what he wanted. Only Mrs. Brown is at the counter.

"Joseph." She smiles. "Now, what can I get you? I've a bit of lovely bacon come in. What do you think?"

He tries to gather himself, grateful for her kindness.

"Lorna was in here earlier to buy some for her grandfather. She's back from Fraserburgh."

He knows Lorna, always a happy word with a wide smile and easy laugh. She works in the bigger ports like so many girls, taking their knitting and their song, coming back to help at home in between. Several of the young men in the village are on her tail, pretty and friendly as she is. But not Joseph. He knows he could get a wife. He sees the way some of the girls glance at him, laugh in a certain way, toss their hair or lower their voices, looking at him sidelong. He likes it. But he isn't interested. Not now.

"Not today, not for me," he says.

"If you say so. You were ever stubborn." Mrs. Brown wraps the oats and tea he places on the counter, and he passes her the coins.

He can feel her looking at him as he goes to the door.

"I've heard Dorothy and William are friendly. Who'd have thought William had it in him, eh?"

His hand drops to his side. He doesn't turn, but he feels a heaviness to his body, as though someone has placed a load on his shoulder. And he knows why Mrs. Brown has told him this.

She is telling him it is time.

He nods, the bell jangles, the door closes.

He's not one for the drink. He never has been, but when he gets home he looks for the almost untouched bottle of whisky that's been gathering dust for years. He pours it into a mug and drinks it in one. He paces up and down, pours another. The strength of his jealousy shakes him. He feels like a ship in a storm. He doesn't know what to do with himself—he can't sit, he can't stand. He wants to bang on her door, he wants to shout at her, he wants to hit William. He slams out of his cottage and strides along the lane. The whisky-fire in his belly burns bright and fierce.

When he gets there, he knocks too loudly. When the door isn't opened, he knocks again.

"Joseph!" Lorna looks surprised. "Have you come to see Grandfather? Do you want to come in?" She waits for him to say something, but now he's there, he can't think of anything. She frowns. "Are you all right?"

He takes a step back. "I'm sorry." His hand goes to his forehead. "I shouldn't have come."

Her voice is warm. "Wait here," and she runs back in.

He glimpses her grandfather in a chair by the fire, sees her put another log in the lively flames, adjust his blanket. She says something Joseph can't hear, and the old man raises his hand in Joseph's direction, then drops it again, already forgetting him.

On the lane, Lorna keeps up her chatter, about her grandfather, about the weather, about working away as a fisher-girl, but once out of sight of the houses, she stops and puts her hand on his arm.

"Now tell me, what's the matter? Why did you come to the house? I've never seen you like this—you reek of whisky."

The fire in his stomach has lessened and has been replaced by a feeling of warm confusion. The world has listed slightly, and Lorna stands in front of him with her kind eyes and gentle smile. He isn't really listening to what she is saying but noticing instead her red cheeks and slightly parted lips.

"Joseph?"

He encircles her wrist with his fingers and pulls her closer, leaning toward her.

"Joseph!" She tugs her arm free and steps back, her mouth a shocked "O."

Suddenly his eyes clear. "My God, I'm sorry, Lorna. I don't know what came over me."

There is an edge to her voice now. "Go home. Whatever it is that is the matter with you, go home and sleep it off. I know you, so we'll say nothing of this, but I must get back to my grandfather now," and she leaves him standing in the cold, in the biting wind, in the hollow ache of his loss.

Lorna is as good as her word and tells no one of Joseph's unaccountable behavior. But she doesn't have to because someone sees them and, in the way of a shared story, it gathers its own shape and momentum till soon nearly all the village knows and at last Dorothy hears too how Joseph might be courting Lorna now, and what a lovely couple they'd make, walking hand in hand up the very lane where he'd swung Dorothy round and kissed her in the rain.

"Your invitation," she says to William the next Thursday in the Kirk. "I'd like very much to come to supper with you and your sister."

William's face brightens. "You'll like her," and right now Dorothy doesn't care whether she likes her or not, though in the weeks and months to come, she really does try, but it doesn't matter what she does, because Jane makes it clear that all her efforts are going to be utterly fruitless.

Dorothy

When William knocks for her, his nervousness is apparent in the way he shuffles from foot to foot. She fetches the tin of mince pies she's made as a gift, and they walk together in the darkening afternoon. A crescent moon hangs over the roof-tops, the soft gleam of the North Star growing in the falling blue dusk.

He clears his throat. "It's the home we grew up in. All six of us children. Not just grew up, but all born there too, but it was Jane, really, who raised me."

He's gabbling, but Dorothy listens politely, wondering what it is he's trying to tell her.

"Mam died not long after the boat went down; of a broken heart, everyone said. That's why it's just me and Jane now." He stops walking and turns to her. "Anyway, you mustn't mind Jane. She's just protective of me. After everything, you understand," and Dorothy realizes this is like him bringing her home for Mother's approval—Dorothy, who any mother would approve of, with her sensible dresses, her manners of a church girl, a schoolmistress no less.

"I'm sure it'll all be fine. I'm glad to be coming."

They live in one of the cottages off Copse Cross Street, and Dorothy glimpses the tidy vegetable garden with its shadowed rows of snow-covered winter kale, the well-kept thatch, the clean whitewash on the old stone.

William lets them in and she follows him through. Jane is at the stove, dark hair pulled back and shot through with gray. She has quick, dark eyes but barely looks at Dorothy, just a nod and a tight smile when they are introduced, before turning her gaze back to her brother. "You must be hungry and tired, William. I'll help you with your boots in a minute."

Irritation flashes across William's face. "It's fine, thanks, Jane."

It's tidy inside, and through the open door to another room Dorothy glimpses a spinning wheel and stool, and a cupboard with a row of small portraits or photos. It is clear from number and likeness that they must be of the brothers who were lost at sea.

"I've made a fisherman's pie—your favorite. It's almost ready."

"You needn't have gone to so much trouble." He glances at Dorothy. "I don't mean it isn't a special evening," and Jane's face falls when she sees the way he looks at Dorothy.

Dorothy tries to think of the right thing to say. "It smells lovely," and William looks at Jane with an anxious frown when she says nothing in return.

Dorothy tries again. "Do you want any help?"

Jane opens a door, bends down with her hands covered to take out a pie, golden and gleaming from the oven. "I've cooked for more than this most of my life. I can manage it for three. Now, William, make a bit of room, would you?"

She and William sit down. Jane sits down too, stands up, takes off her apron, and sits down again. She looks at William, eyebrows raised, waiting.

"Oh, yes, sorry." He shoots a look at Dorothy, then closes

his eyes. "We are grateful for this meal and for the hands that prepared it. Amen."

Dorothy risks a glance at Jane while he speaks, and Jane's eyes are still open and settled on Dorothy.

When William opens his, he looks at Jane and his shoulders tense. He tries to smile. "It looks lovely, Jane," he says and glances at Dorothy.

She swallows hard. "Yes—what recipe do you use?" and while Jane explains, Dorothy sees that she doesn't want to tell her, to give away the secrets she thinks keep William at home.

"You finding it warm enough in the teacher's cottage?" She looks pointedly at Dorothy. "I hear Joseph was there a lot." Her smile is small and cold. "Fixing the windows, I mean, of course," she adds after a pause.

Before Dorothy can say anything, she is loading more food on William's plate, fetching a jug of water, asking William about his day.

The suet pudding, when it comes, has the bitter sweetness of molasses, and too much of it, but Dorothy spoons it in, the talk awkward around her. She is desperate now to be away from this house that is full of ghosts, so that Jane seems like someone who is already half a ghost herself, trying to keep the family together when all the family are dead and she fears the last one going. But as much as she is desperate to escape, her sadness for William grows, her awareness of the way he is torn between duty and want.

When they leave, there is a flash of apprehension in Jane's eyes, their sudden gleam.

"Thank you," Dorothy says. "It was lovely to meet you."

The walk home is silent. Dorothy feels as though she has witnessed something she shouldn't have, something private and shameful. They arrive at her door just as flakes of snow start swirling and turning in the crisp night air.

Dorothy turns to him. "Would you like to come in?"

"I can't. I must get back to Jane—you see how she gets," but he leans forward and unexpectedly places a kiss on her snow-damp hair, then turns and leaves.

She watches him walk away, and her hand goes to her hair. She looks out over the moon-glitter of the sea beyond the houses and pictures Joseph, the Sands, the Steps where they first met. It is all gone now, but here is William who is trapped, caught between two things, and as she watches him walk away, she is inexplicably moved that he trusts her, that he is loyal to his sister and, even more, that after everything that's happened, here is someone who likes her. And it occurs to her that maybe they are both looking for a place of refuge, an escape.

Now

Dorothy

That night, Dorothy is woken by a thump and a crash. She thinks at first the wind has blown in the windows till she comes to her senses and realizes it's coming from downstairs.

The door bangs again, and a gust of icy wind rushes into her room. Dorothy's lamp gutters and leaps as she hurries down the stairs. The boy is standing by the front door, which knocks in its frame.

"What are you doing?" she cries and runs to check the bolts of the door, top and bottom. She turns and raises the lamp to his face. His eyes are staring at something she can't see, and he is making a soft whimpering sound. Her heart beats hard; shadows leap and shrink on the walls, and for a moment it is her own child standing there in the shifting glow of the flame. She shakes her head to dispel the trick of the light.

What is he looking at?

She leads him gently back into the room, placing the lamp on the table, easing him back into bed. His eyes suddenly fix on her face, and he reaches for her. But in the jumping flame, she sees he is still in his waking dream. His arm drops and she tucks the blanket around him. That is all she can do, but she sits in her chair by the hearth and watches him as his eyes close and his breathing deepens into that of normal sleep, before returning to her bed where she pulls the covers up and leaves the oil lamp burning.

The child's wide eyes in the leaping light of the lamp, his soft whimper, keep coming to her mind, because isn't this exactly what Moses did? She'd never told anyone—because who could she tell that her child tried to get out of the house in the dark of the night, eyes wide, talking nonsense about children in the sea wanting to play? It was bad enough knowing what people had said about him when he was born, all that superstitious nonsense about changelings and stolen children, without her feeding it. She couldn't admit to herself, not really, that there had been moments when she'd wondered herself if he were really hers, so little did she seem to understand him. Like this. Like walking in his sleep, like a creature from another realm. The first time he'd done it, she thought it was some kind of childish joke he'd learned from one of the boys at school, though God knows she tried to keep him away from them for his own sake.

"What do you think you're doing?" she'd said, and he'd dropped to the floor, his red ball rolling out of his hand. For a moment she had thought he'd died of fright, lying there, body stiff and unmoving, but then his eyes had fixed on her and the shock on his face told the true story: that he hadn't known what he was doing there either.

It only happened three or four times, but always the same thing, trying to open the door, the talk of the children in the water, his red ball in his hand, once even unbolting the door. And the morning after those nights, his bed linen would be wet, which was only further shame to her.

So she was glad when one day, in the shop, she'd heard Norah regaling the others about finding her husband outside in the middle of the night, his nightshirt flapping around his legs, the wind billowing it out and lifting it like a lady's dress, only what she could see by the light of the moon was nothing you'd find under a lady's dress, and they'd all laughed at the bawdy joke, Mrs. Brown along with the rest of them.

"Well, such things happen, but you mustn't wake him," she'd said. "I've heard it can kill a person—it's only a very lively dream," and Dorothy had hovered, turning a packet of sugar over and over in her hand, listening. Well, the idea that it could kill a person was nonsense, of course, and she didn't want to listen to Norah's chat about a great-aunt who had sleepwalked into the Otherworld and never come back, so she'd left without buying anything, but maybe there was something to be said for not waking him.

She had a bolt fitted, too high for him to reach, which she locked every night to keep him safe, and the next time, she led him by the hand back to his bed, where he closed his eyes, already in deep sleep. And the next morning, his bed linen was dry.

But this night, Dorothy lies awake and wonders at the strangeness of it all, the fact that this new child, this ward of hers, has done something her own child did, and the picture of the woman on the shoreline in a white dress drifts into her mind again, the uncanniness of it. Dorothy turns and turns again in bed. She should never have agreed to this. Her hands are white and clenched on the blanket. She must look forward, not back, or not look at all. It is time she put a bit of pressure on the Minister to hasten the return of the child to his parents.

She hears a small sound at her door. The boy is standing on the threshold in the darkness. She sits up and swings her legs to the floor, and he comes to her, leans his head against her, and cries.

Then

Dorothy

"How are the preparations for the ceilidh coming along, Miss Aitken?"

Dorothy pauses in her sweeping of the aisle. "They're coming along," she says dryly to the Minister. In truth, she would rather not be involved, as it means being part of a small committee with Mrs. Brown and the other women, who spend more time gossiping than preparing. "I didn't go to one back home, but the others seem to know what to do."

"And is it true what I hear?" Dorothy looks up at his change of tone. "Is it true that you're going with William and Jane?"

Dorothy half smiles. "Yes, it is. I'm grateful to them. For not having to go on my own, I mean."

The Minister looks abashed. "I'm sorry, I should have thought. But it is good to see kindness between you and William. They're very fond of him in the village, and he's a wonderful craftsman with the boats. I'm hopeful he'll meet a nice young woman one day. Someone could do a lot worse than William."

Dorothy hears the leading tone of his voice, and after he's gone back into the vestry, she pauses in her sweeping and leans on the brush. She thinks of William's gentleness and kindness.

The Minister is right.

A woman could do a lot worse than William.

The knitting evenings are a reminder of their differences, Dorothy and the village women. She goes now because it's the custom of the village, and she won't have anyone say she doesn't do her bit for the fishermen or for the poor, but she doesn't know how to have the conversations they do, nor does she want to, with their shared intimacies and gossip. But that doesn't mean she doesn't feel the sting of how their talk drifts away when she arrives, becomes more businesslike, laughter drying up with sidelong glances at each other. But as the night of the ceilidh nears, the chat becomes more and more about the music and food, excitement about the dances to be danced and the stories to be told and who will make what and how they will decorate the Hall. Mrs. Brown gives everyone their jobs to do in preparation. "It will be a chance for everyone to enjoy themselves," she says.

Dorothy is dreading it.

One quiet Saturday morning, she takes out her three dresses—four, if you include the one she made for walking on Skerry Sands—and lays them out on the bed. They are so . . . buttoned up. Even Dorothy can see that. And everyone has already seen the one she wears to the Kirk. And then there is the dancing itself. She's never been to a dance, except one at school. Her mother always forbade it, but won't it look strange if she doesn't go?

She recalls a Sunday sermon delivered every year before Christmas and often repeated by her mother. *Dancing is only doing standing up what those with loose morals would rather be doing lying down*, and the girls had giggled and the boys given each other knowing glances, though they were none the wiser either. She has a vision of herself at the school dance in the dress with the mended neck where the lace collar had been torn away, sitting on a hard-backed chair while her classmates danced around her, under the eye of her mother who'd served the girls drinks. Two whole hours of pretending she didn't care, moving her feet when no one was looking, to the pattern of the reels. And this will be the same, while the villagers dance, while Joseph and Agnes dance, or will it be Lorna? She suddenly can't bear it—there is at least something she can do about one of those things.

Mrs. Kildare, the seamstress, lives on a side road, and Dorothy is grateful because she can go the back way without being seen. When Mrs. Kildare invites her in and leads her through, Dorothy sees it is not so much a shop as a room in her cottage. She notes the tidy order of things—the old but polished sewing machine with its well-worn treadle in pride of place, the many-drawered cabinet against the wall, and the side table with spools of cotton, thimbles, needles and pins, measuring tape, and dressing shears. The love for her trade is clear, though Dorothy wonders how much custom the population of Skerry has to offer her. On another table a number of patterns are arranged as well as a pattern book, but it is to the fabrics that Dorothy's eye is drawn, mostly cotton, linen, and wool in serviceable colors of gray, navy, and black, but there is one that stands out.

Mrs. Kildare follows her eye. "You've noticed the green silk, I think. Go on, have a closer look. I couldn't resist it when I saw it, though I have little occasion to be selling or making much out of silk these days!" Dorothy recognizes the shorter vowels of a Lowlands accent and wonders what her story is, though she doesn't pry.

Her mother always told her not to wear green because it drew attention to the red glints in her hair, but she savors the sleek silk as it slips over her fingers.

"Wait a minute, I have just the thing to go with it," and Mrs. Kildare opens a few of the drawers in the cabinet.

Dorothy glimpses an assortment of buttons, lace, and ribbons. Mrs. Kildare returns with a band of cream lace. "What do you think?" A few more trips to the cabinet, and before Dorothy knows it, an array of the drawers' contents is set out before her, along with the patterns.

Dorothy studies some of the drawings, undecided—it's not that she's worried she can't make them, she just isn't sure what the fashion is these days.

Or any days.

"May I?" Mrs. Kildare rifles through the patterns and picks one out. "Now look at this. A friend in Edinburgh sent me this—all the rage, she said—so pretty!"

And Dorothy looks—it really is pretty, the hem shorter than her other dresses; it would swing just above the ankle, and the waist is narrow, with a panel and darts where the skirt flares out. She pictures herself in it, and her heart beats a little faster. She touches the green silk again.

"It's just the thing to go with your hair, you know," and Dorothy feels the stirring of a new feeling.

She feels it as she leaves the shop, clutching the parcel that has far more in it than she intended to buy; she feels it as she turns away from the main road, taking the long way back, and she is still feeling it when alone in her kitchen. She puts the parcel on the table and the kettle on the stove.

It is only then, sitting down with her cup of tea, that she realizes what this feeling is.

She is excited.

All that has changed by the time she is standing in the Hall and it's filling up and the band is tuning fiddles, trying notes on flute and tin whistle, feeling for the quick soft beat of the drum. She doesn't know where William and Jane are. She waited and waited at home, but then it occurred to her that the only thing worse than arriving alone would be to arrive by herself when everyone was already there. The village women are already coming in, some with a husband on their arm, or a suitor, some with their friends. Dorothy in her ridiculous dress comes in alone.

She was only able to glimpse parts of herself in the mirror at home—her hair pinned away from her face in curls. When she turned, she could see the low loose bun at the neck, the wide lace collar with a bow and a ribbon of cream silk following the swell of her breasts under the fitted green silk. She had quickly moved the mirror again, this time to the puffed sleeves, ending just below the elbow, the panel that pinches in at the waist, the slim-fitting boots that are revealed by the swing of the hem. She'd turned on the spot and the dress had flared out, the silk catching the light of the lamp, and she'd imagined the steps, toe in, toe out, another twirl, her arm extended as though linked with a partner, round and round till she was warm, her heart beating fast, and when she'd caught a glimpse of herself in the mirror she'd been surprised at the smile on her face.

But now, smoothing her dress over her hips and looking at the others, she sees it's too much. People are looking at her— are those some of the mothers of her pupils laughing behind their hands? Her mother had been wrong when she said, "Who'll be looking at you?" whenever Dorothy had been nervous about a gathering as a child. People looked. They are looking now. And whereas before she'd not been able to bear the thought of wearing one of her plain dresses, now she can't bear her ridiculous finery. She doesn't want Joseph or Agnes—or any of them, in fact—to see her. If she wants to leave, now is the time.

"It's a good turnout, isn't it?"

Too late. Her heart sinks when she hears the Minister's

voice. He and Jenny are both smiling at her, and she tries to smile back but glances instead at the door—maybe William and Jane will be here in a minute. Where *are* they? "Yes, Minister. Isn't it? So jolly!" And to her horror the music starts up in earnest and the villagers are all smiles and laughter, lining up for a dance that she doesn't know, because she doesn't know any dances.

People are still pouring in and joining the happy throng, and Dorothy is feeling hot in her high-necked dress with its extra lace and silk ribbons, her buttoned-up boots.

"A drink, Miss Aitken?" The Minister presses a glass into her hand.

"Thank you, Minister." She grips it tight to hide the tremble in her fingers.

"Call me Alastair, please. I've told you before, the formality is entirely unnecessary."

She nods, and to look like they're friends and as if she's doing something, having a nice time, chatting with the Minister she can't bring herself to call Alastair, and his wife, she takes a gulp. Too late she realizes it's not the water she expected; it's sour, and the tang of it burns her throat and she's choking and coughing.

She glimpses the Minister's horrified face. "Dorothy, are you quite—?"

"I need some air," is the best she can manage before she goes out of the hall into the shock of the night, where she bends over, spluttering and gasping.

When she straightens up she is looking straight at Joseph, and behind him stand both Jeanie and Agnes, Agnes unable to hide her delight.

Joseph's face, however, is serious. "Dorothy, are you all right?" And this to her seems even more mortifying, to imagine that her condition has invited pity—and from him, of all people.

She straightens herself and her dress. "Quite, thank you."

"I can take you home if you're unwell?" and Dorothy stares at him. His behavior is unfathomable. And judging by the look on Agnes's and Jeanie's faces, they agree.

Agnes puts her arm through Joseph's. "Yes, we could walk you back if you'd like, but I'm sure you'd rather wait for William, wouldn't you?"

Joseph's face tightens. "Dorothy?" he repeats.

Agnes's laugh is brittle and loud. "Come on, Joseph, take me inside. We haven't come to freeze out here, and Dorothy obviously doesn't want our help," and Dorothy has still barely gathered her thoughts as they walk away, Agnes pulling on Joseph's arm.

She stays outside. Even more than before, she wants to leave, but a knot of stubbornness sends her back in to the Minister, even though it is too hot and too loud, and she is starting to feel a little dizzy. The rhythm of the drum, the lively beat, the tunes getting faster, the men and women spinning arm in arm, the women's skirts twirling. She feels a warmth in her belly from the whisky.

In the confusion of sound and color, her eyes find Joseph. He is standing a little apart from Agnes and Jeanie. He is looking at Dorothy. He has the same serious look on his face as he did outside, but he starts to walk toward her and she suddenly can't move.

"Will you not be dancing, Dorothy?" She doesn't know what to say to him, doesn't know how to say no, and the Minister says, "Lovely. You go and enjoy yourself," and she finds herself following while Joseph gently takes her elbow, and then she's in the middle of it all, his arm around her waist, their fingers entwined, and it doesn't matter that she doesn't know the dance because he is leading her. His breath is warm on her cheek, and whether it's the dance or the whisky or something else, she doesn't know, but hers comes more quickly. His hand tightens around her waist, and she realizes the music has stopped but they are still hand-clasped, their faces turned toward each other, and he doesn't try to hide it, the way he looks at her. Beyond him, Jeanie and Agnes are staring at them. Dorothy pulls away, pushes back through the crowd, and sinks into one of the chairs at the side.

Joseph stands above her, but she can hardly look at him in case he sees something in her face she doesn't want him to see.

"Is there something I can fetch for you? Or would you like me to get the Minister?" and she needs this to end. Once and for all, she needs him to stop humiliating her.

She summons her iciest stare. "No. What I want—what I really want, is for you to leave me alone," and she nearly says something, about Agnes, about Lorna, but she stops herself because, more than anything else, she can't bear the thought of him knowing how much she cares, so she holds her face completely still and makes herself watch his expression change from concern to shock as he takes in her words. He stays like that for a moment, then inclines his head once. "As you wish, Miss Aitken," and turns and walks away from her, and she makes herself watch that too, sitting there stiffly and trying not to cry because she doesn't want this either.

"Dorothy, drink this," and it's Mrs. Brown, pressing a glass into her hand, telling her she will be all right, and this time Dorothy knows it's whisky, but she doesn't care now because when she next looks up, Joseph is leaving the Hall with Agnes on his arm and she can't help it, she knows she shouldn't, but she follows them through the crowd to the threshold.

Agnes

Agnes has waited a long time for this moment. She has saved for her new dress for weeks and made a wide collar for it. She is wearing her hair differently. There's been no mention of Dorothy, not since *all that*. There was some rumor about Lorna, but she's seen no evidence of it herself, and maybe it's a good thing anyway. It shows he doesn't care anymore about Dorothy. She turns her mind away from it all and instead dabs a bit of berry juice on her cheeks and then, on an impulse, she uses it to redden her lips too. She has been practicing her dancing, twirling round the kitchen before her father gets home, laughing as her sisters and brother trip over their steps. Agnes has always had an instinct for music, knowing just where to put her feet in all the dances. When she is ready, she turns on the spot and feels the soft swish of the dress against her legs. Her hands keep going to her lace and her eyes to the shine of her shoes. Her heart is pounding, waiting for Joseph who is taking them all, as he does every year.

When his knock comes, she stops herself from running to answer, counts to ten, then opens the door. He is newly shaven, his linen shirt pressed and clean, the collar high on his neck against the line of his jaw.

He smiles. "You look pretty, Agnes. Is that a new dress? Is Jeanie ready too?"

Agnes glows in the warmth of his praise, and she feels pretty, stepping out into the sparkling snow, the cold air tingling her cheeks to further redness. Jeanie hurries out after them, just as her father weaves out of the dark. Agnes pulls on Joseph's arm and glances behind her. "Come on, Mam," hoping they can leave without him spoiling it all, without him seeing the color she's put on her mouth. He mumbles something and the door slams shut behind them. They hurry through the night, but when they get to the Hall, seeing Dorothy outside, disheveled, breathless, brings them up short, and Agnes shoots a glance at Joseph's face, tries not to read the meaning of his expression. Instead, she slips her arm through his the moment she can, putting a stop to his concern and pulling him gently inside where the music is lively, the villagers dancing, leaving Dorothy outside in the cold alone.

Her friends rush to her and gather round. "Has he asked? Has he asked?"

She frowns and shakes her head. "Don't. He might hear."

One narrows her eyes. "What makes you think he's going to anyway? Hasn't he been coming to yours for years? Since his mam died?" Agnes shrugs off the question to hide the anxious leap of her heart, and turns to him, but Joseph isn't looking at her.

She follows his line of sight to Dorothy.

She swallows hard. "Joseph?" but he doesn't hear her.

He's pushing through the crowd, and Agnes can't look away from the tender way he takes Dorothy's hand, the way he leads her in the dance, how beautiful her dress is, how beautiful her hair.

One of her friends pulls on her arm. "Agnes?" but she can't stop watching them, how he's looking at Dorothy, and she wants him to look at her like that so much that it hurts, and she turns away so she doesn't have to see it anymore, gulping down the sob rising in her throat. And then he's back, and in desperation she clings to the wild hope that there might still be a chance for her.

She doesn't let herself think about what she's about to do next but puts her hand on his arm. "I feel dizzy," she says. "Would you take me outside?" and he's not even looking at her, he's frowning and distracted, but she leads him through the throng and out into the cold winter night where she pulls him away from the door. She stands against the stone of the Hall. Joseph's face is lit by the splintered light of the paned window, but he isn't seeing her, just like all the men who don't see her, not properly—like Scott, like her very own father—and she takes hold of his hands and grips them. Only then does he seem to become aware of her and where they are.

"What is it, Agnes? Why are you looking at me like that?" and she ignores the warning in her stomach, in her heart, in all her being, and reaches up and pulls him toward her. She puts her lips to his.

Dorothy and the Children
of the Waves

Dorothy notices from the open door that the snow is falling again now and hears in the unexpected quiet its muffled thud on the roof. She feels dazed. Her hand goes to her chest as to a wound. She doesn't want to see Joseph and Agnes anymore. She closes the door. The band has stopped playing the music and people are all starting to sit, their chat fading, children getting comfortable on laps or on the floor to listen.

A woman has stood up and faces are turned toward her as quiet settles on the villagers. The woman is nondescript, someone Dorothy would struggle to recognize the next day, but when she opens her mouth, the room fades and darkens as the story she tells is woven in the silver thread of her voice.

There was once a fisherman and his goodwife who lived by the sea in their cott. To them was born a child, a boy. He cried little and smiled a lot. One night the sea was angry, great waves pounding the sands, and the fisherman who was out on his boat did not return for his supper. Nor did he return the next day or the day after that, and still the storm raged. The goodwife knew he was gone forever, and she took the boy in her arms and went down to the sands to rage for the loss of her husband.

The sea boiled and seethed around her knees as she wept her grief, and swept her in deeper. In the waves were children made

146

of foam and salt water. They reached for the baby boy but the mother held on to him tightly. She had lost her husband, and she would not lose her child too.

The sea grew higher and fiercer around her, and now she heard their voices, the children of the waves.

Come away, come away.

And just for a moment, the children blinded her, and she felt the boy slither from her hands and heard their laughter. As the wave was sucked back into the sea, she was left standing on the sand again, and to her relief, there was her child at her feet. She scooped him up and ran back to the cott, away from the storm and the children of the waves, because she had heard stories about them, how they were faery children from the Otherworld come to steal human babies.

The child grew into a bonny boy, though he smiled little and cried a lot, and the mourning mother carried on in sadness at the death of her husband, but fed the child and clothed him and put him in his pallet to sleep of a night, all the while weeping her grief into him.

Seven years later, the sea grew angry again, and the boy woke up and heard voices on the wind. He went outside and followed them to the sea.

Come away, come away.

And he laughed because he knew who they were—they were the faeries of the sea come to take him home again, back to the Otherworld where there is no weeping, and he ran into the water till he could see them in the waves.

Come away, come away.

He reached his arms out to them, their hands mingling in the wild water, and he was happy to be with them once more.

The mother never saw her child on land again, though she would often go down to the shore and weep her grief at the sea which had stolen her husband and her child, and sometimes she thought she saw the children of the waves and, playing amongst them, her very own child.

Much later, Dorothy stirs in the night, in that mysterious place between sleep and wakefulness. Many stories had been told at the ceilidh and many songs sung, but as she lies in the dark, she listens for the voices of the sea, and in amongst the hush and suck of the water, breathing in, breathing out, she thinks she hears them, the children from the Otherworld, before she falls back into a deep and dreamless sleep.

Dorothy wakes the next morning and shifts position. She frowns, confused. Why is she in a chair? A blanket is tucked around her and the fire is dead in the grate, though there is a faint breath of warmth in the ashes. She moves to stand up, which is when the pain in her head hits.

And the night before.

She freezes. Blurred images drift back. Sipping, no, gulping the whisky; going outside, Joseph and Agnes. Her head drops into her hand. How much whisky did she drink?

Drinking alcohol is a sin. Abstinence is approved of by God.

Her cheeks flame with shame.

And the dance—what had she been thinking, following him into the crowd? Dancing with him? How must she have looked? Stiff, uncomfortable, deserving of the laughter she no doubt drew when she walked away. How did she get home? And who brought her home? *Brought her home.* And her a schoolteacher. It is then she notices her boots by the hearth.

She lifts the blanket and sighs in relief; at least she is still wearing the dress, with its bows and collar and buttons, but who took off her boots?

She feels thirsty but her head thuds when she stands up,

and once she starts moving, her stomach turns. In the kitchen she gulps water down, then leans her head against the wall.

She notices the cup on the side, and images of Mrs. Brown drift back to her. "A cup of tea will help—you're not the first to have had a drop too much." Mrs. Brown brought her home, then. How she must have loved that. "Though you did drink it like it was mother's milk—I'd never have thought you had it in you."

How will she ever face them again?

Her daily routine will have to be abandoned. She opens the curtains, eyes squinting against the winter light. And then she remembers.

Agnes and Joseph.

The kiss.

Her eyes sting. She goes upstairs and looks at herself in the mirror. She makes herself note every bow, each puff of sleeve, the now crumpled lace and curls in disarray. She makes sure she feels the shame she deserves for every primp and vanity and for caring what Joseph thinks, and only then does she take it all off and lie down.

She drifts fitfully between sleep and horror, headache and nausea. She remembers the woman and the story she told. She turns over. How mysterious and beautiful it had seemed to her last night with its tale of changelings and faeries and children in the waves. She turns again and squeezes her eyes shut against Joseph, Agnes's hands touching his face, the way she'd pulled him toward her with such familiarity.

And all she wants to do is stay in bed, hide from the memory and all the village, but one thought is growing stronger as she lies there, the morning light too brilliant, too loud, and try as she might, she cannot ignore it.

She is going to have to go to the shop and thank Mrs. Brown.

By the afternoon she is washed, newly dressed in a clean frock, hair pulled back into a tight, punishing bun. Maybe she can simply go to the shop and pretend it didn't happen. Staying at home will not do—it'll show she has something to hide. She makes herself think of their raggle-taggle children, coming to school in their caps and boots, some of them dirty, some of them not there at all but down on Skerry Sands helping their fathers with the boats. Anything to lessen her own shame.

By the time she is walking up Copse Cross Street, glad of the winter bite in the air, the fading sky, her head throbs with only a dull ache. There is only a slight tremor in her hands, and she swallows down the rise of nausea.

She wills the shop to be empty, then takes a deep breath and opens the door. The bell jangles too loudly. She enters the fug of warmth and to her relief sees only Mrs. Brown at first, in her usual position, but then makes out by the stove, of course, Ailsa in her headscarf and fingerless gloves, despite the warmth, and Norah with her knowing look. Their chat falls silent. Her heart sinks and for a moment she stands, un-certain if she can do this, before straightening her shoulders and going to the counter.

"Hello, Mrs. Brown." Her eyes slip to the others, who are staring with no attempt to conceal their interest.

Mrs. Brown nods her acknowledgment. "Dorothy. And how are you? A lovely night, was it not?" Is that a smile?

Dorothy has planned what she'll say. "I want to thank you for seeing me home and safe after the ceilidh." She thinks of the blanket, the fire, the cup of tea that must have been made, and clears her throat. "And for seeing me comfortable, of course. I . . . I don't know what came over me—the heat and the noise, maybe—I was a little unwell."

Ailsa snorts and Mrs. Brown's mouth twitches. "Yes, well, the whisky will take you like that if you're not used to it."

This is worse than she imagined. "The whisky? No, I was just—anyway, thank you for your kindness, for the blanket and the cup of tea. I feel quite myself again now, thank you."

"Don't be thanking me for those. I couldn't leave you in your boots and without a fire"—another snort by the stove—"but the tea and the blanket, you can thank William for those."

"William?" and she is so mortified that she turns on her heel and leaves the shop without even saying goodbye, and their chat starts up again behind her with Ailsa's voice.

"So anyway, who'd have thought it! Jeanie was right all along—Agnes and Joseph . . . "

And Dorothy goes faster now because, although she knew it, although she saw it with her own eyes, the women talking about it in the shop makes it even more real, even more certain that whatever she thought had happened between her and Joseph, she'd been wrong, and she hates him for it. In the fading winter afternoon, she knows that all the bright hope she'd had in the summer is lost forever.

By the time she gets home, head down, not meeting the eye of anyone else, Dorothy is just in time to find William standing on her doorstep, a parcel in his hand. He starts talking while she is still walking toward him, so desperate is he to explain. He is sorry that Jane was sick and that he couldn't get to the ceilidh till late and that Dorothy was herself unwell. He blames himself while she shakes her head, ashamed, dazed, unable to think.

"I thought maybe we could walk on the Sands together? It might clear your head if you're feeling under the weather still."

By the time Dorothy is ready, a bright moon is rising.

151

They walk along the cliff and down the Steps to Skerry Sands. Dorothy feels unutterable sadness. William is quiet and gentle beside her, and Dorothy thinks she likes that. She is thankful for his kindness, the way he doesn't ask about the ceilidh and pretends she'd not been well, but she feels her humiliation like a stone in her stomach.

Once on the shore, William feels for her hand in the dark; she lets him, and after a moment she breathes a long breath out, as though letting go of something, and curls her fingers around his.

His proposal comes soon after they get back to her cottage. She sits down but he stays standing. He takes her hand and asks her again. It is a gentle, hopeful offer, and she is comforted by it, grateful.

She turns her back on Joseph, on any doubts.

She accepts.

Jeanie

The news spreads quickly, as it does.

"So that's that. Joseph isn't marrying her, after all." Jeanie notices how Agnes doesn't mention their part in that, not that Jeanie is ashamed of it. She did what she had to do. She also notices that Agnes doesn't say that Joseph isn't marrying *her* either. She doesn't know what happened the night of the ceilidh, but he's not been back, and she knows from the look on Agnes's face not to ask.

Well, it serves Dorothy right, she supposes, to be marrying William. Try as she might, she cannot imagine them together—even she knows you can't make a home of other people, taking your feelings for one person and giving them to someone else, rushing from one roof to another for shelter. *And what's in it for William?* she wonders. Probably anything to get away from Jane.

She tries to talk about it in the shop, but those three, like witches round a cauldron, keep their secrets to themselves.

Mrs. Brown has finished her adding up and tucks her pencil behind her ear, pursing her lips. "No doubt it's good for them both, especially after everything William's been through." If she's surprised at the news, she doesn't show it.

"Jane won't like it. She's always had a strange relationship with that boy—"

"He's a nice lad, Jeanie, leave them alone. No need to bring any more misery to that family."

Jeanie rolls her eyes at everyone pretending to be holier than thou, when she knows full well how they gossip—how they'll probably talk about her, even, as soon as she's left. She isn't going to be embarrassed into not saying what she thinks, so she starts again. "As I was saying, I remember when—"

But the little bell jangles and Mrs. Brown clears her throat. "Morning, Jane."

Jeanie shuts up then, of course, and puts the butter and tea in her basket and smiles as she passes Jane to leave the shop.

"Oh well, I expect they deserve each other," she says to Agnes later as she balances the fresh cup of tea on her knee. She tries to gauge Agnes's mood and decides it's maybe best to keep her thoughts about it to herself today.

Jane must be horrified, she thinks, having always been so keen to keep her brother at home with her, under her watchful eye. What joy can come of a marriage like that, between a man running away and a woman who loves someone else?

And a bit of Jeanie, to be honest, can't wait to find out.

Now

Dorothy

She's only been in the garden a minute, but when she goes inside, he is not in the kitchen where she had left him drinking warm milk, and he's not in the other room playing with the toys the villagers gave.

"Hello?" She hears nothing. "Where are you?" She runs to the window and tries to see through the veil of snow if he's outside on the path to Skerry Sands, though she knows she always pushes the second bolt across, out of long habit. She goes to the back door now, forcing a slow pace, as though there is nothing to worry about. Had he followed her into the garden? The icy air and a flurry of flakes rush in. Not there either.

"Where are you?" She can hear the edge of panic in her own voice now, but then she hears a noise above her.

He's in Moses's room.

She runs up the stairs, sees the open door. It is dark inside because the curtains are always closed, the room not to be seen, not to be entered.

This boy. Who does he think he is?

Who does she think he is?

The toy box is open. She slams it shut and they look at each other in shock.

"These are not yours. Not yours, do you hear?" She can't think straight and grabs his arm, yanks him out of the room and pulls him down the stairs behind her, never easing her grip till they are at the bottom and she swings him round to face her.

He is white and saying something, one word over and over, and she is suddenly utterly exasperated by not being able to understand him. Why are children like this—what do they expect you to give? Moses was the same, and she did everything you were meant to do: He was clothed, better than most of the children in the village, if truth be told, and well fed, and warm, but it was never enough. He would cling to her leg sometimes in the kitchen when she was cooking, and gaze up at her. "Mamma, Mamma, Mamma," over and again, and she knew he wanted something from her, something she was entirely unable to give, and she would prize him off her, but he'd run back and cling tighter. She will tell the Minister that someone else will have to look after the child. She can't. She doesn't understand him. He won't do as he's told, eat what she gives him, stay where he's put, leave her in peace.

Slowly she becomes aware that the child is clinging to her and crying, and she looks down at his curly head and something in her heart unexpectedly opens, and she kneels down, holds his face between her hands. "I'm sorry, I'm sorry," she says and she holds him, while he says something, over and again, and his shoulders shake then gradually become still, and his word becomes clear:

"Ball, ball, ball."

They are both exhausted by what has happened. After supper, Dorothy sits at the kitchen table and drinks tea after tea, the floor unswept, the dishes unwashed. The stitches that hold her life together are coming undone. All he'd wanted was the ball to play with.

She goes into the room where the boy is sleeping, mouth open, little snoring grunts, arm hanging over the side, hand curling and uncurling, holding on, letting go. She sits in the chair by the fire and picks up her knitting. She holds it up to the lamplight. The stitches are too tight or too loose—her work, usually so neat and precise, the tension controlled just so, is shockingly bad. She must unravel it, start again, make it right.

All those men, all needing jumpers to keep them warm at sea. She can't do it, she can't do it, she can't do it, and as she pulls the knitting loose and casts on again, she drops stitch after stitch as she gazes into the fire, the sense of all pattern unraveling, seeing Moses's face in the flames, asking over and over, *Ball, ball, ball.*

Then

Dorothy and William

It is a spring wedding. The Kirk looks beautiful; there are flowers—corn marigolds and meadow cranesbill—and psalms said and everything is properly done. When they leave as man and wife, hand in hand, she thinks how even the Kirkyard looks pretty in the bright spring sun, and she looks forward to crossing the threshold of their new home, away from the crowd, and ready to start her new duties in life as a wife, not a teacher.

Jane is red-eyed all the way through the ceremony, in the Kirk and after, as they are handfasted in front of the village with the rope and knot that slips from their wrists and will hang for many years in the cottage they live in. Much later, when William leaves her, he won't undo it; he will not bring more shame to her. But for today, William looks happy and proud, looking to Dorothy for assurance every now and then, though goodness knows, she understands little enough about these things herself.

The villagers follow them home with gifts—a set of cups, some chairs, linen for the marriage bed. Their home is on the cliff overlooking Skerry Sands, with the path Dorothy walked when she first came, the one leading to the stone steps down to the sea, running in front of her gate. To much hilarity and the expected bawdy jokes, William lifts her and carries her over the threshold, signifying her passing into her new life. He swings her round, and the faces of the villagers blur.

And then one face comes clear.

Joseph's.

Amongst all the faces, drunk and sober, she sees his. He is not smiling like the others, and when their eyes catch, they hold for a moment before he turns and pushes back through the crowd and away down the path to the Steps. Only Dorothy seems to notice. For a moment it is like a thread between them stretches painfully, but at last the door closes on them all as William shuts it with his elbow. Red and laughing, he sets her down in their kitchen, where Dorothy stumbles and, in righting herself, places her hand on the side. A saucer skids and smashes on the floor. At first, Dorothy can't fathom what has been spilt but, bending down, she sees.

It is the gift of lucky salt to bless home and hearth, man and wife, child to come.

Joseph

Joseph leaves the celebrations and goes down to the Sands. The tide is in, the waves hissing on the shore as he pushes his rowing boat out and jumps in. He won't look behind him, up at the cottage on the cliff, although the knowledge of it, of the two people in it, burns the back of his neck more fiercely than the sun. He tries to allow the glinting water, the slow swell beyond the shoreline that lifts the rowing boat, the steady push and pull of the oars, to soothe him, but when he reaches *North Star*, he feels no better, no more soothed than before.

Up on the deck, he still faces away, tries to do the work needed to mend the ropes, splicing, whipping, treating them with tar, but it's hard to concentrate even on these familiar tasks. He finds himself watching the gannets, in full flock, diving and fishing for mackerel, envying the simplicity of a life of such unconflicted purpose. Afternoon fades into evening, and he stays in this place where he feels most himself, with the wide sky above him, the open sea in front of him.

Soon stars puncture the dusky blue of the spring evening and he feels his body tense further. This is it, this is the moment he has been dreading. He imagines, though he doesn't want to, the darkening of the downstairs window as the lamp is dimmed, the blooming of the light upstairs in their—

A sharp pain stabs through his hand, and in astonishment he sees he has sliced into his thumb with his knife. Not in twenty years has he been so careless. He squeezes his eyes shut and curses the rage that surges through him as the blood, deep red and hot, swells out of the cut and flows over his hand.

Dorothy and William

There is no need to prepare food or eat anything at all after the wedding celebration, and so, as the light fades, the larger question looms. She expects shyness now the excitement is over and the door is bolted and they are alone, yet strangely she is ready, and reaches out her hand, for reassurance, for love, for invitation.

"William . . . "

"I'll put the kettle on," he says, and she nods and quickly drops her arm.

Of course, she thinks, and blushes at having seemed so forward.

"Please, let me," and somehow they know each other less, are more awkward, than on that first day. She places the cups on the table while the water simmers on the hob, turns one in the light. "The Minister has been very generous." The words fall into the space between them and disappear.

William nods as though glad of something to focus on. "Yes, yes," but his words fall into the space too.

She pours the tea, opens the pretty tin with the biscuits in it, but nothing fills the space between them, only a sort of dreadful waiting.

Eventually, after they have washed up and tidied up, put the linen on the bed, put things in their place and Dorothy has stood at the window and watched the sea in its dusky blues and shifting grays, the moment can't be avoided any longer.

She goes up first to wash. She undresses, tries not to look at her body, the pale, goose-bumpy flesh, the freckles, the curl of red hair between her legs—is it a lot? It suddenly seems like a lot to her, and her nipples are large—are they normal? She has no way of knowing. She quickly pulls the nightgown over her head, her eyes squeezed shut against her reflection, and gets into bed where she lies, legs together, arms by her side, face to heaven, cool and still like an effigy she once saw in a church in Edinburgh.

She hears William enter the room and keeps her eyes closed.

She saw two cats tearing at each other once, screeching and crying, the larger one on the back of the smaller one, the flash of needle teeth and dagger claws. At first, she thought they were fighting, till her mother came outside and hissed at them, calling them *disgusting creatures*, and in bed later she'd tried to untangle their limbs in her mind, tried to peer where she knew she shouldn't, to understand.

Another time, on the way back from school, she'd passed the alleyway by the butcher's and a movement made her look, and there was a man in the shadow of the meat bins holding something in his hands. She thought it was a plant root. He was staring at her with a strange intensity. The root was red and shining, and then she ran. Somehow, she knows that all of that is tied up with the Wedding Night, with the sly looks, the half smiles, the sniggers and bawdy jokes, and she starts to feel frightened.

Yet in amongst her fear there is curiosity too. The thrill of a mouth against hers, of another's body.

When she opens her eyes, William is standing by the window, and in his hands he is holding a root.

Dorothy freezes. She realizes she is staring. She feels her stomach lurch and her hand goes to her mouth. He is tugging at himself, then sees her eyes are open and his hand drops; the root wilts. What is she meant to do? In the underwater light of the room, she sees her own fear in his eyes and thinks it is connected with the way he won't look at her when they kiss, and how he often holds tight to her after, head on her shoulder, somehow more like a repentant child than an ardent suitor.

But now he is pulling her nightdress up—it's tight on the back of her thighs and hurts her. She says nothing, and then he's tugging at himself again, the root heavy against her leg. His hands push her legs apart, accidentally pinching the skin; he is hot and gasping on top of her now, eyes squeezed tight shut, and then he's pushing it between her legs, actually into her flesh, her flesh that is whole, and she cries out in pain as the flesh tears and stings. He shudders and sinks into her. Her muscles are stiff, her teeth gritted against the pain, and finally he pulls away, slithers out of her, and there is a new smell, mingled with the smell of the ocean and the tinny blood and the clean linen, and she thinks it must be the smell of what had come out of the root the man was gripping in the alleyway outside the butcher's shop back home.

Afterward, they lie in the dark, side by side in the uncomfortable intimacy of each other's breath and awkward joining. Dorothy slows her breathing as though she is falling asleep, remembering how, when she and Joseph kissed on the lane behind the almshouses, she'd felt it with her whole self. She waits and listens to the sea, adjusting her rhythm to its rhythm, until at last she notices that William is asleep, his limbs soft and heavy next to hers. It is a relief to get out of the bed, to go and wash the blood from between her legs where her torn flesh is stinging, with water from the ewer. She creeps downstairs and outside to pour away the liquid with its blush of red. She returns then to the strangeness of the shared bed. She, Dorothy, a bride, a wife now, with a new duty.

The next day starts with the lighting of the stove in the morning for William's breakfast. She is grateful for something familiar to do. She sees the apology in his face when he sits down at the table, and she feels sorry too. In their mutual regret, they make an effort with each other, and she is glad to present him with his parcel of bread and cheese and sweet wrinkled apples for the day's work.

Later he comes back, and that night they try again to do what man and wife must do. But the nights never do get any better, the desperate grasping at himself that doesn't often work, her ignorance of what she should do to help. He is kind and holds her hand; he brings her gifts—wild geraniums and soon summer roses that smell of hope.

But later, they will smell only of disappointment.

One night her hand creeps to the warmth between her legs; she feels the painful tension on touch and slips her fingers inside her salty flesh, and the tension starts to build then releases like a wave rushing her onto the beach, where she lies, gasping, hand slick, lips parted.

And then there is the awful night when the exquisite tension builds and Dorothy pulls up her nightgown, actually climbs on him. She tries herself to pull at him, to make him hard, to push him into her, and is weeping with frustration when she catches his glance of open horror at the hair

166

between her legs, her gleaming thighs. That night she cries herself to sleep in shame for what must be wrong with her, and he lies next to her in silence, surely knowing there is nothing to be done to comfort her.

They don't try again.

Agnes

Scott is a regular visitor now. Agnes doesn't bathe in lavender for him. She gathers the clothes for washing and thinks about his offer. Maybe there's something in what her father said. *No airs and graces.*

His passes are clumsy but affectionate. "You and me," he says, following her from garden to stove, table to fire, standing over her while she bakes and stirs and chops, "we could be happy together, Agnes. I'd give you lots of kiddies. Fertile stock, us Mackintoshes," and he beats his chest and laughs, grabbing her about the waist.

Agnes doesn't smile. And that's easy at first. There's a sore place that makes her weak, makes her hold on to the table and shut her eyes as she hears Joseph's voice, again and again, the night of the ceilidh.

For one mad moment, she'd thought he wanted her to kiss him. He hadn't moved his mouth from hers, but then he'd pulled away sharply, rubbing his hand across his lips. "Agnes, what do you think you're doing?" and he'd stepped backward, the shock in his face vivid in the light from the windows, and suddenly she wasn't a woman anymore, she was just a stupid little girl. She squeezes her eyes shut against the memory of how his expression had changed to something even worse—kindness.

No, not kindness. Pity.

"Agnes, you don't mean this. I am not the man for you. That man will come, if you're patient. You are the little sister I never had, you know that. You're family." His expression had been appalled. "If I've ever led you to think otherwise—"

But she hadn't listened to the end of his sentence, covering her ears instead. "I hate you!" she'd said, like the child she is, and then she'd run, to hide her humiliation in the darkness of the night. When she'd got home, she'd torn off her dress with its stupid collar and thrown herself on the bed. What had she been thinking? What had made her think a man like that would be interested in a woman—a girl, really—like her?

Shame burns her cheeks.

She takes a deep breath and brings herself back to the present, checking the clothes for tears that need mending before sinking them in the water. At least she doesn't have to pretend with Scott to be something she isn't. And he's a hard worker. Yes, he likes a drink, but she's used to that, isn't she? Would it be so bad? And she's not her mother—she'd be going into it with her eyes wide open.

If she had children, they'd always come first; she wouldn't see them frightened, and she knows how to give love—her heart is full of it.

If she says yes to Scott, and it's only an if . . .

She pauses in her washing, thinking of the children she'd have, her hand drifting to her stomach as though one were already with her.

. . . it will all be different.

Now

Dorothy and the Plover

They start to spend their mornings in the garden—there are still vegetables to be found belowground, turnips and potatoes, and some hardy kale growing above, and while she digs in the snow, he plays and tends to the small snowman he's made with twigs for arms and stones for eyes, or peers at the hens in the coop, fluffing themselves out for warmth. This particular morning they've not been out there long when he cries out.

Dorothy straightens up slowly, knees aching a little, and leans on the spade, one hand in the small of her back, wiping away the snowflakes that alight on her cheeks and lips.

"What is it? What have you found?"

He's crouching at the far end of the vegetable garden at the base of the apple tree. It had only been a sapling when she'd wed, but is now sturdy and strong, though bent by the wind. He waves her over, and she guesses from his excitement it is an animal of some kind. She sighs and trudges through the snow to see.

Under the branches, where the snow lies in patches amongst the layers of crisp frozen leaves, is a bird. At first, she thinks it is dead, but then its eye flutters and one of its wings moves weakly. The child looks at her with agitation.

Dorothy leans in closer and glimpses its brownish-gray back and white belly. She gently brushes away the leaves. It is a ringed plover, one of the many that visit Skerry Sands when the tide is out. The boy moves to pick the bird up, but she sees now how it is injured, its wing twisted and broken. Dorothy puts her hand on the boy's arm and shakes her head. "Leave him be."

The boy understands her meaning, if not her words, and looks horrified, as though she has killed it herself, then and there. She knows the bird will die. It will not survive the winter. These things have to be accepted.

The boy looks up at her, stubborn and pleading at the same time. Dorothy considers the child's curly head, his quiet stance, and the plover in the dead leaves.

She sighs. "Stay with the bird. I'll be back," and goes into the house. It is against her better judgment, but she puts the kettle on the hob and looks in the pantry for the basket she keeps eggs in. Inside she places a clean linen cloth. Outside in the garden, she kneels beside the boy and cups her hands to show him how to pick it up. He is gentle. He cradles the frightened bird in his palms and lets it slip into the basket, and they bring it into the kitchen. Dorothy feels the kettle, and when it is the right temperature, she takes it off the heat. The boy is peering into the basket, which sits on the kitchen table. Dorothy goes upstairs to fetch the stone pig, and when the boy sees it, he nods excitedly, smiling, as she fills it with the kettle water.

She wraps the stone pig with a drying cloth and places it near the stove. He knows what to do and places the basket on top of the stone pig, and smiles.

She gives him a piece of linen to lay over the makeshift nest and then leads him, finger to her lips, to the table, where she puts the kettle back on the hob to make them a cup of tea and leave the bird to die in warmth and darkness.

Later, she makes supper. She can't keep him from the stove because all he wants to do is crouch by the fire to be near the plover. It is less cold now, but when she pulls back the cloth, she can see the wild fluttering beneath the feathers of the bird's plump chest, the frightened spin of its eye.

And suddenly, like a book that is accidentally knocked off the shelf—a story from childhood you'd forgotten about till that moment—she remembers the hoglet.

Moses and the Hoglet

Moses finds it in the garden near the henhouse one smoky autumn morning when they're picking up windfalls from the apple tree.

"What is it?" she asks.

He's squatting on his haunches, his face very close to the grass and fallen leaves. It hardly even looks like a hedgehog it's so small, its new spikes just starting to darken.

"Where's its mam?" His voice is quiet and worried, and he looks up at her, a small crease between his eyebrows. "Where's its mam gone?" and together they search for the nest, under the tree, under the henhouse.

"Maybe a bird dropped it," she says.

"Or it went for a walk and got lost." He reaches out his hand and the hoglet curls up to protect itself.

"Don't touch it, Moses, it might have ticks. Come on, best to leave it. There's no saving them at this age."

Moses looks up at her, horrified. His chin is set. "No."

She is used to his stubbornness and puts her hand under his arm. He shakes her off and drops into a cross-legged position in the damp grass and folds his arms. "No," he repeats.

"Suit yourself, but I'm going into the warm to stew these

apples for a pudding." She waits for him to take the bait, but he just folds his arms tighter and stays by the hoglet.

A bit later, the apples softening in butter, Dorothy goes back out into the garden where Moses has covered the hoglet in leaves and bits of grass. He can't stay out, not on a morning like this, with a fret coming in and a veil of fine drizzle hanging in the air.

"All right, you win. Go and get a cloth and the basket on the table that had the apples."

Moses smiles and leaps up, running into the cottage and back out a moment later. Squatting back down, they use the cloth to gently lift the hoglet into the basket. They place it near the stove in the kitchen, where Moses crouches over it.

"Can it eat porridge?"

"No."

"Can it eat apple pudding?"

"No."

"What about bread?"

"No, it can't eat bread. Now go and play somewhere else."

"What can it eat, then? It must be hungry."

Dorothy sighs in exasperation, stops what she's doing, and wipes her hands on her apron. There's no point in it eating anything. It's too small and it won't live.

"I'll stew a bit of apple on its own, but for now it can probably have a bit of warm water if you make a teat with the cloth."

"How do I do that?"

Dorothy purses her lips, pours warm water from the kettle into a cup, and kneels by the stove with him; she shows him quickly how to twist the end of the cloth and dip it in the water, to drop into the hoglet's mouth, then returns to her cooking.

Moses stays with it all day. He takes his job seriously. He laughs with delight when the hoglet sucks at the soft apple on the teat and puffs itself up with pleasure. He changes its cloth, which Dorothy notices has spots of blood on it. He feeds it and keeps it warm by the stove, but Dorothy hears its tiny sneezes, sees how dry its skin looks.

After a supper of haddock and stovies, Moses disappears upstairs and brings down a blanket and puts it on the floor by the basket. He curls up on it. The hoglet is wheezing now; its nose is running.

"I'm going to sleep here."

"No, Moses. Just let it be. It's not very well. Can you hear the sound it's making?"

"He's snoring. I'm going to stay here and look after him."

They argue and Dorothy wins when she promises to build up the fire and fetch an old jersey for him to put over the basket to keep it warm overnight. Moses stomps his foot on every step up to bed, then slams his door.

Dorothy wakes before dawn. Creeping downstairs, she finds Moses exactly where she expected, wrapped in the blanket next to the stove and the basket. The hoglet is dead, its little body already rigid, its legs outspread and reaching for nothing, mouth open. She looks at the sleeping boy and regrets her impatience the day before. Sighing, she covers him better with his blanket and leaves the basket outside the door into the garden, where a frost is stiffening the grass and the sky is turning soft pink with the coming day.

Inside, she heats the porridge, then gently shakes him awake.

At first, he doesn't believe her, so she takes him outside where he lifts the cloth and looks at the body. When he cries, he covers his face.

Between sobs he asks her, "Why did he die?"

"He was just too little to be on his own for so long," she tries to explain. "It was too cold and he needed his mother."

They dig a small grave under the apple tree and bury its body, and Dorothy helps Moses to tie two sticks together for a cross to mark the place.

Much later, her words come back to haunt her on the nights she places her stone lantern on the ledge and peers out of her window into the night.

He was just too little to be on his own for so long. It was too cold and he needed his mother.

Then

Dorothy

A day comes when her courses don't. She only realizes when she feels sick one morning and has to rush out of the kitchen while making William's porridge. She retches in the vegetable patch, a vile, sour taste in her mouth. She assumes this is what it means, because her mother was sick all day with the child who came after her, her cloths for her monthly blood no longer in the washing.

She stands back up, breathing in the fresh sea air. She leans against the wall, suddenly faint. Maybe it's too soon to tell; she will wait a few days to see.

As the days in which she is dry and sick continue, she starts to be sure. She can feel there is something different about her body and often looks at herself in the mirror to see if it is visible.

She feels reluctant to tell William, as though it is a secret to be kept for herself alone. She stands at her window and looks out to sea, at the hazy line of the horizon in sunlight, and places her hand on her belly, which has the merest hint of roundness. The women of the village seem to pop them out like kittens. Is it this miracle, this fear, for them each time too? She wants it to stay like this, she and her dream child and their mysterious unity.

One morning when she comes back into the kitchen after leaning against the back door, clutching her stomach, he asks.

"Dorothy, can it be? Are you—" His voice stumbles.

Dorothy nods. "I think so. I think I am," and she feels a surge of hope, and they smile at each other; it is the first piece of happiness they have shared for some time.

William comes to her and puts his arms around her, lays his head on her shoulder, so happy that somehow, their awkward coupling must have been enough.

"I'm so glad," he says, and in those words are so many things—apology and forgiveness, regret and relief, fear assuaged. And behind all of that, an uncertain, emerging joy. He kisses her hair. "I'm so glad," he says again.

Dorothy is grateful for his gentle pleasure. And she is glad too; there is a life inside her, and this is maybe where her life—their life—can begin as well. But in her gladness there are other feelings too, uncomfortable ones, now that the dream child is not just hers. She leans into him and shuts her eyes.

Later, Dorothy is lying awake. Her sickness is starting to pass. Next to her, William is softly snoring. Sometimes he snores before he has even shut his eyes, and she wonders at his ability to fall asleep so quickly and stay asleep till dawnlight. She knows he does because she wakes so often, especially now. She finally feels her eyes closing and drifts into the liminal space between wakefulness and sleep. She feels like the sea, the ebb and flow of her breathing, the rise and fall of her chest, her hair seaweed on the pillow.

Something moves inside her. It is only a small movement, a small creature flipping over in her belly. Her hands move in wonder across her skin, feeling for the life deep inside, feeling for the way they are both one and two. She feels as though she is expanding out till she is all the oceans of the earth containing the whole of life within her.

Her belly grows and she has to let out her dresses; her back and hips hurt, feel looser. There are times when she stands at the stove and the stabbing pain down through her thigh locks her in position. On these days, William is very attentive, insisting she sit down while he brings a pot of tea to the table. Sometimes she sleeps for too long and comes downstairs to the oats thick and lumpy in the pan where he's tried to make his own breakfast and leave some for her. On these days, guilt pulls at her, but they muddle through. When she presses her hands to her skin, she can feel the baby's twists and turns, watch her skin undulate. When William feels and sees this, he smiles in wonder and pride. Dorothy smiles too, but her uncomfortable feelings are growing.

One night she wakes and thinks.

What if I won't love it? What if I don't know how to look after it?

What if I am my mother?

Now

Dorothy and the Plover

That night Dorothy dreams she is running from room to room, searching in cupboards, under beds for something; she hears a call, fluting and melancholy, but cannot find where it comes from.

When she wakes up, she thinks of the boy's eager, worried face as he tended the plover, of Moses's quiet crying when the hoglet died. Why hadn't she tried harder to keep it alive? Had she really been so like her own mother?

She hurries downstairs in her nightgown and checks on the boy first. The dawn-light is gray and cold. The boy is still asleep, but on his stomach, in the cradle of his arms, is the basket. She pulls back the linen coverlet. She's too late. The bird is dead, one dull dark eye open, unseeing. Dorothy's eyes sting—though she is relieved at least to have found it before the boy—when she sees a rapid rise and fall of its breast. She places her fingers gently against the feathers to be sure, and there it is, the beat of a tiny heart.

She goes back upstairs and comes down dressed to sweep the grate and light the fire in the other room, before warming the oatmeal through with milk. In another bowl, she tears some bread and adds a little warm milk. Outside, the trees on the cliff, already blasted, creak in the wind, which blows the snow against the windows of the cottage. When she calls him, the boy appears in the kitchen, carrying the stone pig. After she's filled it, she shows him the bowl of bread and milk and a cup of water.

"For the bird," she says. "To eat," and mimes putting food in her mouth. "Bread and warm milk, that might do it." If it survived the night, maybe there is a chance, after all.

She places the bowl on the table. She starts to mash it up and then hands him the spoon, which he uses to finish the job, then nods, smiling, as though they have done a particularly good piece of schoolwork. They take it through with a cup of water. When he feeds the plover, he is extraordinarily gentle. He shows the tenderness that children naturally have toward animals and birds, recognizing their vulnerability, approaching them without fear. Afterward, Dorothy watches him take a corner of cloth and dip it in the water, twist it into a teat. He drips the water into the bird's open beak and she observes his concentration, his assumption of the trust they have in each other, and turns away to make the fire. He pulls the cloth over the basket again and comes through to the kitchen for his porridge. As he eats, Dorothy notices the bloom of his cheek, the brightness of his eyes. Looking after the bird, trying to make it better—it must be good for him.

The bird survives the day, but on the occasions when they look under the cloth, its feathers are still fluffed out, its beak open, its breath panting and panicked. She shows him how to change the cloth when it's soiled without lifting the bird out. She can see his feeling for it, how strong his desire to bring it back to life is.

At supper that night, she says, "Well done, you've taken good care of the bird. I think we can give it a second chance, I really do," and he looks up at her, tilts his head, and smiles his small, quiet smile.

Then

Dorothy

It's a white winter morning when her pains come. They catch her unawares, crouching by the hearth, almost unbalancing her. William is only just able to support her upstairs before her waters break, soaking her and the wood of the floor. Once she's on the bed, he hurries out to fetch the midwife. Two come, an old woman and a younger one. They are entirely unfussed by her agony, her fear, chatting away to her and each other. Boiling kettles, fetching towels, putting cool flannels on her forehead, making tea while William waits downstairs. Dorothy doesn't know how anyone has ever done this before, surely no one has felt such pain; it takes over her body; she tries to walk around the room, bends over, clutching the window ledge, crouches on all fours, while the midwives try to keep her in the bed, but she's like a wild animal and can't keep still.

She has no idea how long has passed, whether it's hours or minutes, but they've got her on the bed at last, and between each clutching, tearing wave of agony, she falls into a dazed silence while her body labors.

Someone is shaking her. "Dorothy, time to push! Push!" and she pushes, when pushing is an impossibility, when it is both an agony and a necessity; she pushes through her split, torn flesh, and then as the baby slithers out, a rush of blood and relief. She lies back, exhausted.

Outside, snow is falling in soft flakes against a dusky sky.

The midwives rush to tend to him. "It's a boy, Dorothy. A healthy boy," the older one says. "He's . . . " Her voice trails away.

"Quick, get it off him," the other says. "Cut it so he can breathe."

Dorothy tries to raise herself to her elbows, panting and sweating. "What's wrong?"

"It's nothing, dear." But they're leaning over him, touching him, pulling at something, speaking in hushed, urgent voices.

"What are you talking about? What's the matter with him?"

"There," the younger one says, lifting him. "Nothing's the matter with him," and she's slapping his back, and at last he makes a choking, gurgling cry that rises to a wail. "Hear that? That's what we want to hear. I've never seen it myself, but it's nothing to worry about. Some even say it's good luck," but the more she says it, the more panicked Dorothy feels.

"Give me my baby, I want my baby."

The midwives glance at each other, then reluctantly pass him to her. She clutches the little swaddled figure and cries out. Across his head and cheeks is a hood of membranous skin. The women have tried to lift it from his nose and mouth, but it clings to his scalp, is hooked over his ears, presses his eyes, mistily visible through the membrane.

Dorothy's heart pounds, her voice a breathy sob. "What's that? What is it?"

"It's just the caul." The younger midwife tries to smile. "Just a part of what he grew in. Now, we'll need some paper to gently rub the rest off. You have paper?"

The older midwife leans in. "You should keep the paper. It protects the child against drowning. Like a talisman."

Dorothy recoils. "I'll do no such thing." She turns to the other one. "So it comes off?"

The younger midwife touches her hand. "Of course it does. Now, shall I get this paper?"

Dorothy is so relieved, she goes weak. She quickly explains where it is, and the younger midwife runs downstairs.

The older one comes closer to the bed. "Are you sure you don't want to keep it? The child that wears the caul is a special child, the birth a special one. A fey birth."

Dorothy clutches her baby tighter and turns away from the woman but can't look at him again, not yet, not with this hideous aberration on his head.

The younger midwife is back in the room. "Don't go filling her head with those old superstitions."

Dorothy passes her the baby quickly. "Please, just take it off," and it's the work of a few minutes, a gentle rubbing and, "There. He's all ready for you now. I'll just pop this on the fire downstairs," but Dorothy isn't listening, she is already holding him close, gazing at the face that is now fully revealed to her; it's like a wrinkled apple, eyes clear and squinting and gazing back into hers. She presses her cheek to his, breathes in his sweet smell. Her heart steadies, her limbs relax, and the most extraordinary peace suffuses her body.

He is perfect.

She is barely aware of the midwives tidying the room, washing her, rolling her from side to side while they expertly change the linen, taking away the sheet that is soaked in blood and sweat. The younger one sits on the bed and shows her how to put him to the breast, and then they call William upstairs. When he comes in, Dorothy is lying under the blankets she has knitted herself, holding him to her, in quiet and warmth, she and the child both exhausted in their struggle to separate and be together, already drifting in and out of sleep. William is tender. He kisses the top of her head, then the top of the baby's. There are tears in his eyes as he sits next to her.

"Well done," he says. "Well done." And she doesn't tell him about the caul, doesn't want him to think the child is anything less than perfect, doesn't want anyone to, ever. He tucks them both in, plumps up the pillow, kisses her hair again, and strokes the baby's cheek.

"Now, wait there," he says, as though they might go some-where, and he brings her broth, holds the child while she pushes herself, wincing, into a sitting position to eat. He holds the baby like he's the most fragile thing that ever ex-isted, his face alight with wonder.

Afterward, he places him next to her in bed, takes away the bowl, and she and the boy sleep until she awakes much later, just before his shivering cry, his face ancient and crum-pled, his hands curling and uncurling, grasping at her nightgown.

When she feeds him her womb cramps; her breasts ache but soon the first milk comes and she does what the midwife showed her, till he is noisily suckling, both of them learning, his hands gripping her flesh, his eyes fixed on hers, till she has the strange feeling that the birth didn't separate them at all. Her body relaxes to accommodate him, and his skin is the same as hers, their gaze one gaze.

When William comes to bed the baby is put into the simple crib next to Dorothy. She feels cold without him. In the dark she turns on her side and reaches out to place her hand on him, to feel him breathing, and she stays awake, waiting for him to be hungry, or wet, or to cry for loneliness so that she can scoop him up and be one again.

Now

Dorothy

The dream comes again. The frantic running from room to room. It is the plover; it is out there somewhere in the cold. It is suffering. There is no one to feed it, no one to mend its wing, no one to make sure it is warm.

She hears its sorrowing call.

Mamma, it says. *Mamma*.

And she wakes up.

"Moses," she cries.

Dorothy is sweating, the blankets are twisted, and there is terror in her heart as she stumbles out of bed and into that terrible night.

She'd known as soon as she'd woken up, the way you know when you knock at a door that no one is home—Moses wasn't there. The storm was howling, the house a ship torn loose of its mooring, the wind buffeting every window, every door. She doesn't know how she knew, but her frantic glance into his room had confirmed it.

Not tonight, not tonight. Not in this.

And she'd run through the two rooms downstairs, eyes widening in horror. His boots were gone . . .

. . . and there it stops again, where it's always stopped, although it's been years since she's tried to get herself past it—because why would anyone want to remember a night like that? But something in her is yearning, and Dorothy rises and goes now to the cupboard in her bedroom, the one that she never opens, and she lifts the catch of the door.

They are still there, after all these years, and as one slips, they all come tumbling out, the jumpers and hats and socks and gloves and scarves she'd knitted since that terrible night, and none of them are for a fisherman.

They are too small.

They are for keeping a child warm, one who is always six years old.

There hadn't been enough time. She hadn't had enough time with him.

Dorothy sinks to the floor, surrounded by all the clothes she'd made for Moses, for her child, night after night, even though he'd left her, and closes her eyes. She scoops them up in her arms and holds them to her face, and she opens the locked box of her heart and finds inside the tiny hope that had never died, the one that told her that there would be a day when Moses would come back to her. He would come back and God would give her another chance with him.

And a sense of wonder steals over Dorothy as she sits there for a long time, the room lightening with the coming day, and thinks about the sleeping boy downstairs and how God works in mysterious ways.

The Postboy

Tom Carnegie pulls a chair close to the fire to eat his morning porridge. He tucks a whole drying cloth into the collar of his shirt and smooths it over his top and trousers. His mother looks at him and smiles.

"Who'd have thought it! You, Tom! A postboy!" She lifts the iron off the stove top and spits on it. It sizzles and, with a satisfied nod, she returns to pressing his jacket. "That Mrs. Gray always said you'd make something of yourself if you put your mind to it. Patience of a saint she had with you."

Tom thinks of the hours she spent, teaching him to read and write, and agrees between mouthfuls. It's barely light outside, his younger brothers and sisters just starting to stir in the sleepy warmth of the bed they all share.

"Hurry up now, Tom, before the rabble get up."

He does up the jacket, the stiff fabric still hot from the iron, polishes the buttons with a cuff. "What do you think?" He turns on one foot.

"Same as I have every morning for the last two weeks. Proud as punch." Her eyes gleam, and he steps forward to hug her. "Don't go messing that jacket up. Now go, or you'll be late."

Tom brings the bicycle through from the garden. It is his pride and joy, and the hours he spends cleaning it of dirty snow show in the bright reflection of the fire on the metal frame and spokes.

Outside, the snow has finally stopped falling. The villagers have come to their windows and to their doors to look. For the first time in weeks, the Tops, the sea, the other side of the street, are visible. As he pushes his bike up the hill past them, hat firmly on his head, they greet him and each other, almost in a festal way, commenting on the change, how it couldn't come too soon, how at last, maybe this terrible winter is coming to an end and normal life can finally begin again.

As he passes Brown's Grocers and Confectioners, Mrs. Brown herself is standing in her doorway.

"Morning, Mrs. Brown," Tom calls. "Lovely morning." He clears his throat and repeats the phrases he's heard the grown-ups say, trying them out for size. "Couldn't come quick enough!" and "Spring'll be here before we know it."

She looks up at the sky, and Tom looks up too, trying to see what Mrs. Brown can see.

She sniffs the air, then tightens her shawl around her shoulders before turning back to the shop. "I wouldn't speak too soon, Tom. Could be this winter is just gathering its strength."

Then

Dorothy and Jane

The days and nights and nights and days blur and merge in a kaleidoscope of feeding, changing, sleeping, hurting. She is still bleeding and the midwife comes and gives her ergot to stem it. William goes to work, the winter always a busy time for boat repairs and building. Sometimes Dorothy is downstairs to make his breakfast and lunch, Moses in a crib on the table or asleep upstairs, but while the blood still comes, William insists she rest with the child.

But in amongst the exhaustion is their shared joy when the child grips William's finger with his tiny ones, when his eyes follow their faces, when he first smiles at William's homecoming, arms and legs wriggling in excitement. But their favorite time of day is the evening, when they pick Moses out of his crib and have him in bed with them, playing peek-a-boo with the blanket and singing nursery rhymes, while Moses smiles and coos and reaches for them with his chubby arms and then falls asleep between them. On these times William kisses Dorothy's hair and says, "Well done," after another day when she has been too tired to clean or make bread, but he never seems to mind, so proud is he of his healthy son and his wife.

One morning, when Dorothy wakes, the cottage is full of the most delicious savory smell. She comes downstairs with the child to look for William. The bleeding has finally stopped, but she still feels weak and sore, so she takes it slowly, the child clasped to her chest. She can hear movement in the kitchen, but when she opens the door, it is to Jane.

Dorothy's heart jumps and she feels the blood rush from her head.

"What are you doing here? Where's William?"

Jane turns, takes in Dorothy's unbrushed, loose hair, the hastily pulled-on dress, still unbuttoned for ease of feeding. Ease! The pain has become excruciating, like tiny knives slicing into her nipples where the blisters pop and reform, pop and reform with his urgent, relentless sucking.

Jane's lips tighten. "He left an age ago. Someone needs to take care of him. Of you both," she corrects herself.

Dorothy sinks into a kitchen chair. Jane is right. William can't keep going to work and looking after her while she looks after the baby. The other women do it all. She tightens Moses's blanket around him and places him on the table. "There's no need, Jane. I can do it. I'm just a little tired."

"Sit yourself back down, Dorothy, I'll get the crib. I've been up cooking before sunrise this morning, there's a pan of chicken broth heating now and a partan bree for tomorrow. We'll get you on your feet again—after all, an empty pot can pour no tea!"

When Jane appears with the crib, Dorothy is cradling Moses in her arms, gently rocking him. "No wonder so little is getting done around here if you're always mollycoddling the baby. Give him to me," and reaching out, she plucks Moses from Dorothy's arms.

Dorothy's eyes widen in alarm. "What are you doing?"

"I'm putting him in the other room."

Dorothy's distress makes her voice weak. "No, he's happier here with me. Jane. Please. Give him to me."

"Happier? Babies need quiet," and Dorothy hates herself for being too exhausted, too afraid to stand up to her.

Soon Moses is swaddled in the crib in the other room by the fire and Dorothy is sipping at the hot broth Jane has said she needs to keep her strength up, while she fusses round the kitchen. Dorothy listens all the time for Moses, for the first sign he needs her and she can go through and pick him up. When everything has been washed and wiped and cleaned down, Dorothy sighs a little silent sigh of relief. Jane can go home now, and she's right, Dorothy needs to pull herself together and keep things in order. Look after home and hearth.

"Thank you, Jane, this has been such a help," and she tries to sound like she means it, though all her thoughts are with the baby and how she will rush into the other room as soon as Jane has gone and clutch him to her while she waits for William to come home. "You must have your own things to see to now . . . " She leaves the words hanging.

Jane looks at her as though puzzled, then her face clears. "Oh, I shan't be going home. I've made up a little bed in the box room; I'll be staying for a bit." She flaps a drying cloth, deftly folds it. "William asked me—just to help, you know."

The tears, so readily available since Moses's birth, spring to Dorothy's eyes.

"William asked you?"

Moses begins his shivering cry, rising to a wail, and Dorothy heaves herself up, wincing.

"And we'll start here, I think—no need to be picking the child up every time he cries—you can't let him be the master of you. He's just exercising his lungs, is all. The Gray boys didn't turn into fine young men by being pandered to, you know."

And Dorothy thinks, *What do you know?* But the thought is quickly followed by, *What do I know?* Her breasts hurt as the milk rushes in and Moses's wail becomes more urgent, more piercing. She steps forward, ashamed as milk soaks through her dress. Jane stands in front of her, her eyes dropping to Dorothy's chest, to the darkening fabric. "Why don't you go and get changed," she says with barely concealed disgust. "I'll see to the baby."

"No, he needs me, Jane," and she can't believe she is begging Jane to let her feed her own child, and she wants to push past her, to tell her to leave her house, but Jane hurries into the other room before Dorothy can. Dorothy follows. Jane is leaning over the crib, staring into the child's face. She reaches into the crib and folds down the blanket and tightens it around him.

Dorothy wants Jane to leave him alone, to stop staring at him. Moses's crying is an agony to her, and she moves toward the crib to push Jane out of the way, but just as quickly Jane looks up. The look she gives her reminds Dorothy of the look she gave her the first night she went for supper.

The hostility nearly takes her breath away.

Dorothy steps back, feels the blood drain from her face.

Because she can see that Jane knows.

She knows it isn't William's baby at all.

Dorothy and Joseph

It happens one of those dreadful nights when they are lying awake pretending to be asleep. Dorothy tries to talk about it with him again.

She places her hand on William's shoulder, who is turned away from her. "William?"

He doesn't move. "What's the use of talking?"

"Maybe it would help."

"Some things just can't be helped," and he pulls the blanket further over his shoulder to let her know the conversation is over.

Dorothy's anger flares. "Well, they can't if you won't tell me what the problem is," because she really needs to know what is wrong with her that this act, which must come so easily to others, does not come easily to them. What do other women do—how do they know what to expect? Who tells them?

"Just go to sleep, Dorothy," and she turns away but she can't sleep, staring instead into the darkness, and when his body relaxes next to her and his soft snoring begins, she can bear it no longer. She slips her legs out of bed; the cold bites in a different way to shame and anger. William, if he hears her, doesn't ask where she is going as she wraps her shawl around herself, and she doesn't bother waking him to tell him. Once downstairs, she puts her feet into her boots but doesn't lace them in her desperation to get out, to feel something other than this appalling disappointment.

Outside, a bright moon is rising over the black sea; clouds drift across it like smoke. Moonlight silvers the vetch along the cliff top as she hurries down the Steps, nightgown flapping, skin tightening with cold beneath the shawl. The white-foamed waves rush up the beach and then suck back in, and she allows her anger and disappointment to bubble up until she is standing in the icy, painful water.

Joseph doesn't know she's there until he hears a cry of rage. He has come down to check he secured the boat, and is now tying the last rope. The rain is already spitting. At first he thinks it is a bird screaming, or an animal injured on the cliff, so he is shocked when he sees Dorothy, boot-shod in the water, hands pulling her shawl tight, hair whipping her face.

"Dorothy?"

She turns, and he's never seen her so exposed, so raw. She can't gather herself, simply stares at him, not seeming to comprehend his presence.

She hates him, she hates him. Why is he walking toward her? Why is he down here at all? He is always where she needs him not to be.

Dorothy watches him come closer. She doesn't move; a great stillness comes over her, and she lets out a long sigh. There has not been a moment of decision, there has been no gateway through which she has passed, but here she is, and so is Joseph. It seems very natural that he should take off his jersey and pull it over her head. She breathes in the smell of him, and some of the heat of his body seeps into hers. He wraps the shawl around her, then reaches behind her and frees her hair from the neck of the jumper. It is wet from the squall that is picking up. He lifts a lock and brings it to his face. It is the most tender thing anyone has ever done. She wraps her hand around his and they walk across the wet sand, footprints vanishing behind them.

When they reach the shelter of the cliff, he turns her to him and wipes her face dry. She's not sure if his is wet from sea spray or rain, but she wipes his as well. When his mouth touches hers, she is surprised at its softness and then its heat when he opens it. She opens hers too. His tongue is searching and curious; his hands hold her face.

She wants to touch him; her hands feel cool on his skin, which is smoother than she thought it would be. She feels down all the length of his spine, from the back of his neck to the hollows at the base, fingers tracing in wonder. Her palms follow the curve of his muscles. His skin is beautiful. She unbuttons her nightgown beneath the jersey, and his hands explore her flesh. He bunches her skirt around her hips and pushes her legs apart; he lifts her, pinching her by accident; the pain is exquisite. There, in a cleft of the rocks, in the rain and the cold, he enters her, and she is wholly transformed, holding on to the thrust and weight of him as he rocks against her, his hands in her hair. She can feel his urgency now and her own desire rising like the tide to meet his, higher and higher, till it breaks like waves over them, the sea pulsing, their breath gasping.

Afterward, they cling to each other, their faces, mouths, hair, hands, legs entangled. They cling to each other like they are lost, like they are found.

"Dorothy," he breathes.

"Don't say anything, don't say anything."

"Look at me."

But she doesn't want to, because then it will be over and

she will have done the most terrible thing. She opens her eyes. His are warm and steady. He strokes her cheek and kisses her hair, but it is just as she feared, because now she is on the other side of it, a different person, someone who has betrayed every rule she was brought up to believe in.

Her voice is ragged. "We can't—" She steps away from him, painfully aware now that she is wearing only her nightgown, her boots, and his jumper.

They both bend to pick up her shawl, and bump shoulders.

"Don't leave," he says. "Not yet."

"Please, Joseph," and she's terrified, because he will have to be a stranger to her all over again, and she doesn't know how she will bear it. She takes off his jumper and, not looking at him, thrusts it back and takes the shawl to wrap around herself. The exchange is awkward, clumsy.

He holds her arm. "What happened to us?"

But she doesn't want to have to talk about any of it, because it's too late, and she pulls away. "It's done," she says. "I can't undo it. Not now I am married. I'm sorry," and she is, for him, for them both, because where marriage to William had once seemed to her like a refuge from pain, she knows now it is a yawning loneliness. "I wish—" She looks at Joseph, and the despair she feels is reflected in his eyes.

His grip on her arm tightens. "You wish what?"

But she can't show him how she feels, it is too painful for both of them, so instead she walks away, first slowly, then faster, running up the Steps to the path.

Up ahead, on the cliff top, a shadow moves from the silvered vetch into deeper darkness. Dorothy stops, breathing hard.

"Who's there?" The words are torn from her.

Her nightgown gleams in the moonlight and, down on the Sands, Joseph stands alone on the shoreline. Who has seen them?

"*Who is it?*" she calls again, more desperate this time, but the only answer is the cry of the wind.

The Shop

"It's nonsense," says Ailsa. "And even if the old stories were true, I thought it was supposed to be good luck—to protect against drowning."

"Not the old stories I know." Jeanie purses her lips. "A child born with the caul is a changeling. Mark my words, they'll come back for that child, the water faeries. Wouldn't be the first time, in these parts." She places her goods on the counter.

The women look uncomfortable.

Mrs. Brown breaks the silence. "You may not like her, but that is a wicked thing to wish for."

Jeanie looks defiant. "I didn't say I wished for it, only what the old stories say. Remember what Lizzy Fisher always said? And anyway, I'm not the only one who doesn't like her, with her hoity-toity ways."

The women look even more uncomfortable at this.

Mrs. Brown hands Jeanie her change. "Lizzy Fisher just couldn't face the fact her child had drowned. And who can blame her? Went quite mad with grief, that one."

Norah chimes in. "Always said her sister's child was her own boy come back to her. Remember? When she came back with that baby after working away?"

Mrs. Brown tuts. "Like I said, Norah, quite mad with

grief. I think we can guess very well how Lizzy's sister ended up with a baby and no father to show for it." She turns back to Jeanie. "Now, how is Agnes?"

Jeanie's voice has a brittle brightness to it. "She's taken to married life, as I knew she would—one less mouth to feed for me." She can't quite hide the way her face sags at that. "It won't be long till the kiddies come, I'm sure. Some people don't catch straightaway." She puts her parcels in her basket, then looks at Mrs. Brown, eyes narrowed. "I know what you're thinking, but he would have asked her if it hadn't been for that woman."

The women swap glances.

Mrs. Brown sighs. "No mind. I'm sure Agnes will be very happy, Jeanie."

Jeanie holds her head high as she leaves the shop, the bell jangling briskly.

"That Scott's a bad apple. No better than his father," says Norah, pursing her lips. "And Joseph was never going to ask."

Ailsa shakes her head sadly. "You know what they say— first the man takes the drink, then the drink takes the man, and there it is."

Norah nods. "Remember when Scott was trying his hand with Lorna? She soon put him in his place. Said she didn't want to end up black and blue like his mother—and she wasn't just blaming his father for that. That's what she said."

The women stand shaking their heads at this new piece of information.

Mrs. Brown wipes down the counter. "Well, Lorna's engaged to a young man in Fraserburgh now, I heard. No need for her to be worrying about the nonsense of Skerry men anymore!"

"There may be truth in what Jeanie said about Dorothy,

though—that she's the reason Joseph never asked." Norah pokes the stove. "Has anyone seen this child, then? What's his name—Moses? Is he healthy? I've heard a child born in a caul can be terribly afflicted—"

"I'm sure he looks like every other baby does, and will grow just as well as they all do," Ailsa says, then falls silent at a glance from Norah. "I'm sorry, I—"

"Pot of tea with something stronger?" Mrs. Brown says briskly, and disappears into the back of the shop.

Norah puts the kettle on the stove. "You always say the wrong thing, Ailsa. And don't be so sure about those old stories either. I hope to God Jeanie's wrong, but they say a changeling child brings nothing but grief. And anyway, who's to say they're stories at all?"

Agnes

Agnes huddles in bed. Another night she can't face working at the alehouse. All she's doing is earning back what her husband drinks anyway. The windows rattle in the wind, which finds its way through the rotten frames. How many times has she told Scott about them? He's useless with that sort of thing. How soon their first excitement faded. And she doesn't want to tell Jeanie what it's really like, hear her say, *What did you expect?* And *Look at the father if you want to know the son*, and he isn't like his father, not really. Yes, he's pushed her, but he wasn't to know she'd slip and crack her cheekbone on the table. He hasn't hit her, and there are times when he's kind, affectionate even, especially when he stops the drink. And then it's almost like the life she'd hoped for, with a good meal on the table and a husband who brings his money home.

Almost.

She curls around herself for warmth, pulls the blanket over her head. If she's asleep, or pretending to be, when Scott gets home from the alehouse, he might leave her alone. She can't face his pawing, not tonight. It's been months and, good God, he's tried, doesn't she know it? But every month the blood comes.

Even under here, the blanket scratching her cheek, the chill seems to get in. She does what she did as a child and rocks gently. She summons a sunny day. She's on the drying green, a swaddled baby in the grass by her feet. No, she's on the Sands and he's in her arms, wriggling. She's kneeling at the water's edge, lowering him to dip his toes in the foaming frill of the waves. He's pulling up his legs, squealing, curling his toes away as the waves rush in and rush out.

It's always a boy, a boy without a name.

A gust of wind shakes the window, calls her back to the bed and the blanket, where the barren winter of her body freezes her marrow, where her womb is empty and cold, frog-like.

It's not fair. Why, when it's the thing she has wanted most, to be a mother, is it the thing that is denied her? And why are children gifted to those who don't deserve them? *Damn you, damn you.* Her balled fists push into her stomach. *Why not me? What's wrong with me that I can't have the one thing, the only thing, I ever really wanted?* And her thoughts gather, thick and dark, around one name, the name of the person she tries not to think about, the one who stole her happiness.

Dorothy.

Dorothy

Jane says nothing in those first few weeks of staying, and Dorothy doesn't dare say anything to her. William hasn't changed toward Dorothy or the baby, his delight in Moses and his kindness to her never wavering. Nighttime is no longer the trial it once was, not now Moses has come and William believes himself the father. They still bring Moses into the bed, play the same games, sing the same songs, but Dorothy can't share the same joy, not now Jane is in the house, knowing what she knows.

Dorothy knows now who'd seen her on the cliff top and Joseph down on the Sands. And she sees how Jane looks at William when they take supper together, how she scrutinizes them both, eyes unreadable.

It's the day after a night when Moses has spent much of the time awake, crying. William has gone to work and Dorothy lies in bed, listening to the sound of a blackbird on the thatch, singing its song of spring. Moses is asleep on her chest. They breathe together, his fists clutching her hair; his skin is warm against hers.

When Jane comes in, she slams open the door. "Give me that child."

Dorothy sits up.

"Give him to me. Nothing is going to change round here

till there's a routine. He'll be as lazy as—" She doesn't need to finish the sentence.

Never in her life has anyone called Dorothy lazy, and she leaps up after Jane and follows her downstairs. "It was William who insisted we both rest—you heard the child overnight."

"William would say anything to keep this shambles going."

Dorothy stops still. "What did you say? Did you call our life a shambles?"

Even Jane looks stricken by her words. "I shouldn't have said anything. I'm just trying to help. Let's both calm down and I'll make tea."

Dorothy sees that this game of hide-and-seek cannot continue, and she gathers her courage. "I know you know, Jane."

Jane's mouth drops open. It's a moment before she can speak. "And William? Have you spoken of this to William?"

Dorothy is silent.

"I see. My poor brother." She looks at Dorothy for a long moment, lips pursed, then sighs. "Well, maybe it's best to keep it this way."

Dorothy goes upstairs and washes and dresses and comes back down to empty the bowl of water and the ewer. She takes Moses and changes and dresses him too, then puts him to rest in his crib in the other room and comes through to the kitchen and chops vegetables and makes bread and cleans and does all the things a new wife and mother should do. And she does it day after day, trying to ignore Moses's crying, just as Jane likes. Anything to stop her changing her mind.

And after a few weeks, Dorothy is stronger, it's true, and she knows now that you can leave a baby to cry while it's exercising its lungs and you mustn't feed it whenever it demands it, because it will get fat and greedy, and she is

208

learning to sleep through the cries, like the other mothers Jane has told her about. She is rested and feels better, her body is healing, but when she does pick the baby up, his skin doesn't feel like hers any more. They have separated, and she's no longer sure of how she should hold him or touch him. After a time he doesn't cry but lies in his swaddling blanket, eyes open, staring, hands curling and uncurling, and Dorothy wonders what it is he sees or feels.

She has no idea.

Now

Dorothy and the Child

Dorothy is very quiet the next day. She feels like a blackboard covered in chalk that has been wiped clean. Her movements are careful, deliberate, thoughtful. She watches the child, thinking of the way he'd looked for a ball, how he drew a picture of Skerry Sands with Dorothy in her nightdress on the shore. She doesn't understand it, can't look at it directly, but there are stories you hear out here on the edge of nowhere. There are mysteries.

He looks up at her and smiles, head tilted. Silver hair, green eyes.

Dorothy smiles back.

On a whim, she puts on her walking dress—it really is time to let it out by a few stitches now that her waist is starting to thicken—and goes back downstairs. The boy is kneeling on the floor by the basket.

She lays out the clothes on the end of the bed. "Get dressed. We're going out," and she moves her fingers to show and points to the sea. The strip of beach Dorothy can see from the window glows gold in the sunshine; the light flashes on the water and the sky is blue and clear, and everything in that moment looks new and fresh.

The boy nods and suddenly smiles, and her heart stirs with his pleasure.

When the boy comes into the kitchen, the light is behind

him, catching the silver in his hair, his face in shadow. Same height, same build. Time blurs.

When she opens the door, the cold takes her breath away. There is a crystal clarity to the light, a sparkling crispness to the thick snow. Down on Skerry Sands the wind is fierce, the sea breaking in clouds of spray and spume on the Rocks, and he fair pulls her along toward the water. Back then she thought she was doing it the right way, the way her mother had—Moses's boots taken off before he came in the house, his clothes still clean, leaving any crabs or crayfish that had been put in the bucket at the spring.

The tide is out, leaving stretches of shining dark sand and seaweed and rock pools, and this is where he is headed, pulling her like Moses tried to, till she makes herself do it—she lets him go. He picks up pace and so she does too, to make sure he's safe, lifting up her skirts a little and running after him. Running! The quickening of her blood, and her breath is released in a laugh, and when the boy sees she is following, he laughs too, and goes faster, till they have passed the tide line, their boots squelching in the sucking sand, bent over, gasping for breath.

There is plenty to find in the new rock pools now the moon has pulled the tide back into the belly of the sea—a crayfish, waving its spindly legs and antennae, a starfish that curls and uncurls like a child's hand, and in another, even a sea snail. The child moves from squatting on his haunches to kneeling, and Dorothy fleetingly thinks of the dirt, the washing, but stops herself from saying anything, and then, hesitantly, she copies him. The wet soaks through her skirts to her knees, and they watch the sea snail together, its slow, lumbering movements, catching each other's eye; she sees the joy in his, how easily it springs up, and her heart opens.

Dorothy stands up and holds out her hand. The boy

stands too, and they walk together to the tide line, then run at the waves as they're sucked in, and away from them as they rush back out over the ripples of the sand, and Dorothy can hardly take her eyes off his face and his look of happy excitement. She stops, and he looks up with the disappointed question in his eyes—*Are we leaving already?*—but she can't speak, so she just shakes her head and stares out at the distant line of the horizon, the fresh salt and green seaweed smell of the sea, and lets the wind blow and blow and buffet her, dress flapping around her knees, face stinging, appalled at how easy it would have been to give her child joy if she hadn't been so frightened always.

She grips the boy's hand, and they walk to the Rocks. This time, after they have harvested some mussels, the bucket is carried up the stone steps, the water with its starfish and crayfish sloshing and tipping, the boy holding on to it tight with one hand while the other finds Dorothy's. They lift out the mussels, then leave the bucket outside the front door, but Dorothy has decided they'll take it back down to the sea the next day and release the creatures back into the water at high tide, because if something is still alive, especially when you thought the hard winter had killed it, then you must keep it alive, allow it to live, give it a chance.

When they get in, she puts the kettle on the hob, reaches for the tin of biscuits. One of the kitchen chairs scrapes across the stone floor. Dorothy turns. It is the child settling himself at the table.

"Home," he says.

Later, Dorothy is making bread. The boy stands next to her, watching her hands pull and stretch the dough, folding it, pushing her fists into it, and the yeasty smell fills the kitchen.

"Pull up a chair—we can make it together," and she points. He drags it and kneels up.

"Like this," she says, and they pummel it and pull it together first, then he does it on his own with fierce concentration, and Dorothy opens her mouth to say well done, but something else comes out instead, as though it was a story she had started a long time ago.

"And the midwives—they came to the house because my pains came on very suddenly and William sent for them. They said the baby was coming and when he did, I was on the bed and—" She gives the boy a sideways look, but he looks as uncomprehending as always, so she carries on. "When he came out, it was—it was like a great weight slithered out of me, and the midwife, well, she gasped. There was something on his head, a—a caul," and her words come faster now so that she doesn't have to stop to think about what they mean, "and the midwife said what a lucky child, for a child born with the caul will never drown, that's what she said, that is truly what she said. She said I should keep it to protect him." Dorothy's hand flies to her mouth. The boy has stopped kneading and is watching her. "But I saw them look at each other, and I knew what they were thinking, because there is another kind of child that is born with the caul too and, God knows, round here they all know what that is, and I know they all talked about it, up in that wretched shop. But what if I'd kept it, what if they were right all along, would he have . . . ?" and her voice breaks on a breathy sob as the fear she's always felt that it was her fault rises in a rush like a wave breaking on a rock, and her breath comes quickly.

The boy lays his hand on her arm. She looks down at his face, sees the kindness and worry in it, and she puts her hand over his. She leans her head against his silver hair.

"Thank you," she says. "Thank you," because isn't all of it

really what she thought she deserved? And that is why she doesn't talk and share like the women around the stove, because when you talk, you find things out, things about yourself, like the creatures in the rock pools you hadn't known were there till the sea let you see them. Till you crossed the tide line of the water flowing backward.

Joseph

Joseph prepares the new caulking for *North Star* and warms the iron on his brazier. Farther along the beach, some of the fishermen's lads are kicking a ball on the harder sand where the tide has retreated, blowing into their cupped hands to keep them warm, their breath smoking on the air.

He notices a movement on the path to the Steps. His heart jolts when he sees it is Dorothy and the child. He remembers the shock of how like the child is to Moses when he found him, washed up amongst the seaweed and the driftwood, but nothing prepares him for this. The morning sun glints on his silver hair, and from this distance he is the same height, the same age. He could be the child that was lost. Dorothy is taking great care with him, steadying his fumbling steps. The child stops and looks out to sea and points while she says something to him. Joseph cannot look away.

They are on the Steps now, and the child places his feet carefully, looking from them to the sea. She is standing a little straighter than the last time he saw her, and when she bends to the child, there is something softer about her.

They rest at the bottom of the Steps on a boulder, and some of her old stiffness comes back—the boys are shouting and swearing, calls of "Bampot!" and "Bawbag!" followed by friendly pushing and shoving, and she is ever looking at the child, who is rapt, watching the game.

One of the boys notices her and calls something to the others, and they turn to look and laugh and touch their caps. "Sorry, Miss!" and "Will you be coming back to school soon, Miss?"

To Joseph's surprise, Dorothy smiles at them, a whole-hearted, engaging smile, and suddenly he is in her kitchen all those years ago.

It was one of the Saturdays when he was meant to be mending the windows. He'd helped her outside first, clearing garden waste, gathering it for the autumn burning, before coming in for a pot of tea.

It was the first time she'd set out two cups and had sat down with him. The chat had turned to the Minister and one of his well-meaning but slightly hapless misunderstand-ings, and they had unexpectedly caught each other's eye and laughed, and she'd tilted her head and smiled at him, a warm, natural smile. And he'd known then that her cool resistance to him was thawing. Later, he'd cut his hand on a pane of glass and wrapped some cloth around it. She'd come back from the garden and had seen it.

"Let me."

He'd waved his hand with the now-bloodstained make-shift bandage around it. "It's fine."

"It's not even clean. Sit down."

He'd glimpsed in that moment how she might be as a teacher, but he'd hidden his smile and sat down and put his hand on the table. It was throbbing now and more painful than he wanted to admit. She'd fetched a bowl and clean cloth, hot water and salt, and gently she'd unwrapped the bandage. She'd dipped the cloth in the salt water and cleaned the wound and the blood and dirt from his hand. He'd gritted his teeth against the sting. Her usual slight wariness had gone in the focus of her concentration, and her quietness enveloped him. He'd watched her, bent over her work; her lowered eyes, the shadows of her face, the faint scattering of freckles across her cheek—it all enchanted him.

After she'd dried his hand, she'd expertly wrapped and tied the cloth.

He'd not wanted her to let go and had tried to find something to distract her. "Where did you learn to do that? Your mother?"

To Joseph's surprise, Dorothy had laughed, though her smile had faded quickly. "No, she wasn't really that kind of mother. They teach you at college. How to treat minor injuries, that sort of thing."

He'd cleared his throat. "My mother wasn't that sort of mother either," though that was an understatement. Say what you liked about Jeanie, but she'd been a kinder force in his life than his mother. But he'd said none of this, though he'd pulled up his sleeve to show a badly healed scar, an uneven ripple of white skin on his brown forearm.

She'd gasped and reached out with her free hand and run her fingers along the bumps and grooves. "How did—?"

"Glass again—put my arm through a window messing about with my brother. Got a thick ear for that," and they'd looked at each other then, and something had passed between them, an understanding. A loose lock of hair had slipped over her cheek and, without thinking, he'd looped it around her ear.

As though she'd suddenly become aware of herself, she'd let go of his hand and stood up, flustered. But the look had happened, and it had changed things.

How close the past feels sometimes.

He stops his work now and moves to a part of the boat where he can watch them better. Dorothy leads the child away from the boys' game and their rowdiness, and over to the Rocks, tightening their coats against the cold. The closest rocks are black and wet and covered in mussels. They tug off their gloves and pull the mussels off, filling a bucket with them. He carries on watching her face, the way she is with the boy.

The football game wanes, and the children drift to the boats to help their fathers or up the Steps to help at home. The boy starts to tug at Dorothy's hand, leading her along the Sands and to the shoreline. Dorothy is rigid. The boy tries to pull her, but she has seen Joseph. He can't pretend he wasn't looking, but her expression is so far from his warm memory of her that it is like a physical blow, and everything that has happened since returns to him. Dorothy leans down to say something to the child and, tightening her grip on his arm, she makes for the Steps, while the child turns his head to catch Joseph's eye. His hands are clenched so tight, his nails dig into his palm.

Yes, how close the past feels.

Yet how utterly beyond reach.

Dorothy

Dorothy is shaken. She hasn't seen Joseph since he stood in her house and tried to tell her how to look after the child. She builds up the fire when they are home and heats up the broth for the midday meal. What was he doing watching them like that? And after all this time, why should any of it matter anyway?

And she's angry because it does matter to her, he matters, even now, and she clatters in the kitchen, pokes the fire too hard. While she cuts bread, the boy shows himself adept. He finds a knife and prizes open a mussel at the table, scooping the glistening pink flesh out with the other half of the shell. The first one goes straight into his mouth with its tiny ocean of salt water. He tips his head back and gulps. He has done this before, and she has a picture of him, on some beach somewhere with his mother, prizing, opening, scooping, and gulping, but the thought makes her heart clench and she pushes it away. She doesn't want to know.

Today the plover is standing up. The boy picks up a tiny bit of the mussel meat and puts it on the cloth. The bird pecks at it, then returns to its defensive position, cocking its head to look at them with an eye that is brighter than yesterday. Like this, the injury to its wing is more visible, but there will be no way of getting to it, not yet, and without

both wings it will surely die. Again she pictures Moses looking at the body of the hoglet, the way his shoulders shook as
he cried, and she feels a sudden yearning, an ache like hunger.

This time, it must be different.

The bird must survive.

Then

Dorothy

Late one night, when she's feeding Moses and trying to stay awake so she can put him down after, she hears Jane's voice downstairs, its angry hiss. She strains to listen. She hears her own name and Moses's. She tries to interpret William's hushed protestations but can make nothing out. When he finally comes up, she pretends to be asleep. He doesn't kiss her hair as he usually does, doesn't bend over the crib to kiss the baby's forehead, but pulls the blanket over himself and turns away. Dorothy's eyes are wide in the dark, barely blinking, her body rigid. She is terrified of Jane and the power she has over her.

But when she gets up the next day, there is barely a sign Jane was ever there, only her bed linen neatly folded, a Cullen skink on the stove.

"Where is she?"

William doesn't look at her. "She's gone. I told her to go."

Dorothy searches his face but doesn't dare ask why. "I see. I'll make your lunch to take."

"Jane made it." At last he looks at her. "She said some things—" But he doesn't finish the thought, and they both try to pretend everything is good between them.

But over time, Dorothy notices a change in William. She catches him sometimes staring into the cot and when he realizes she's near, he turns, eyes overbright. Dorothy finds herself searching for the evidence that he knows, almost wishing he would just come out and say, but somehow neither of them can.

Sometimes he's almost his old self, picking Moses up and peering into his face, laughing at every new expression, every babble that sounds like *Mamma* or *Dadda*. He's proud when the boy starts to walk and then to run, especially when William comes back from the boatyard, though that is becoming later and later. But sometimes as William looks at Moses, his smile is sad or he'll reach for Dorothy and pull her down to sit next to the crib beside him, holding her hand, trying to share a moment as a family. But this is almost worse. Her heart flutters when he looks at Moses. What can he see? How much, exactly, has Jane said? Dorothy always finds some reason to pick Moses up, to take him away to change or feed him, anything to break the agony of the moment. Her only relief is that Jane stops visiting and she feels released from her scrutiny, her barely hidden judgment.

At night, she and William lie side by side, sometimes holding hands, though he turns away more often from her now. She wonders if a new child, one that is his, will mend things between them, and so she tries again, letting him know with touch and soft words that she's willing, but this seems only to make things worse, so she busies herself instead with making good food, with keeping the home clean, to weigh against what they can't be in the marriage bed, what Moses can't be to him, what she can't. She wants to protect them both from the shame that should be just her own.

One day she goes into the little room Moses sleeps in now, drawn by a strange, muffled sound. William is kneeling by the bed, hunched over. It takes Dorothy a moment to realize he's crying, hands covering his face.

She rushes in, crouches next to him. "William?"

He turns to her, face red and swollen. "I can't do it. I'm sorry. I've tried, but I can't do it, Dorothy."

Dorothy can hardly breathe. "No, no. Don't say sorry. All of this is my fault," but still neither of them can name it. She reaches for his hand.

He grips it tightly in his. "I wish I was enough for you. For both of you." He bends his head over their knotted hands and quietly sobs.

Dorothy can't speak. She is blown open, and all she can do is shake her head, over and over, her chest tight with tears she can't shed—for William and their pitiful nights, for her betrayal, but most of all for her desperate yearning for Joseph.

He can barely look at her now, and the small gestures of affection have stopped, the held hand, the kiss on her hair coming home or going to bed. And worse, they have stopped for Moses too. One evening, she thinks to take the stew to him at work in a covered pot. The yard is behind the family cottage he once shared with Jane, and Moses holds on to her skirts now he is walking. She's about to pass the turning to Jane's front door and go straight to the entrance of the small yard itself when something halts her step. Warm light flickers in the cottage window. The curtains are not quite shut, and she peers in from the shadows. William is sitting in his old place at the head of the table, Jane standing to his side, ladling stew into his bowl, a hunk of bread in his hand ready to soak up the gravy. Dorothy is very still as she watches.

She sees how it is. Far from working late at the boatyard, he has been going to Jane's, Jane who seems always to be somewhere she is not wanted in this sad family, straining the ties that bind them together.

She watches for a little longer, wonders what she is saying

to him, then swallows hard. Moses catches a glimpse of William and points.

"Daddy!" and for a moment William and Jane turn and look at the window, but Dorothy pulls Moses into the shadows and then hurries him home, where they sit in the kitchen alone and eat their supper.

He has his bath in the tin tub by the fire and then to bed. When William comes home, she pretends to be asleep. The next morning, she doesn't ask him about the night before, nor does she say what she saw; who can blame him for not wanting to be with her and the child? What does she think she deserves? So when he tells her he is taking a job in a bigger boatyard, in a busy port where the work and money are, not here in Skerry, she is not surprised.

William does not so much leave her as never return. The job is a good one. His money arrives on a Friday, and she knows she's lucky; it always comes, whereas she knows the Carnegie mother—she taught some of them, a raggle-taggle band of ruffians they were too—never sees the inside of a wage packet. It's been spent down the alehouse before suppertime. Everyone knows, but Mrs. Carnegie closes her door and curtains on those nights so the children don't have to smell the fish and potatoes, the stovies, the pies, and broths warming in other houses. But not William. He is never like that.

She'd hoped to create the family she'd never had, where love holds the center together, but she'd failed before it ever had a chance to begin. And in fact, as the days become weeks become months, she finds she is relieved, because at least they don't have to keep pretending anymore.

Agnes

Another month, and Agnes's belly tightens painfully as the blood comes again in a mockery of labor. She leans her head against the privy wall. She saw them again today. She squeezes her eyes shut. Such a beautiful child. A child of silver and green, like the sea on a bright spring day. He had turned his head and looked at her, a shy smile curving his lips, but *she* had pulled him farther up the hill. She's rocking gently now. In her mind's eye, it's *her* walking up Copse Cross Street with a child's hand in her own. He is looking up at her with trust, and she squeezes his hand. Perhaps, instead, they each squeeze the other's hand at the same time and laugh. It's sunny and Mrs. Brown's door is open, the window stacked high with jars of—

Scott bangs on the privy door. "What're you doing in there?" He swears and bangs again.

Agnes sighs, pulls up her undergarments, tries to get rid of the blood. She doesn't want to talk about it, not tonight. Pinning a smile on her face, she opens the door.

"What have you been sniveling about?"

Agnes's hands go to her face. She hadn't realized she had been. Her face is wet.

"Oh, don't tell me. It's your—" He can't bring himself to say the words, and as he pushes past her, he smacks her against the privy wall. Her head jolts backward and hits the cold stone. "Call yourself a wife," he says, and the privy door slams shut.

Later, when Scott has gone to the alehouse, Agnes sits at the table. This isn't desire or want—she knows what they are. They are what she felt for Joseph, or for a ribbon she saw in a dressmaker's shop as a child. This is something else. This has teeth. It gnaws at her. This is an open wound of longing that has festered into an agony of need. She feels like half a person, hollowed out. Her grief is the grief of loss, as though her child has died. She moans softly at the kitchen table in the empty house with its empty rooms.

She could reach out and touch him, her dream child, he's so real, the roundness of his cheeks, his dimpled knees, his smile with its missing teeth. Her face is wet with tears that won't stop. If only she could will him into being. If she just tried hard enough. *Please, please*, she says. If she could just open her eyes and he'd be running in from the garden, flushed, arms outstretched toward her, the sun caught in his silver hair. Her child, her little boy. Oh, she would give him a name, a name as beautiful as him.

Her mouth forms the word, the one word to conjure a child like that.

Moses, she says.

Now

The Shop

Mrs. Brown has suggested the back of the shop for the meeting she usually does in the run-up to Christmas, for the warmth—the Village Hall is always comfortless and too big for the few who turn up. She brings down some chairs from upstairs and a fruit loaf she's baked that morning. Norah and Ailsa arrive together. Norah is already knitting, for her father, her husband, her brother, her sons, wooden sheath at her waist to hold whichever one is the current work. Her designs are the envy and pride of the village, the green and ochre stripes on the sleeves and shoulders, the raised anchors she makes with a special combination of knit and purl stitches that are her own distinctive style. Her needles move so fast, it's a wonder to them, though they all spent their girlhoods learning from mothers and grandmothers. So afraid is Norah of losing her men, of not burying them if the tide were to give them back, that she knits their initials into the ganseys to recognize them by. So far she has been lucky, not a one lost of her five sons, but every time *The Maid of Skerry* goes out in stormy weather, she prays God grants them smooth passage and a safe return. Mrs. Brown tries not to think of her lost brother, but always knits a small imperfection in the village wave design now—just in case the sea takes one of the others, so far away in the southern ports.

Mrs. Brown has the kettle on the stove and a trestle table

unfolded and dusted off for the cups and cake. With the steam from the kettle and a lively fire, it is cozy. The women take off their headscarves, apart from Ailsa, who tightens hers, so badly does she always feel the cold. Mrs. Brown pours the boiling water in the pot and puts the cozy on it.

Ailsa raises her eyebrows. "You got something stronger for us?"

Mrs. Brown winks and goes to the sacks of flour that sit below the shelves full of stock for the shop. She reaches behind them and dusts off a bottle of whisky. When the leaves have steeped a bit and Norah has poured the tea into the mugs, she adds a good measure to each and returns the bottle to its hiding place.

Ailsa looks disappointed.

As they settle into their chairs, arranging their heavy skirts and shawls and first blowing, then taking small, burning sips of whisky tea, one chair sits empty.

"She'll not be coming, then," says Norah, nodding toward the empty chair and wrapping her hands around the mug.

"Has anyone seen her—or the child?"

"I heard the Minister wasn't sure about it at all—has anyone been down?"

Mrs. Brown rolls her eyes. "The Minister has been down, Martha has been down—there's plenty that have seen them, but the boy still sleeps a lot. Building up his strength, I've heard."

"Has Joseph been down? Seeing as he found him, I mean," and the women give each other sidelong glances, since they all know that Joseph and Dorothy don't speak and they all know of the argument.

Norah takes another sip, then picks up her needles again, leans forward, has even opened her mouth to share some morsel of gossip when the shop bell jangles, footsteps are

230

heard, and Dorothy comes into the back room, bringing a rush of icy air into the fug of warmth and whisky and tea.

Quick glances are shared.

Ailsa does a little shiver. "Shut the door, quick now, Dorothy, no need to let the North Pole in."

Mrs. Brown pulls the empty chair out from the table. Dorothy sits and arranges her skirts. Mrs. Brown pours another cup, then fetches the bottle, holds it up, the gesture a question, though she already knows the answer. The fire catches the golden liquid and Dorothy holds her hand up.

"No, thank you."

"I'll not say no to another drop," says Ailsa, and Norah holds up her mug too.

As the women knit, they discuss village business, Christmas parcels of food, the gifts for the poor on Handsel Monday in the new year. As always, Dorothy does what she must, though she never takes part in the gossip and lowers her eyes to her knitting, as though she can't hear it when the whisky loosens their tongues and they talk about Ethel's husband catching her with Harold. They are scandalized when Norah says she doesn't know who was more distressed, the Minister when he came knocking or Harold when he came flying out, bare-arsed, trying to pull his trousers up. They rock in their chairs, silent with laughter; it's impossible not to with the picture Norah paints, true or not. Mrs. Brown wonders if this is how Norah is trying to tell them that she's heard the stories of her own husband and the postmaster's wife, by finding so much gratification in Harold's humiliation. She wipes her eyes, tells Norah to stoke up the fire. As they recover themselves, Dorothy speaks.

"Will there be something for the children again this year? A party for Hogmanay to bring in the new year?"

They all turn to look at Dorothy. Dorothy is knitting a

jumper for a child this evening, her first in a long time, and her eyes are brighter. Looking after the boy, making him better—it must be good for her, though now Mrs. Brown is looking more closely, the bloom on Dorothy's cheek is almost feverish. Something tugs at Mrs. Brown's memory, but she can't quite place it. She shakes her head and loops the wool over her needle.

Probably nothing.

Then

Joseph and Moses

It's taken Joseph a while to conjure up the courage. He hesitates just out of sight of Dorothy's window. He knows she's still married, but what happens in situations like these—when a woman is left like this with a child for so long? How long has it been? Two years? William has not visited, not as far as he knows. And she's let her child come down to the Sands—he's sure she knows it's to him Moses comes. And a boy needs a father—if not a father, he corrects himself, then someone like a father, a man—to show him the way.

He goes up the path and knocks on the door.

Dorothy looks tired. "Joseph."

It is neither a question nor a greeting, but he is not going to be put off now.

"Hello, Dorothy, I—" He holds up the things he's brought with him—a bucket, string. "I thought the boy might like to catch crabs. I thought maybe—"

"No, Joseph."

He gently presses her. "All the boys do it. I'm not meaning anything by it." He glimpses unwashed pots in the kitchen and hears, from further inside, the sound of a ball bouncing against the walls. "You could do the things you need to do, and I could just keep him busy a while."

He's surprised by how quickly she gives in. She calls Moses and helps him with his boots, and he knows she is watching them from the door as they hurry along the cliff path, Moses

233

excited. Joseph raises his hand as they start down the Steps, and she disappears from view.

Once on the Sands, they clamber out onto the Rocks. The tide is just right, breaking against the ones jutting farthest out. There is a spot there that is perfect for crabbing, a cleft between two rocks not even a hand's width wide, and when the sea is just far enough in, as it is this day, you can dangle a broken-open mussel on a string to tempt a crab.

Moses watches carefully as Joseph cracks the black shell open. "Only a little, just enough for the crab to smell it," and he shows him how to tie a reef knot. "Right over left, and tuck it underneath." He guides Moses's fingers gently. "Now do it backwards—that's it—left over right and—"

"Tuck it underneath." Moses smiles up at Joseph, squinting against the sun.

Together they pull it tight, and Moses lets the string slip through his fingers and down into the water below them, leaning over to watch the mussel disappear into the sea, which gently surges into the cleft and sighs on its way out, dragging the mussel and the string with it.

Joseph puts his arm around the boy's middle as he leans over farther. "Careful, lad, the sea's a dangerous thing. Don't be coming out here on your own, now."

It isn't long before the string pulls taut and Moses's eyes grow wide and his mouth round in excitement.

"Careful, now, bring him in gently," and Moses tugs on the string, and clinging to the shiny black shell is a big red crab.

"My crab!" Moses looks at Joseph's face. "My crab!"

Joseph smiles at his excitement, helps him bring it up without knocking it against the walls of rock. They put it in the bucket and this time, with only a little help, Moses prepares the next mussel and ties the knot himself.

Soon they have three crabs in the bucket. "We could take these up to show your mammy? Would you like that?"

Moses tilts his head to the side and looks at the crabs, their waving legs, their snapping pincers.

"You could eat them," Joseph adds.

Moses looks horrified. "I want to put them back," he says. "Back in the sea," and Joseph ruffles his hair and laughs, and they tip the crabs back in, swill the bucket, and clamber back over the Rocks to the Sands and up the Steps.

As they get closer, he sees her through the window, hands tangled in her apron—maybe wiping flour dust from them, some still on her cheek—and Joseph is suddenly in another life, where he walks up the path with a child and opens the door and good smells of cooking breathe out of the warm kitchen and a wife comes smiling toward him.

Moses pushes the door open. The stove is burning brightly, the kitchen is clean and tidy, and Dorothy is bringing a pie out of the oven.

"Oh good, he's brought you back just in time," she says, and then turns and sees Joseph standing there too. Her tone changes. "Thank you." She puts the pie on the table and straightens up, reaching back to take off her apron.

"Can Joseph stay for some pie?" Moses's face is all innocence, and an awkward silence follows, then they both speak at once.

"No, lad, I better be—"

"I'm sure Joseph has—"

Moses goes round the table and pulls on her skirts. "Please."

Dorothy frowns, then sighs. She looks at Joseph but just off to the side so she doesn't quite meet his eyes. "You can stay if you want. There's enough. Though if you'd rather—"

"Thank you." Joseph reaches out his hand. "Come on,

let's wash our hands. Thank you," he says again, and he means it.

Around the table, Joseph and Moses do most of the talking. "Joseph wanted to eat them, but—"

"Well, I didn't mean then and there—I meant cook them first." He notices Dorothy's mouth twitch as though she wants to laugh.

Moses looks horrified all over again. "It was better to put them back."

Dorothy is quiet, but Joseph can tell she is listening carefully to the talk about their time on the Rocks.

Moses turns to her. "Do you know what a reef knot is? I could show you. What you do is—"

"Eat up, Moses," but Dorothy is looking at her child, and there's a softness in her eyes and a half smile on her lips that gives Joseph a little confidence.

"He picked it up very quickly. I could take him again some time, maybe—"

Dorothy stands up and starts to clear the table.

"It'd be no bother to me." He's watching her face, trying to read what it is she is feeling.

The moment stretches between them. "Let's see," she says finally.

And for Joseph, the perfect afternoon light that is slanting across the table, and Dorothy saying *let's see*, is enough.

Dorothy and Jane

It's late when the banging at the door starts. Moses is asleep and Dorothy is sitting by the fire, the kettle warming. She jumps up at the noise and undoes the bolts. Dorothy can see there is something wrong with Jane as soon as she opens the door—she is disheveled, her face swollen, and her eyes red. She doesn't wait to be invited in but comes brazenly into the kitchen. Dorothy is astonished. She hasn't spoken to Jane in—she can't even remember how much time.

It takes her a moment to find her voice. "Jane—what is it?"

Jane does not even pretend to be polite. "I've come for something I should have got a long time ago."

"I see," says Dorothy, not seeing at all. "And what would that be?" but Jane gives her a look so haunted that it silences her.

Jane makes for the stairs.

"There is a case of his in the cupboard in my bedroom. Don't go up there, let me—"

But Jane already has one foot on the stairs, climbing. Dorothy is trembling. It's all happening so quickly, and she can't hear anything, doesn't know what Jane's doing, and starts to follow her.

But then Jane's foot is on the stairs, already coming down,

her breathing short and ragged, and Dorothy looks up to see what it is Jane had been looking for.

In her arms, looking straight at her, wide-eyed and frightened, lip quivering, is the child.

Dorothy's fear is sudden, visceral, all of her senses engaged in this one moment. "No, Jane, no—what are you doing?" She takes a step toward her, arms outstretched.

Jane holds Moses more tightly, turns her whole body away from Dorothy. The look in her eyes is wild, maddened. Moses's cry starts up, high and piercing, as it was when he was very small. It used to shred Dorothy's nerves; she never knew what it was he wanted, but she knows now. He is frightened. He wants her.

Dorothy drops her arms, tries to steady her voice. "All right, it's all right, come and sit down. Let's talk. Give him to me, Jane," but Jane is at the bottom of the stairs now, she is near the door, her hand on the handle. Dorothy's voice sounds far away. "He hasn't got his coat on—it's too cold outside. Please, give him to me."

"This child is still a Gray boy, despite everything. Do you hear me?"

Dorothy thinks she might be sick.

"Don't you come another step closer, or I swear I'll—" She doesn't finish the sentence; she's opened the door, the flames of the fire leap and quiver in the surge of cold that comes in on the wind. Moses's mouth is open but no sound is coming out.

Dorothy is weak with fear. "Please don't hurt him," she tries to say, but Jane has gone.

At the slam of the door, sound comes back, wind rushing in off the sea and whistling through the grass, waves crashing on the Sands, and she can move again. She runs to the door, out into the night, onto the path to the Steps.

"Moses," she cries. "Moses, Jane." Which way did they go? She runs one way, past the cottage toward Copse Cross Street, but there's nobody there. Below, on the Sands, a shadow moves in the ragged light of the moon.

"Jane!" she cries, running back toward the Steps, and then she sees them ahead on the path, and she rushes toward them, but the figure from the Sands is there already.

"Give him to me now, Jane. You're frightening him," and Dorothy almost cries with relief when she recognizes Joseph's voice.

There is a struggle, but then Joseph comes toward her, carrying the child. Beyond him, Dorothy catches a glimpse of Jane's face—livid in a glance of the moon, stricken, till she turns and is gone.

Moses is already reaching for Dorothy, leaning his whole body toward her, and then she is clutching him to her, his face buried in her neck, and around both of them Joseph wraps his arms. Slowly Dorothy's breathing steadies, the world settles down. Joseph's arms loosen, and he leads her back down the path into the cottage. Dorothy can't let go of the child. Joseph closes and bolts the door. The kettle is hissing. All of that in only the time it took for the water to boil. Dorothy's eyes are shut, she is rocking the child from side to side, she is breathing him in, and in that moment he is a baby again, when she knew what he wanted, when they felt whole. She doesn't know how long they are like this, but she feels Joseph gently lift the child away from her. He takes him upstairs.

He's gone a little while, and when he comes down, he comes to her and holds her again. "He's asleep. Why was Jane here? What happened?" but Dorothy can only mutely shake her head. She stands in the circle of his embrace while he kisses and strokes her hair. He lifts her chin, and in the distress and displacement of the moment, she puts her hands around his head and pulls him toward her and they kiss, and in that moment they are as wholly engaged with each other as the night on the Sands. Joseph leans her against the wall. Her hands are under his jersey against his skin; his are opening her dress. She can't get close enough to him, but then, unexpectedly, Joseph pulls away, and Dorothy's feeling had been so strong that it hurts when he releases her.

"Joseph?"

"Not like this, Dorothy. I'll come back and we'll talk. Get some rest." He holds her for a few more moments, then breaks free and, without turning back, he lifts the bolt and leaves.

Dorothy hasn't even said thank you. She stands for a while, staring at the door, then sinks into a chair. On the table is the empty pot of tea and a single cup.

It isn't till later that Dorothy starts to shake. What brought Jane to her door, to her house, in such madness? What was she going to do with Moses? She goes upstairs to Moses's room, to check his quiet breathing, and then downstairs to check the bolts, top and bottom. After all this time, the realization that Jane still feels such anger toward her makes her weak. She sinks down onto the side of the bed. But why shouldn't she, after all, after what Dorothy did to William? Time doesn't lessen a sin, a wrongdoing.

She can still feel Joseph's touch on her skin and closes her eyes in shame. Time doesn't stop her being married either. What did she think she was doing? What did she think could happen? If anyone had seen them—she can't finish the thought. She is suddenly terrified of what Joseph wants to say to her. Whatever it is, she won't listen, she mustn't. No, whatever it is, it cannot happen again. And he mustn't see

240

Moses again either; it has to stop. She has a husband, even still—for better or worse—and she can't face what the villagers would think if they knew, can't face what she did to William, can't face herself.

And so it is that when Joseph comes back, daring to hope, with a gift for Moses—a boat he has made, like his own steady boat, with sails and even its name painted on the side—Dorothy opens the door but doesn't quite meet his eye.

She leads him straight through the house and into the garden. He glimpses Moses with his toys by the fire. When he sees Joseph, Moses's eyes brighten, but such is Dorothy's hurry that there is no time to say anything to him or show him the boat he's made, as he'd hoped.

Laid out between neat rows of carrot tops and kale are a trowel and a basket with some onions in. "You don't mind if I carry on, do you? I want to get the last of these up before the frosts come," though she doesn't wait for an answer, but kneels on a strip of grass and picks up the trowel.

"Actually, I do, Dorothy. I want to talk to you. There are things that need to be said."

She bends her head and sighs before putting down the trowel and standing up to face him. She wipes her hands on her apron and waits.

He gathers his courage together and asks the one thing, the only thing that really matters between them now. "I'm going to go straight to the point. What is to stop us being together? Wait," he says as she goes to speak. "I think you like me. I think we understand each other and, God knows, you must know my feelings by now."

He sees the shock in her face at the directness of his question, quickly replaced by bewilderment. "I'm married, Joseph. I'm still married. How could we? It would be impossible."

He puts out a hand toward her, as if to calm her or stop her from saying more. "I know. I've thought about this. We could go somewhere—away from here. I have a little money set by—"

"Leave Skerry? And go where?" Her cheeks are flushed now. "And as what? We'd be living in sin."

"I know it wouldn't be easy, but who would know?"

She frowns as she looks at him. "Who would know? Everyone in Skerry would know that we'd—" She can't finish the sentence. "And when we got to wherever we were going, everyone there—" She stops. "Or do you mean we would lie? You want me to *lie*? To *pretend* we are married?"

It is not going as he'd hoped, but he notes that she hasn't actually said she doesn't want to be with him, that she doesn't have feelings for him. She hasn't denied it.

He tries again. "If we don't do this, what are you going to do? I know you're married, but where is he? Where is William?"

Dorothy closes her eyes. When she opens them again, he can't read their expression. "Don't talk about William. I won't talk to you about him."

He can't stop, not now he's here, not now it's this conversation or nothing, ever. "And what about Moses—he needs a father, he—"

Her voice is breathy, he doesn't know if with anger or fear, or what it is she is feeling, but she stammers over her words. "You need to leave, Joseph. You need to go now. It can't happen, none of it—and you mustn't ask me this, not again, not ever."

And he knows there is something else there, underneath, but she won't show him.

"Dorothy—" He reaches for the words he needs to show

her that they could do it, to change her mind, but he has no more words.

He stares at her in silence for a moment, then turns and goes back through the house. He passes through the kitchen where they had all sat together around the table. In the winter of her voice, already the memory of the warm afternoon light is fading, along with Moses's chatter, Dorothy saying *let's see* by the brightly burning fire, till by the time he has closed the door and walked home, carrying the boat the child didn't even see, it's as though it had never happened at all.

He sits in the darkness of the evening with its autumn chill, but he doesn't light a fire. Maybe he always had it wrong; maybe she is, after all, the woman the villagers say she is. Cold. Prideful. Maybe he doesn't know her at all. But he knows something about himself.

He is not a man who needs telling twice.

Now

Dorothy and the Minister

When Martha and Ailsa come with more provisions, Dorothy is ready to tell them to thank the Minister and Mrs. Brown and just take the basket, when she sees that the Minister is standing right behind them.

She stiffens and her heart flutters—maybe they've found where the boy's home is, have even contacted his parents. She hesitates on the threshold but knows she will have to let them in.

She wipes her hands on her apron and steps aside. The Minister removes his coat and hangs it on the shoulders of a kitchen chair, sitting down and making himself comfortable. He looks exhausted, though Dorothy bets he isn't as exhausted as Jenny. Martha and Ailsa help her put the things away—haddock, cod and potatoes, scones, and sweet bannocks made with raisins that Ailsa has baked, even some cockles the schoolchildren have gathered as a gift—and then they're gone, leaving just Dorothy and the Minister. The boy is in the garden playing quietly. She chooses not to examine her desire to keep him away from the Minister.

She stays standing. "How is the baby?" Dorothy surprises herself with this question she hasn't been able to ask before—not just about the Minister's child, but about any baby, or pregnant woman or child.

The Minister's face brightens, then sags again. "Thriving,

thank goodness, though I leave the mysteries of it all to Jenny."

And she feels the familiar pang of sadness when she thinks of how William tried to help where most men don't because, like the Minister, they think babies are a mystery only a woman understands.

"And Margaret? Is she managing the extra days at the school?"

"Margaret is quite happy with the arrangement for now. You have no need to worry about that. It's the boy I've come about. How is he? Where is he? Is he speaking yet?"

Dorothy has hoped to delay the question a little longer, and she hovers for a moment between the truth and the lie, then sidesteps the question altogether. "He's in the garden—I'll call him in."

The child comes in and stops dead when he sees the Minister. Dorothy sees him through the Minister's eyes—brighter, plumper, cheeks red from the cold. He is holding the ball that had been in the box of toys the villagers donated.

The Minister smiles at the child. "Now, we are trying our best to find out where your home is and who your mummy and daddy are."

The boy stares at him, lips pulled in.

The Minister turns back to Dorothy. "I have finally managed to get a telegram through to the Police Authority. They will know of any missing persons, and I have also sent one to the Coastal Authority. We're trying to get messages up and down the coast to fishing communities too—to see if a child has been lost at sea. It shouldn't be long till we hear something. Someone is bound to have reported what's happened." He sips his tea and gives a reassuring smile. "He won't be here much longer—" He cuts off, frowning. "What's that?"

The bird gives its fluting call again, and the child runs out and into the other room.

Dorothy is glad of the interruption to the talk of telegrams and authorities. "It's a plover with a broken wing. We're looking after it."

The Minister goes to get up. "May I see it?" and Dorothy feels an unexpected reluctance. In fact, she realizes she doesn't really like him being here at all. She steps between him and the door to the other room.

"It's very nervous, as you can imagine, it's still recovering—I wouldn't want—"

The Minister raises his hand, takes the last gulp of tea, and shrugs his coat back on. "I understand, I understand. It's a shame there's no sign of his memory coming back or even any speech." She thinks of the boy's drawing and the few words he's uttered, but it is a statement the Minister has made, not a question, and Dorothy waits to see how long she can let it rest there between them.

"As soon as he does, as soon as he remembers anything that might help, be sure to let me know," and then the door is shutting and Dorothy's heart is beating hard as she discovers her truth-telling habits aren't quite as ingrained as she thought.

"The lad looks well"—he pops his head back round the door—"and so do you," and she can hear the surprise in his voice, on both counts, and then he's gone.

Before the Minister leaves, he can't resist getting a glimpse of the child, and he goes round to the side of the cottage and looks through the window. The boy, with his new haircut, is playing with some tin soldiers. There is a spinning top tilted on its edge in the middle of the room too, and these must all have been Moses's toys because they're certainly not the ones the villagers donated. The Minister smiles at the scene that could have been conjured from the past.

As he walks up the hill, he reflects on the visit. Dorothy looks well; the kitchen is tidy and clean again. And the Minister thinks what a good idea it was to have chosen Dorothy; what a light it has brought into a life that was surely lonely. He has always been grateful for her sense of duty and diligence but maybe found her a little stiff at times. She seems much softer now, and the child too is thriving.

Later, Dorothy lies awake. The wind has picked up again; it is wailing outside, and she can hear the keening of some creature in the night. It gets louder, and in a shift of awareness she realizes it is coming from inside the house. She hurries out of bed, wraps her gown around herself, and quietly goes downstairs.

In the darkness she sees him, hunched over on the bed, head on his knees, arms wrapped around them.

"Mamma," he is crying. "Mamma," and the word goes to the very heart of her. The power of it brings her to him and she sits on the bed. She puts her arm around him, and without changing position he leans into her.

The wind is louder now, whistling through the thatch and the branches of the apple tree out back.

He wraps his arms around her, sobbing.

"Mamma," he says again.

Joseph and the Plover

When the Minister tells him about the bird with the broken wing, Joseph can't stop thinking about it, about the boy he rescued and how much he wants to see him again. As he hesitates at the door, he hears the sound of Dorothy's laughter inside and a ball being bounced on the floor.

She is flushed when she answers, but her smile fades when she sees him. "Joseph? Can I help you?"

"It's about the bird. The plover. The Minister mentioned its broken wing. I thought I could help." He holds up a bag of tools by way of explanation.

She hesitates for a moment, looking back into the cottage, then steps aside to let him in and leads him to the room with the bird, calling the child. When the boy comes in, he frowns at first as if he's not certain who Joseph is, then smiles. Joseph proffers his hand toward the bird. "May I?" He mimics its broken wing and shows the child the bag he has brought with him, the narrow sticks of wood inside and linen for padding and securing the splint. The bird is watching him, head over the rim of the basket, tense and afraid.

The boy nods and picks the bird up gently, not touching the injured wing, which it is holding out at an awkward angle.

"Hold him carefully but firmly," Joseph says, hoping he will pick up the sense of it, which he seems to, so gentle is he with the plover. Joseph feels along the bones, light under his fingers.

The bird struggles, but the child murmurs soothing words. Joseph turns to Dorothy, who is crouched next to him, biting her lower lip.

"It's a clean break. The worry is that it'll hurt the wing more if it keeps moving it."

"Can you help?"

Joseph is surprised at how much it seems to mean to her. "Yes, I can make a simple splint now that will hold it in the right position to heal," and Dorothy's body relaxes.

"The bird will be all right," she says to the child. "It's good. Good!" and the boy understands and repeats the word, smiling.

Joseph takes a thin stick of wood and measures it against the plover's wing. "It needs to be just a bit longer, but not so much it'll catch on things." He cuts it at the right point, then winds a strip of linen around it. "So it doesn't hurt him." The boy helps to hold the wood and padding in place while Joseph bandages it carefully around the wing. "Not too tight," he says. "It needs to be comfortable. There." He leans back on his heels. "That'll do. It'll help anyway," and the boy beams, first at Joseph, then at Dorothy.

"Tea, Joseph?" The offer surprises him and he almost accepts, but as he packs the wood and linen back in the bag, he is reminded of his visit long ago when he'd stood in the garden and searched for the words needed to reach her, and failed.

He stands up and picks up his bag. "No, thank you," he says, but he can't look at her, and when he says goodbye, it is to the boy, who he sees isn't really like Moses at all.

Later, when Joseph has left, Dorothy goes into the kitchen and thinks of an afternoon many years before, when the light was golden as it spilled across the table where she, Moses, and Joseph had eaten all together. Even now, the pull of her feelings is like the pull of the moon on the tide as she remembers how close she'd come to letting herself have what she'd really wanted.

She gathers the silver-haired child to her as though no time has passed, as though it is still not too late, and, "I'm sorry, I'm so sorry," she says.

Dorothy

Dorothy doesn't look directly at what the boy's desperate cry of *Mamma* meant, but it has changed things between them: She kisses his head when she gives him his breakfast; he reaches for her hand when they go out and looks up at her with trust in his green eyes. She starts to sleep better. They look after the plover together. Since Joseph made the splint to help the bones knit back properly, they share moments of delight as it hops on the furniture round the room, and excitement when it shows signs of trying to use its wing. They play on the Sands, chasing each other and the waves.

A few days before the children's party, Dorothy holds up the trousers and jumpers the villagers so generously gave. She tilts her head. Maybe the trousers are a bit short, and without wanting to be rude, she has made better jerseys herself. She stands outside Moses's room for a long while, then takes a deep breath and turns the handle. Inside, she opens the drawers and pulls out a pair of warm trousers, a jersey he'd loved that the moths haven't eaten, and some undergarments, and looks them over. Yes, they are the right size, she gauges, and takes them downstairs to be washed and mended.

While the boy feeds the plover, Dorothy tidies up. It all feels a bit crowded in the room downstairs with the bed in it, as well as the bird and the toys. Afterward, she goes back upstairs. She has only a moment's hesitation before she opens the curtains and looks out at the view of the Sands and the Rocks below. She puts fresh bed linen on the bed and plumps up the pillow. There's a blanket in her room that she knitted a long time ago, just waiting to be put on a child's bed, and Dorothy goes to get it, then places Arthur on top, leaning against the pillow. She stands back to admire her handiwork.

She feels a tiny stir of something, a feeling of sort of waking up or a fret lifting. A small smile curves her lips. She can't wait to show the child.

Mrs. Brown and the Children's Party

When the day of the children's party dawns, Mrs. Brown has already been up several hours, baking scones and filling paper bags with sweets from the shop, though it's not been easy now no deliveries are being made and the temperature has dropped and nothing can get in or out of the village. She'll be the first one up there to get the Hall ready, though *Hall* is a grand name for the building where the village meets on occasion, with its corrugated roof and stone floor. There is at least a wood stove at one end, and it is to this she hurries first. It's bitter cold, and occasionally the wind shakes a slump of snow off the branches of the oak that leans over the roof, and it slips and echoes through the ripples of the iron. Ice rimes the inside of the windows.

She crouches by the flames once the kindling catches and runs through the day's plan—a psalm with the Minister, some games, singing and dancing, a floor picnic, another psalm, then each child leaves with their gift. Soon the fire is giving out warmth with the sweet smell of alder and the chill in the room starts to lose its bite. She puts up the trestle tables and starts to unpack her basket when Ailsa arrives with branches of holly and, as on every Hogmanay, her black bun. Mrs. Brown breathes in the rich aroma of the fruit cake encased in buttery pastry as she places it in pride of place on the food table. Ailsa's daughters come to help too—grown women now, with their own families—and Norah comes soon after with the hats and scarves she's knitted with the village wave pattern, but also some of her own designs of stripes and anchors. Her husband, Nicholas, comes too, in his endless search to get back into her good books and to make up for his transgressions with the postmaster's wife, setting up his ladder to fix bunches of the holly in the corners of the ceiling. The gift table is starting to look more exciting with the growing number of donations: picture books being passed on as children grow older, marbles, dolls, skipping ropes, and kites. The kettle is hissing on the stove now; by the time the Minister and more of the village women have come, Mrs. Brown is pouring tea into mugs as they gather round the fire and look at their handiwork.

"It's hard not to feel excited for them, isn't it?" says Norah.

Through the high windows, the sky is hard as stone, with no sign of a thaw. The flames have chased away the winter chill and the Hall is welcoming with its holly, its laden tables, the crackling of the fire.

Ailsa nods and tries to smile, her mouth full of Mrs. Brown's scones—*some for the kiddies, some for us.*

They discuss the psalm the Minister has chosen—*a reminder of the Lord who is so easily forgotten on a day of lightness*—and the Minister places his hands together and recites the opening lines, eyes closed in earnest devotion. The women glance away from him and each other in case they laugh, and Mrs. Brown is grateful when she hears the rise and fall of excited chatter, the shouts of the village children, and then the door opens and the first few step in, round eyes, round mouths, till they are crowded around the tables full of food and presents, pointing and happy.

They're all in now, voices bouncing off the roof, and she is about to push the door shut when she sees two more arriving. It is Dorothy and the child. They are caught in a dazzle of snow-light, and Mrs. Brown catches her breath. She hasn't realized, not fully till then, how the past has come back to Skerry on this turning of the year when we look forward and back.

Once Dorothy and the child are inside, Mrs. Brown watches them. They are playing a game where Norah's husband plays a fiddle and whenever he stops, the children drop to the floor and the last one's out. He is shy, the child, and staying close to her, while she is gently pushing him toward the others, nodding reassuringly. It is the opposite of what Mrs. Brown remembers from all those years ago, when Dorothy didn't seem to want anyone's attention on Moses.

Finally, he lets go of her hand and steps toward the others just as the music starts up again—the children are thundering around the Hall, and Norah's granddaughter grabs his arm and he's in the throng and running with the others, falling breathlessly to the floor when the music stops. It seems a miracle that the child who Joseph carried up the hill, almost dead that day after the storm, is this child so full of quiet delight. She is busy wrapping the gifts and placing them so she knows which are sweets, which are scarves, which to hand out where most needed—jumpers for the Bannons, no mother to knit for them, some toys for the Carnegies, God knows the father drinks all the money in that house; she sets a kite aside for them along with some of the marbles and books. As the children all drop to the ground again, she glances at Dorothy, and her hands fall still.

Dorothy is like a child who has seen something beautiful for the first time. Her hands are held in front of her, palms close, fingertips touching, a look of wonder on her face as she watches him run and play. Mrs. Brown looks between

256

her and the child and back again, and at first she too feels wonder at the transformation in this cool and distanced woman. But then she looks back at the boy again—at the way his hair has been cut so like another's, at the ironed stiffness of the trousers. It troubles her.

At that moment the door opens and, with a rush of cold air and a swirl of snow, Joseph comes in. He has a sack with him and brings it to the table where Mrs. Brown is working. He starts to unpack it. Inside are wooden toys, simple and lovely—a soldier, a boy, a boat. When he sees him, the child leaps up from the floor where they are all meant to be sitting and runs to Joseph and stands in front of him. Joseph's face lights up. He reaches into his pocket and pulls out another wooden toy and crouches down to show it to the child. The other children are still playing and Mrs. Brown is still wrapping, but she's also watching Joseph and the boy. The toy is a plover, with its distinctive rounded belly and head, its short beak, of the sort seen down on the Sands all through the year. But the head is a separate piece, and when Joseph puts the plump body on the table and shows the boy the different ways he can angle the head, the bird looks by turns quizzical, then shy, then bold. It is ingenious, a little miracle of craftsmanship, and the boy's face fills with joy as he turns it and changes the bird's expressions, looking at Joseph with his quiet smile.

Later she and Ailsa hand out the gifts they've organized for the children, and Dorothy brings the child to the table, where he chooses a bag of sweets.

"Come now," Dorothy says. "Let's go home," and the child is smiling and Dorothy is looking only at him, the way a mother looks at her child, and Mrs. Brown frowns, her own smile fading, because there it is again—the high color, the bright eyes—and the memory Mrs. Brown hadn't been able to put her finger on at the knitting evening rushes back to her. And it's a memory of her own self.

It had been after Fergus died. Her arms had still ached from holding and rocking him, even though she'd had no baby to hold and rock anymore; her milk had still come through at the times she'd fed him, and she'd never told anyone but had carried on washing his clothes and his bed linen, taking comfort in the routines that had started to form the pattern of her motherhood. And then, during the terrible loneliness of the nights without him, she'd started to hear him cry. At first, she'd hurried out of bed to the cold, empty crib, bewildered by what cruel dream made her hear her lost child.

But then she'd started to hear him during the day too.

And it had got worse, till there were times she'd run frantically from place to place in her home, looking for her baby, mad with the grief and loss of him, and on one of those times she'd caught a glimpse of herself in a looking glass, her hair wild, her cheeks fever red, her eyes too bright.

Looking at Dorothy now, a shadow falls across her.

Maybe looking after the child is not so good for Dorothy after all.

Dorothy

A few days after the party, Dorothy walks up Copse Cross Street with the boy. He is wearing Moses's good coat and a green hat and scarf Dorothy has knitted. It is cold and bright, ice glittering in the footprints made by the villagers, the frozen snow crisp and hard underfoot. Over the years, Dorothy has trained herself not to care what others think or to try to close the distance between herself and others. When William stopped coming home, she didn't want to hear their questions, see the doubt in their eyes when she answered—and some things become a habit—but today Dorothy feels exposed. The way Mrs. Brown looked at her in the Village Hall did not escape her notice, and now everyone they pass seems to look at her more intently than usual; she passes the bakery and some of the customers are facing away from the counter and looking back out of the window. Even Ailsa, usually more warmhearted than the others, seems to hurry away from her up the hill toward the shop. Her heart beats faster. Up ahead, the Minister's wife, Jenny, is walking toward her. She stops and looks at the boy.

"My, doesn't he look well!" She bends down till they're face-to-face. "Do you remember me?" He smiles a bit, gripping Dorothy's hand more tightly. Jenny straightens herself.

"Alastair said how well the child is doing. It's good to see. He said to bring him up to the Manse."

"Yes—he'd like that. He could meet the new baby," and she tries to engage in the small talk that seems to come to others so easily, though really she wants nothing more than to get away from here and what she is sure is the small frown of puzzlement on Jenny's face. They smile and say goodbye, but Dorothy's feeling of unease has deepened.

She swallows hard and opens the door to the butcher's. It is a small shop. There is not much in stock but some scrawny-looking chickens, some sides of pork and slices of bacon. Pig carcasses hang from hooks out back. Dorothy recognizes Agnes at the counter paying the butcher.

"That's how it took my Scott. Just like that, upright one minute, face down the next. He recovered, though. It's hard to kill a bad thing, as they say," and she laughs, but grimly. "I heard Norah's Nicholas isn't so good either."

Their conversation dies away when she comes in. Dorothy waits for Agnes to turn, even considers saying something, but Agnes hurries past her, eyes down, and out the shop.

Is that the butcher seeming clipped with her now? Everywhere she looks she sees accusation, or narrowed eyes, or unaccustomed curiosity.

She has hoped to show the boy the village with its Kirk and Schoolhouse, take a walk to the Tops where you can see right out over the thatched roofs with their curls of smoke, and beyond the black rocks of the bay, right out to sea, but instead she puts the wrapped bacon in her basket and hurries back down the hill, almost pulling the child.

As soon as they're home, there is a knock at the door. Dorothy jumps. She seems to be startled by everything at the moment. When she unlatches the door, Mrs. Brown is standing on her doorstep in one of her loose-fitting dresses and a huge shawl she is wearing as both headscarf and coat, stomping the snow off her boots in expectation of coming in. Dorothy's alarm must show on her face, because as though by way of explanation, Mrs. Brown holds up a bundle of clothes and steps over the threshold without invitation. Dorothy steps back, remembering herself. Mrs. Brown seems bigger now she's standing in Dorothy's kitchen. Not just bigger in size but somehow more impressive, and Dorothy can feel herself shrinking with doubt. She tries to stand straight. She looks again at the bundle of clothes that Mrs. Brown has now put on the table and wonders why she is really here.

"I'm making tea if you'd like some?" She is hoping the offer will prompt her to leave. After all, what will they talk about? But Mrs. Brown pulls out a chair.

"Thank you. Black and strong, if it's no bother." She sits down and spreads out her skirts, making herself comfortable.

Dorothy is recovering herself now. She knows how to play the other half of this game, the one where people try to find something out about you while pretending they're not. She's played it for too many years. She sets the kettle on the hob, scoops the leaves into the pot, and brings it with some cups to the table and sits down too. *If we're going to do this, let's do it.*

"That's a good bundle of clothes there. For the boy?" Dorothy is pouring the tea as though she is neither surprised nor curious about the visit and merely thinking of something polite to talk about.

Mrs. Brown warms her hands on the cup. "Just a few things from the villagers that should have had more use over the years, instead of being left in a drawer. Best to let the past go, I always think."

"Well, thank you. I had a few things here myself, but no doubt these will come in useful too."

261

Mrs. Brown puts her cup down again without taking a sip. "Moses's things? He wears Moses's things?"

The question catches Dorothy off guard. "Yes, well, as you say, no good being left in a drawer where they're no use to man nor beast."

"How is the boy?" She doesn't wait for an answer. "The Minister is working hard now to trace his family." Mrs. Brown's eyes are fixed on Dorothy's face.

Dorothy's heart beats faster and her mouth feels suddenly dry. She drops her eyes and takes a sip of the tea, saying nothing.

Mrs. Brown continues. "I expect it will be a relief to get things back to normal. And the boy must miss his mother terribly."

Dorothy flinches and recalls the night when she'd comforted him and he'd leaned into her and called her Mamma. She swallows hard. "Of course, yes."

"Terrible for the mother too. It will be nothing short of a miracle for the family to discover he has survived. They are very lucky. The sea is a cruel beast, as we know to our cost in Skerry."

Dorothy stands up abruptly, her chair scraping loudly on the stone and nearly falling backward. The noise brings the child in; he stops in the doorway looking solemnly at Mrs. Brown, who goes to him, crouches down with a bit of difficulty and pats his cheek. "You're a good lad. We'll find your home for you." The boy smiles.

Dorothy wants to scream, she wants to pull her away from the boy, she wants her out of here. How dare she touch him? How dare she come into their home uninvited and talk her rubbish, dropping hints about him leaving her?

"Well, thank you for the visit and the clothes. I'm sure it is very kind of you, but if you don't mind . . . ?"

Mrs. Brown groans slightly as she stands up. "This cold gets into my bones." She turns. "I'll be glad of the thaw and the roads reopening and life going back to normal for a bit." She waits for Dorothy's response but, getting none, goes to the door. "Well, I shall see you soon, I have no doubt." As she opens the door, Dorothy notices that she'd never even taken her coat off.

Mrs. Brown smiles at the boy one more time before she closes the door behind her. Dorothy sinks into a chair.

I'll be glad of the thaw and the roads reopening and life going back to normal for a bit. When she looks up at the empty doorway where the boy had just been standing, Mrs. Brown's words echo in her heart, and her heart is full of dread.

The Minister's News

The next day, Dorothy and the child have barely turned into Copse Cross Street when Dorothy sees the Minister a little way up ahead. He is with Jenny, who is pushing the pram. Dorothy tugs on the boy's hand to cross the road. She doesn't want to talk to him or hear about the investigation Mrs. Brown has mentioned. She has much to buy and organize and not much time. She pretends she hasn't seen them and crosses the road.

"Dorothy! Dorothy!" The Minister is waving his arm and crossing too, racing toward her.

Dorothy is irritated but forces a smile and nods her head briskly, then returns to looking pointedly at her shopping list.

In a moment, he is standing in front of her, breathing heavily with the exertion. "I need to speak to you," he says, trying to catch his breath.

Dorothy goes very still, holding the shopping list out in front of her, unable to move.

The Minister continues. "I don't want to get your hopes up, but the investigation is progressing." He leans forward, excited and pleased with himself. "I received a telegram this morning."

Jenny has almost caught up with them now, the wheels of

the pram sticking in the snow. "It's good news, Dorothy, isn't it? For everyone." She pauses and frowns a little as she looks at Dorothy's face.

Dorothy nods. She can't speak, so she keeps nodding and gathers the boy's hand into the crook of her arm.

"Will you be coming up to the Manse? To hear the details, or shall I—?" but Dorothy says something about leaving a pan on the stove and says goodbye to the Minister, to Jenny who has taken the baby out of the pram, her own baby in her arms.

She hardly remembers leaving. She can't walk straight; she just wants to take the boy back to their home and shut the door and the whole world out.

She is still breathing heavily when they get back. She sits at the kitchen table with her head in her hands. She hadn't really taken in what the Minister was trying to tell her as she walked away, something about a family whose son had gone missing the day before the child had appeared on Skerry Sands. She doesn't want to take it in.

There hasn't been enough time.

When the Minister comes later that evening, full of apologies, he is surprised at Dorothy's appearance, at how tired she looks. *Haunted* is the word that springs to mind. He knows how much she likes tidiness; he's seen it often enough in the Kirk and in the vestry where every time he goes in after Dorothy has been, he has to look again through the orderly pile of papers he usually spreads out on his desk. But today the dishes are unwashed and her hair is not her usual neat—no, tight—bun, but instead her graying hair has worked loose and hangs about her face.

He feels even more terrible that he has to deliver bad news. It is clear to him now that Dorothy has hidden her struggle well and that he has perhaps been mistaken in his reading of the situation. Far from the child bringing joy to her and a purpose, it is clear she wants him gone. She doesn't offer him tea, even when he settles at the table, so instead he asks her to sit down.

"I am very sorry, Dorothy, but I have received a further telegram this morning." Her face sags. "It is, I am afraid, not good news." He is tempted almost to reach out for her hand but stops himself—he's never been fully sure of her. "It would appear that our child is not the child we had hoped he was. Certainly not the one from up the coast anyway. Tragically, a body has been discovered. They think the boy was swept off the beach in the storm, and from items of clothing"—he clears his throat discreetly—"it is clear it is the body of the missing child." He notices Dorothy's white face. "Anyway, I'm afraid it may still take some time."

Dorothy's eyes gleam with tears, and the Minister feels worse. There is noise in the doorway, and when they turn, the child is standing there. The Minister wonders if he has heard and understood their conversation. A thought occurs to him, though he ought to check with his wife first. She is coping so well with the baby, though, and doesn't seem to need as much sleep as she used to, so maybe it wouldn't make so much difference, especially with Martha there. He turns back to Dorothy. This time he does extend his hand toward hers.

"Dorothy, I know how hard this has been for you. Your actions are seen and valued. We can take the child to the Manse now, and he can stay with us while we wait."

Dorothy snatches her hand back. "No. No, he must stay here. He—it's his home."

The Minister is a little taken aback by her vehemence but, he thinks, as he says goodbye to them both and closes the door behind him, he has to admire the woman's sense of duty.

When the Minister has gone, the child comes into the room. His face is alight and, almost unbelievably, he speaks. Not single words, like *ball* and *Mamma* and *home*, but a whole string of words. Dorothy's mouth drops open.

Dorothy kneels before him and grips his arms. "What did you say? Say it again." She shakes him. "Say it again!" and he does, his words more garbled and urgent than before, his lip wobbling at the vehemence of her voice. Dorothy isn't sure what he's saying, but the word *home* is there again, and suddenly she can't breathe. It's all happening too quickly.

She can't lose him.

Not again.

Dorothy and the Child

That night, Dorothy lights a lamp and sits in the kitchen, wrapped in a shawl by the fire, the kettle on the stove. While she waits for it to boil, she tries to think it all through.

The Minister's investigation has come to nothing. And what had Mrs. Brown said? That it would be a miracle for a child to survive the sea in such a storm? And hadn't the doctor said the same thing? Well, he *had* survived. He had not only survived—he had come to her. However you look at it, God had sent him to her. There is no point in not admitting it to herself anymore. The child called her *Mamma*, and there is only one person in the world who can do that, use that word, and it doesn't matter if the Minister doesn't know it, or Mrs. Brown doesn't know it, Dorothy knows it.

Deep in her heart, she knows that the child sleeping upstairs is her own child, given back to her to put things right.

And it is, indeed, a miracle.

Because her child is home.

The Kirk

The Minister is ready to leave for home. He has stayed too long as it is; it's just that the baby simply isn't settling. Every evening he screams inconsolably. Colic, the doctor said. He shuffles his papers, stares at the lists of figures, realizes he's taking nothing in. A glance at the clock tells him it's past seven. He slips his fingers under the lenses of his glasses and rubs his eyes. It's no good. He knows what he's doing, sitting here, delaying. It's just that he didn't realize babies were quite so upsetting, with Jenny tired all the time, the baby hungry and crying or hungry and feeding and, in truth, when he's at home, he's just not quite sure who he is anymore. He blinks and tries to focus on the figures again. The clock says half past now. He stands up; he can't put it off any longer.

He opens the vestry door and is about to step into the Kirk itself when a small sound draws his attention to a bowed head in a tightly tied headscarf, barely above the pew, deep in prayer. There is an intensity in this moment that swells into the cold empty space. Even being here feels like an intrusion on the lone figure whose prayer fills the Kirk.

Quietly he steps back inside and closes the door. He waits what feels like a long time for the heavy front door to fall to rest against the lintel. He hurries then, out of the vestry, down the aisle, and out into the snow-blue night where the lowering clouds press down on to the village. All the way home, across the Kirkyard and under the lychgate to his kitchen, where he sits quietly eating the supper Martha has left for him, and even when he climbs into bed where Jenny is sleeping, one arm over the baby in the crib next to her, he is thinking of the woman in the Kirk and wondering who on earth it is in the village who has such a weight on their conscience.

And not only that, just as he'd stepped back into the vestry, his eye had caught on something. Even in the gloom he could see it. The woman's hand, pale and thin, and clutched within the cage of the fingers what looked for all the world like a red rubber ball.

The Shop

She wants to go to the shop, but not when it's busy. She doesn't want the prying eyes, or to see the Minister. She doesn't really want to see Mrs. Brown, but flour and soap can't be bought anywhere else. Dorothy helps the boy on with his gloves and scarf, and they take a shopping basket and start out. The light is already fading and Copse Cross Street is nearly empty. Nevertheless, holding on to the child's hand, Dorothy looks neither right nor left as they go up the hill. When she reaches the top, she stands on the other side of the road from the shop and tries to see who's in there. She's not going in if it's Ailsa and Norah, but as far as she can tell they're not around. Mrs. Brown is handing a parcel to someone who is leaving now, the door banging shut behind them. She comes out from behind the counter, and Dorothy sees her moment. If she is starting to tidy up, it must be empty, and Dorothy hurries across the road and opens the door.

Mrs. Brown looks up from sweeping when the bell jangles. "I'm about to shut up the shop now, Dorothy." But when she sees the child, her face softens. "Well, if it's not much you need, I suppose," and Dorothy nods her thanks and goes straight to the shelves with the items she wants, bringing the boy with her. The soap is on a higher one than

271

usual, and she tilts herself up on her tiptoes, letting go of the boy's hand.

"Oh, Mrs. Gray, I was hoping to catch you."

Dorothy drops her box of soap in surprise. The woman picks it up and puts it in Dorothy's basket.

"It's me, Fiona, remember? You taught my Eliza. Well, along with all the others! I just wanted to tell you, she's started at one of those colleges in Fife that train you to be a teacher. Always looked up to you, she did." Her face shines with pride. "I thought you'd like to know. Will you be going back to the school when the child goes home?"

Home? What does she mean?

When Dorothy doesn't answer, Fiona frowns a little. "Are you quite all right?"

But Dorothy is looking around her. Where is the child? She hears his voice, the garbled talk he has started to do at home, and hurries along the aisle to the front of the shop, where Mrs. Brown has stopped sweeping and is staring intently at him. He's looking up at her with a tin of cakes in his hands.

"Is that—?" Mrs. Brown frowns. "Is he speaking—?" She steps toward him, bends a little to his height. "*Norge?*" she says, and his eyes widen, a smile brightening his face.

He nods. "*Ja, Norge.*"

Mrs. Brown straightens up and turns to Dorothy. "This child is not from Scotland at all, Dorothy. He's from Norway."

Dorothy nearly laughs. Norway? What is Mrs. Brown talking about? She lowers her basket to the floor and comes to stand by the boy.

"Dorothy, did you hear what I said? He's not from round here at all." Mrs. Brown puts her hand on Dorothy's arm. Her voice is gentle, soft. "You've gone very white. Let me get a chair. You stay there," and she turns to the boy and says something, and he replies, but it's all too far away for Dorothy to understand.

As soon as Mrs. Brown has gone out the back, Dorothy grabs his hand. "No," he says, "no," but she's not listening. She can see Fiona coming toward her now, a concerned smile on her face, and she pulls on his arm. He plants his feet in a widened stance, his bottom lip sticking out, and tries to pull his arm free. With a frantic look at Fiona, at the back of the shop, Dorothy ignores his protests and picks him up.

When Mrs. Brown comes back, Dorothy has gone, there is just her basket with its box of carbolic soap where she's left it on the floor, and Fiona standing over it with her mouth open.

At home, Dorothy bolts the door. She pulls the curtains shut. She can't understand what Mrs. Brown has said. It makes no sense. She's heard the words he uses, the way he calls her Mamma. She needs to make them understand. Aren't they the ones who believe in the old stories about children being taken and then coming back? She goes into the other room. He's sitting on the floor by the fire, playing with the wooden plover Joseph made. The toys from the toy box, the top and the tin soldiers, are scattered across the floor. Arthur the bear, who the child has brought downstairs, watches him play from a chair.

Can't they see? The firelight gleams on his silver hair. It's not a scene from the past; it's happening now.

Her heart nearly stops when the banging at the door starts.

Mrs. Brown calls out. "Dorothy, Dorothy. Let me in." The boy tries to rush into the kitchen, but Dorothy holds his arm and puts her finger to her lips. Mrs. Brown's shadow looms at the window now as she tries to peer in. "Dorothy," she calls again.

Dorothy realizes she's holding her breath, as though Mrs. Brown might hear her. She keeps completely still. The boy listens with her, eyes wide, then pulls away quickly, and Dorothy tightens her grip, shaking her head. "No," she whispers.

Mrs. Brown knocks on the window now. "Dorothy. I need to speak to you. It's important. I only want to help."

And the sound Dorothy makes is halfway between a laugh and a sob. Help? She knows what that means. It means taking him away from her, just like the Minister wants to. Well, she won't let it happen. Even after Mrs. Brown gives up and goes, Dorothy still doesn't move, still doesn't let go of the child's arm, in case it's a trick.

When she's sure she's gone, she sits down, shaking. She's not stupid. She needs to explain everything to the Minister, make him see. She can imagine what nonsense Mrs. Brown will tell him about what happened in the shop. She puts her hand to her hair; it's loose from its bun and falling about her face. Perhaps she won't go now, though—not like this. And she hasn't eaten today. No, she'll feed the child and they'll go to bed, and first thing they'll go up to the Manse and she'll clear everything up.

The next morning, heart fluttering, unsure of what it is exactly she is going to say, Dorothy and the boy are on their way to the Manse. The shops aren't open yet, though the windows above them glow with lamps lit, and the butcher is in the back of his shop with his cleaver. He doesn't look up as they go up the hill, and Dorothy hurries past. Only the upstairs windows of the grocer's flicker yellow, the shop below still in darkness. The moon is still in the sky, delicate and translucent, the last stars paling with the coming day.

As they turn at the top of the hill toward the Manse, there's the frantic ringing of a bell and a "Look out!" and Dorothy swings round, just in time to pull herself and the child out of the way of the postboy. His cap is pulled down low over his eyes and he swerves to avoid them, wobbling and trying to balance with his knees out, but he can't recover, and they watch, the child wide-eyed as the bicycle slowly tilts.

"Bawbag," he says as he sprawls on the ice, and the child can't help it—he laughs, a big burst of mirth, and then the postboy sits up and laughs too, and Dorothy recognizes him as Tom, the oldest Carnegie boy. She's glad he has a job to help his mother and she says, "Are you hurt? Can I help you?"

"No, Mrs. Gray, I'm fine. It's not the first time. I just can't get the hang of the thing," and he puts one hand on the bicycle and goes to stand up. He winces as he puts weight on the one leg and looks down at the bloodied rip in his trousers. There's a crimson smear in the snow too. But worse than that, the front wheel is bent completely out of shape. He's crestfallen. "Oh, Lord, they're not going to like that," and the years roll away as he looks at Dorothy. "What shall I tell them, Miss?"

"Tell them the truth. That I got in your way. Now, Tom, I can't stop, I've got to get to the Manse, but you tell them that, and I'll pop in later and tell them the same."

"Did you say you're going to the Manse?" He bites his lip. "I know we're not supposed to, but could you take this?" He reaches into his satchel and pulls out a telegram. "It's for the Minister—it's urgent. I think I need to get this back to the Post Office and . . . " He gestures at the icy stretch of road still to go.

Dorothy looks at the piece of paper fluttering in the wind. It's in the postmaster's handwriting. The word *Norway* catches her eye. Time stops. She looks back at Tom, his eyebrows still raised in question.

She steps forward and takes the paper from him and puts it in her handbag. "I've got a moment—let me give you a hand up?"

"If you wouldn't mind?" and so she helps him get to his feet, to right the bicycle, then watches as he limps away from them, pushing it on its back wheel, and as soon as he's out of sight, she turns back toward the village, where the shops are just opening. She buys bacon and cheese, some more tea, as though it is a normal day and this was always her intention. She hasn't consciously thought *I shall steal the telegram* or *I shall obstruct the Minister's investigation.* In fact, she tries not to think of the piece of paper at all and what it might say.

Later, after supper, Dorothy goes upstairs. She takes the telegram out of her bag and doesn't even read it. She opens a drawer and buries it beneath her undergarments, then lies on the floor of the bedroom and reaches under the bed for her leather case. She would have liked more time to plan, to gather together what they'll need, but she has a little money hidden away. They'll go somewhere where no one knows them, rent a house. Maybe they'll go to Edinburgh. Yes, she thinks, at least she knows it there; they can get lost in its crowds and busy streets.

When she pulls the case out, a spring day years before and the smell of gorse come back to her for just a moment. How long ago it all was, her hopeful arrival, that first summer full of bright promise, of Joseph and the beautiful thing she'd thought was growing between them.

How much has happened since.

Now that it's in front of her, the case is smaller than she remembers, the past and its hopes shrunk to an empty case gathering dust, but she won't think about that. She doesn't need to take much anyway—some clothes, the money, the

tin soldiers. She pulls a few things out of drawers and cupboards, folds them, and fastens the straps.

There is a clatter of footsteps on the stairs, and the child
appears in the doorway and spies the case. His face lights up
and he says something in words she doesn't understand.

"What did you say? Say it again," and she tries to hear
what Mrs. Brown did, but Mrs. Brown has definitely got it
all wrong. She knows the doctor said he'd suffered no injury
to his head, but as his speech is coming back, things are
bound to be jumbled. She gets up and puts her hands on his
shoulders.

"We're going to find a new home. A new home for you,
for us," and he wraps his arms around her and leans into her
embrace.

Then

Agnes and Moses

It is a chance meeting. The wind is brisk and cold, and Agnes pulls her coat around herself as she goes up Copse Cross Street. She's not really even looking ahead but more at the cobbles and the worn leather of her boots. She doesn't think the bruise on her cheekbone is showing much and there's a bit of powder on it anyway—a trick she's learned from her mother.

As she passes the butcher's, she catches sight of Dorothy and Moses inside. Dorothy is crouched down by the counter, and when she stands up, a red ball is in her hand. She says something crossly to Moses, and Agnes steps away quickly as she sees her pull him outside.

"Now, just wait there till I've finished. And no more nonsense with the ball!"

When she goes back in, Agnes waits till a quick glance tells her Dorothy is at the counter again, with her back to the door. Seeing Moses, here, like this, is meant to be, of that Agnes is sure. Out of sight of the window, she crouches down.

"Moses?"

He looks at her solemnly.

"Do you know who I am?"

He shakes his head.

"We've waved to each other, haven't we?"

He nods uncertainly.

"We're friends, I hope?" though her heart yearns to use a different word. Out of the corner of her eye she sees Dorothy is finishing up, putting the parcels in her basket and looking for the right coins. When she turns back, Moses is showing her what's in his hand—the bright India rubber ball. She smiles.

"Look at that! Aren't you lucky! Would you like to play with it sometime—with me?" and he nods, more certainly this time, and smiles, and she knows it's wrong but she says it anyway. "It can be our secret," she says and puts her finger to her lips. "You could come to my house." She points up the side street. "That's mine," she says, and she's only got a couple more moments. "You could bring your ball and we could play," and she stands up and quickly walks away, hearing the butcher's door open and shut.

Her heart is pounding and the wind is picking up. She looks up at the sky, at the gulls flying inland. A sudden gust makes her pull her coat tighter around herself. Above her, the gulls are screaming.

If she's not mistaken, there's going to be a hell of a storm tonight.

Now

Dorothy and the Child

She waits till dusk. They'll take the road that skirts the village and walk to the train station in the next town. They'll be fine if they are well wrapped up; it's only a few miles. They can wait overnight, get the dawn train to Edinburgh. She runs back upstairs and fetches a blanket she knitted and rolls it up and puts it in a bag. There. They can put that around themselves if the waiting room is cold.

For the first time in days, Dorothy's hands aren't shaking. A strange calm has taken over her body. She'd stayed in Skerry for this very reason, waiting and hoping for her child to come back. All those nights she'd lit her lamp and put it in the window to guide him home, and isn't that just what she did the night before he was returned to her? There is no need to stay now, not when staying means they could be pulled apart and someone take him from her again.

Back downstairs, she sees to the plover. He needs more time, but there isn't any. He will just have to take his chances like they are. She brings down the case and puts it in the kitchen, then goes through and picks up the basket. By the time she gets to the back door, the boy has caught her up.

"No," he says, hanging on to her skirts. Her heart leaps at his spoken word. See? Even though his voice has a strange slant, it's all coming back now.

"He's ready," she says, going into the garden and placing the basket under the apple tree. "We can't take him."

The boy pulls in his lips and frowns at her, shaking his head. "No," he says again, his eyes filling with tears. He grips the handle of the basket.

Dorothy prizes his hand off. "He's ready—look." She scoops the plover up in her cupped hands, and it hops onto the snow. It tries to stretch its wing, hops again, lopsided and ungainly with its splint.

The boy is crying now. She tries to reassure him. "He's used to the winter, he'll survive," she says. "I promise," and she pulls him into the house and closes and bolts the door, refuses to think about the plover out in the growing cold of the waning day. She hurries through to the kitchen so she doesn't have to hear its melancholy call.

The boy looks mutinous. He stares at the door to the garden, his breath coming in tearful little hiccups now, but she dries his face, bundles him into an extra jumper, two pairs of socks. They both have hats and scarves on, gloves and coats.

Outside, they take the path leading away from the village and up the lane that skirts around it. The moon is fat in the darkening sky and glows dusky blue on the snow, pooling in the hollows of its frozen drifts and icy ridges. An owl hoots from the trees on the Tops, and somewhere in the village, a dog barks and another answers. The sounds ring out clearly in the winter night. As they leave behind the warm lights flickering in the windows of the cottages, the cold deepens. Dorothy grips the boy's hand, at the same time trying to hold her case and stop it dragging and slowing them down. A bitter wind slices her face, and she buries her chin into her scarf and toils with the child up the hill.

The snow lies thick and frozen. Soon Skerry falls behind them. When they get to the Tops, they stop. Dorothy won't listen to the voice that tells her to go back, that this journey is madness. She stops to check that the child is warm enough. She pulls his hat down over his ears, and her breath catches at the bewildered look on his face. She places her hands on his shoulders. "It's for your own good—for our good," she says, hoping he can understand. She puts her arms around him and he leans into her, though she tries to ignore the distress still visible in his face when she lets him go.

The road out of Skerry is clearer than the lane to the Tops—an effort had been made before the great freeze to dig a path through the snow. Drifts of it tower over them on either side, but the track between is treacherous. Clouds darken the way, and the boy grips her hand in silence, head down into the wind. She stops every now and then to give him a warming sip from the flask she packed.

After a while, the clouds clear and the wind dies. The sky is huge, the stars icily bright. The world beyond the banks of snow disappears. The wind has sculpted the snow into an eerie, alien landscape of hollows and ridges, ripples, and waves. With one careful step after another, she feels somehow outside of time in the moonlit landscape of drifts and shadows, valleys and peaks, under the wheeling starlight.

A creeping, sleepy warmth steals over her. Maybe they should stop for a while and rest. She crouches down. The boy seems almost asleep too. His eyes are nearly closed, his lashes frosty. If only she could work out how far they've come, how long they've been walking for, she'd know whether to stop. When she stands up again, a light up ahead flickers and dies. They make it to the brow of the hill, and at last the moon glances on the tower of a kirk and a few lights glow in a fold of the valley below as the town finally appears in an expanse of silent, white beauty. She lifts him onto one hip and drags the case with her other arm and sets out again, but the town seems to get farther away, not closer, and after a time, the last lights flicker out. Hours pass, or is it minutes? She has no way of knowing; time is stretched and dilated by the heavy rhythm of her steps, the strange drowsiness, the pale ghosts of the drifts.

By the time they come at last to the outlying houses, her arms are numb and the boy's head lies on her shoulder. She feels as though she is walking in a dream. Soon they are passing through the little town itself, the only figures in its empty streets, past the alehouse with its shuttered windows, past the kirk with its lonely graveyard, past the sleeping cottages. Dorothy remembers the way—she's used the train a few times over the years—but it is not until they are on the empty platform and opening the door to the waiting room that she realizes this is exactly where she'd sat, so many years before, waiting for the Minister to arrive to take her to Skerry. There is the very bench, in fact, along the back wall, in an otherwise empty room. She lets go of the boy and sits him down, sinking beside him. With numb hands she manages to get out the blanket and wraps it around them both and opens the flask. She wakes him up just long enough to make him drink, and then, leaning into each other, they fall asleep in this place that isn't a place at all but only a waystation between worlds.

Dorothy and the Stationmaster

"Miss? Miss."

Dorothy is at the bottom of a deep, dark lake.

The voice comes again. "Miss?"

Slowly she swims up to the surface and blinks in the half light. She is confused at first, uncertain where she is, and then the strange night comes back to her—the drifts, the drowsiness, the cold.

The Stationmaster is leaning over her, frowning. "Miss, what are you doing here?"

Against her arm the boy lies heavily, still asleep. She moves him slightly and sits up straighter. The Stationmaster looks familiar. "I'm waiting to get the Edinburgh train."

The Stationmaster looks baffled. "The Edinburgh train, Miss? There's been no trains in or out of here for weeks. The lines are frozen."

Dorothy swallows hard. "You don't understand, we have to leave. We have to leave today."

"There'll be no leaving, Miss. Not till this snow thaws. Where have you come from?"

"From Skerry last night. We walked."

His eyes widen. "*Walked?*" He clears his throat. "Are you quite well, Miss?" He scratches his head and looks at the boy.

"You must both be frozen." He turns toward the door. "Wait here. I'll be back."

Dorothy pulls the blanket tighter around herself and shivers. Surely it's not the same stationmaster who helped her with her case all those years ago? Who waved her off to her new life in Skerry?

When he comes back in, he is carrying a tray and places it on the bench. There is a steaming pot of tea and two cups and a plate piled high with toast.

"You busy yourselves with that, now, and I'll be back when I've sorted something out."

"But what about us leaving? Is there nothing you can suggest?"

He shakes his head wonderingly. "Yes, there is something I can suggest. Home. That's the place you need to be going to, home." He leaves, still shaking his head, before she can say anything else.

When the crying starts, it is very quiet. She turns to the boy. The weak dawn-light catches the sheen of tears on his cheeks. In between his soft sobs, his eyes keep closing, as though he can't stay awake.

Dorothy feels the skin of his cheek and his hands inside the gloves. They are cold and white. She arranges the blanket around him. "Come, wake up now. Have some tea. You need to wake up," and she helps him into a sitting-up position, tries to help him sip the tea. He turns his face from her.

"Mamma." He says it again. "Mamma." The word is a sob.

Dorothy pulls the blanket tighter, adjusts his hat, but he pulls away from her and says it more insistently. "Mamma."

Dorothy's heart flutters with fear. She reaches for him.

This time he turns to her. His face is angry and he pushes

her hand away. "Mamma! Mamma! Home!" and then he collapses into sobs.

Dorothy goes cold. She feels like she's been slapped. She wants to say his name. She reaches out her hand again, then pulls it back. When he looks at her, he says something in that garbled speech he has started to use, and the growing light picks out the gray of his eyes. Dorothy starts to feel faint. The walls and door of the waiting room bend closer; the packed case at her feet looks new and, for a moment, past and present elide.

Outside, there is a jangle of harness and the creak of wheels in the snow. The Stationmaster reappears.

"The cabbie has come, Miss. None too happy to be woken up, but he says he'll take you as far as he can." He picks up her case and waits at the door of the waiting room for her to follow.

Dorothy rises and the boy does too. They cross the empty platform, back to the road. The horse's nostrils are puffing out smoky air, and he stomps his hooves and whickers. The cabbie stares at her in open curiosity. They climb up into the back of the cart, and the Stationmaster passes up the case, then tucks the blanket over their knees.

"You keep warm now," and he smiles but the stitch between his eyes remains, "and I wish you good luck, Miss," and with a flick of the cabbie's switch and a *walk on*, the horse pulls away, the Stationmaster watching after them with a worried frown.

Dorothy won't think ahead or back. She stays quiet and stiff as they bounce over the rutted snow. Maybe it was the journey, maybe it's exhaustion, but none of it feels real, back amongst the drifts, the glitter of the ice crystals. After a while, the horse's broad back is steaming with the effort. Finally, as they get close to the Tops, the cabbie calls and pulls on the reins to bring the animal to a stop.

"That's as far as I can take you, Miss. Best get the lad home and warm." His face has the same puzzled frown as the Stationmaster's, but Dorothy says nothing other than thanking him for his trouble and giving him the coins for the journey and a tip.

It's not long before they're slipping and sliding back down the lane that skirts the village. They follow the hollows and ruts of their own footprints back home, back to some growing inevitability. And all the while the boy's face in the dawn sun keeps coming to her, the gray of his eyes.

Gray? She thought they were green.

When they get back, the boy rushes out to the garden. The plover has survived the night, and he brings it into the kitchen, where Dorothy is stoking up the fire. Her movements are automatic, unthinking. She puts the stew she hadn't even thrown away, such had been her hurry, on to warm. The boy sits at the table, shoveling in spoonfuls of it, one hand possessively on the basket with the plover. Every now and then, a shivery sob shakes him. He won't look at Dorothy. After, she puts him to bed with the stone pig, but he won't let go of the basket and she can't fight him, can't fight whatever this is anymore.

When she leaves him, she stands outside her room. Some great truth is gathering to break over her head, and it is on the other side of that door. She has tried for so long to keep the past from entering her house, but at last, with the same otherworldly feeling she has had since setting out the day before, she goes in and stands in front of the chest of drawers, takes a deep breath, and feels amongst her clothes for the telegram.

The Minister

He's sitting in the vestry, head nodding, eyes closing, then startling awake again. He has a flask of tea that Martha made for him, and he sips from it now, though it's lost most of its warmth. He's mid-yawn and stretch when there's a shuffle outside the door. He quickly sits up straight, places his hands on the table.

"Hello?"

Another shuffle.

He stands up to go and see who it is, when the door opens and he sees Agnes standing there, thin and tired-looking in the gloom of the Kirk behind her.

"Minister?" and as soon as the word leaves her mouth, she staggers. "Minister—it's Moses." She starts again. "It was me. Moses died because of me," and just in time, he catches her before she slips, a red ball falling from her hand.

Dorothy and the Telegram

Her head is throbbing, she can't take in the words. She makes herself read it twice. Makes herself do it again.

Boy missing *STOP* Norwegian *STOP* Fallen overboard presumed dead *STOP* Johan Anderson *STOP* Please check *STOP*

Johan Anderson.

She reads it till the words blur. She balls her hands into fists and pushes them against her eyes and takes a few deep breaths till her breath is no longer shaking. In his room, he is half asleep, one hand protectively on the basket. She watches him for a few moments, his rounded cheeks, their childish fuzz, his beautiful hair. And then she speaks.

"Johan," she says, praying it isn't him. "Johan?" and he opens his eyes, his face slowly transforming in the recognition of his own name.

Then

Joseph

He comes across it when he's clearing out, looking for rubbish to burn on the bonfire with the garden waste. After he
dusts it off, the paint is still bright, though chipped in places,
but there it is—the model he made of his own boat for Moses
a year ago, with its long keel and two masts, its vertical bow
and stern, its broad beam for stability. He'd even made the
sails and painted the name, *North Star*, in black on the hull.
He wonders whether to put it on the pile with the rubbish.

He sighs. There is no future for him with Dorothy; he has
accepted that. But he still feels sad for the lad. Perhaps he
should give it to him anyway; there's no harm in that. And
he doesn't want to keep it.

When he gets to her door, he raises his hand to knock,
then pauses. Is this the right thing to do? He looks at it balanced in his hands. He tries to remind himself that it's not
for Dorothy, it's for Moses. And he can float it in the rock
pools and the shallow waves. He stands a while, unsure what
to do, then cursing himself for his lack of courage, he leaves
the boat by the door, sheltered by a stone trough from the
wind that is picking up.

Agnes

It's strange how a life can turn on a moment, on the smallest thing. For Agnes, it is finally speaking to Moses outside the butcher's shop, asking someone else's child to come and play. Walking away from him, the wind makes her cheeks cold. All the way home, the tears rush down her face and are still coming in the kitchen where she leans against the shut door. She doesn't want to do it anymore—it's too hard to return to the childless house, to know, month after month, that no baby is coming, hard to see this beautiful child and his underserving mother. Hard to wait for a man who doesn't love her, whom she doesn't love, to come back to this house without tenderness, without warmth and kindness.

She sits at the kitchen table and thinks about her life. *It's the soil, not the seed, that's barren.* Isn't that what Scott always says? She doesn't know how she's going to accept it, she doesn't even know how she's going to let go of the daydreams and hopes that have allowed her to escape the miseries of her life, but she's going to have to find a way.

After a while she sits up straighter. What she is thinking makes her heart thump, but she wouldn't be the first woman to leave her husband, would she? There are no children to stay for—and could anyone blame her? They all know Scott beats her, however much she tells herself otherwise, just as they knew about Jeanie. She could go home, help more with the little ones. The wind rattles the door in its frame, and Agnes tightens her shawl around her. With any luck, Scott will be in the alehouse already and back late. She has a lot of thinking to do.

She puts some more wood on the fire and hangs the kettle from the hook. A vicious gust rushes down the chimney, making the kettle swing and sparks fly into the room. Outside, the wind rises to a wail as the storm builds.

Jeanie

It is Jeanie who sees the argument, sitting in her rocking chair by the window, waiting for her daughter to come with the soup. Not even late afternoon, but might as well be, the clouds low and heavy, the gulls flying inland screeching. She can't see the Steps down to Skerry Sands but makes out the figure of Joseph down at the water's edge, tying down his boat. The other boats are already secure, pulled up the beach for safety.

It is an unexpected movement that catches Jeanie's eye, and she knows it's Dorothy immediately. It is obvious from the way Dorothy's arms are moving that she is angry, and Jeanie is surprised, for she's never seen any passion in her before. The child sits on a rock a little way behind her. They have their backs to Jeanie, so it is only Joseph's face she can see. Her Agnes had set her sights on him a long time ago, handsome as he is and a fine, strong fisherman. But everyone knew he'd only eyes for the schoolmistress.

But never mind all that now.

He is shaking his head, and Jeanie squints because the day is dying, the last glisk of yellow light glinting through the clouds. The wind is flattening the grasses on the cliff, and Dorothy wraps her arms around herself. Joseph is saying something, and Jeanie wishes she could hear it. Maybe

294

Dorothy is angry that the child goes down there. Oh yes, she's seen him often enough, bothering Joseph. Or maybe he is the one who is angry—she wishes she knew. But then, unbelievably, Dorothy slaps him clear across the face. Jeanie's face is a picture of thrilled shock.

She feels the stunned silence that follows the slap all the way up here on the cliff behind the window. Joseph has hold of Dorothy's arm and is gesturing with the other, and Moses has run to Dorothy, but she is trying to push him behind her. She breaks free of Joseph and, turning, runs back toward the Steps and out of Jeanie's sight.

She pulls back from the window now; she doesn't want anyone to think she's a busybody. She hopes Agnes won't be long—it's getting late for supper. Lazy girl. She can't wait to tell her daughter what she's seen. And so she does, and Agnes of course tells somebody, who tells somebody else, so that by the time everyone is trying to understand what happened the night the child goes missing, they can't help noticing—in their muttered whispers and sidelong glances—Joseph's own role in the whole thing.

Joseph

Joseph knows the storm is coming. He's seen the yellow glow of the halo around the moon and the ice-glitter of the winter sky. He's securing his boat, the wind snatching at the ropes as he ties them to the posts sunk into the sand above the high tide mark. The waves are already building. The gulls have flown inland. He heard them screaming earlier, flying low over the thatch. Something makes him turn, and Dorothy is there and, a little way behind her, Moses sits on a rock. Can't she read the signs? He should be warm at home, they both should. He finishes tying the mooring knot, before facing her.

She still has to raise her voice to be heard. "I want you to leave Moses alone." At first he thinks he's got it wrong. He is about to say something, but the distress in her face silences him. "I told you, Joseph," she continues.

He steps forward. "Is this about the boat I left for him?"

The wind is picking up and whips a lock of hair into her face. She tucks it tightly behind her ear. "You know it is. I mean it. Do you hear me?"

"But it'd do him no harm to have it. I made it for him, after all."

"No."

Joseph feels his anger rise. "Apart from that one time

296

crabbing, it was the lad that used to come to me, not myself looking for him, Dorothy."

"Mrs. Gray."

The sky is livid with the sunset. The wind smells different; the storm will make landfall soon.

"What are you so afraid of?" and he starts to turn away— he has another rope to tie.

Her shout when it comes shocks him. "Afraid? Afraid? Who do you think you are to say that to me?" and he turns back and sees it right there on her face. The fear she has of him.

"Don't you understand? Someone will guess."

"Is this because of what happened between us that night?" And he sees now that it is—she cannot forgive herself, because she'd wanted for it to happen as much as he had. How pitiful it is that this one night when they'd found each other, so many years ago, had come to be the great romantic adventure of his life, and he hates her for it, for the memory of her scent, her skin, the taste of her sweat, the welcome of her body forever denied him since.

"It meant nothing," and he's never meant anything less, "nothing. Forget it. I barely remember it," he says, remembering her breath, the smell of her hair, damp with sea spray and rain.

The slap when it comes takes his breath away. Moses runs forward, and as the stinging recedes, he notices it—the way she tries to push the boy behind her, her agonized *no*, the distress on her face, caught in the violent light of the oncoming storm.

And at last he understands what it is she is afraid of people guessing.

He kneels down, takes hold of the boy's arm, pulls him gently toward him.

Dorothy's voice is a whisper, "No, no . . . "

He looks into Moses's face, his voice full of amazement. "How can you be sure? There's only one way." He looks up at her. "Are you telling me that you and William . . . ?"

The cry that is torn from Dorothy is part animal, and she pulls on Moses's arm too, and the few seconds while he and Moses stare into each other's faces, before Dorothy drags him across the sand to the rocky stairs, are the only moments in his life when Joseph looks upon the child and knows himself to be his father.

Now

Agnes and the Minister

The Minister settles Agnes on a chair, guides her head to rest between her knees. He feels a little peculiar himself. Of all the things she could have said to him, he could not have anticipated this.

He pulls his chair up next to hers and waits, wondering what to say. After a while she sits up but covers her face with her hands. He gently moves them. "Come on, Agnes, start at the beginning."

And falteringly, she does. She tells him about her father, about Joseph and his kind manner. She tells him how she thought they would marry till Dorothy came along, and that whatever she did to try to make him choose her, she must have been doing it wrong because he kept choosing Dorothy until she and Jeanie did their best to ruin it. How after she married Scott, her longing for a child stayed as just that—a desperate, grieving longing—and maybe she was being punished for what she'd done, but it wasn't fair that Dorothy had Moses, a beautiful boy, and she had nothing at all, and that she'd lain in bed and planned over and again how she could get him away from her, how Dorothy didn't deserve him—in fact, how she deserved to feel the very grief that Agnes felt because, somehow, in the other life that Agnes should have lived with Joseph, there would have been children, and the moment that was taken away from her, the moment Dorothy took it away, her future, her barren, childless, miserable future with Scott was decided.

As the words rush out, tears streak her face, and she pulls at her hair. The bruises on her arms—thumbprints, scratches—peep from her sleeves, and the Minister feels such a welling of grief, of compassion, of godly love for the torment of her life that it is a moment before he can speak.

He puts his hand on hers. He remembers seeing her praying in the Kirk, clutching the ball. "You must tell me what you did."

Her voice is a low moan. "I—I spoke to him, I'd seen them in the butcher's. He'd dropped the ball. It had rolled under the counter. She was so angry with him. She made him stand outside. I told him he could play with his red ball with me, that he could come to me." Her face is a mask of horror. "I never meant—I got home and I knew it was wrong—I didn't mean to bring harm to him. I would never have wanted that, not ever. I just wanted to see him and to teach Dorothy a lesson, I suppose. But that night he—oh God, it was the night of the storm." She puts her hands over her face.

The Minister swallows. "You mean this—" He picks it up with shaking hands. "This is Moses's ball?" It's pitted now, its color faded. He looks back up at the figure, small in the chair, her rough, red hands covering her face, nails short and ragged from biting. He struggles to speak. "So he came to you, that night? What happened then?"

Her hands drop from her face. "No!"

He shakes his head. "I don't understand." He holds up the ball. "Then why have you got this?"

She's crying now. "I slept through it all; I don't know how. The whole thing. The men that helped—they were fetched from the alehouse, so Scott didn't come home. I didn't know what had happened till he came back almost at daybreak and told me—after Joseph had found his boot."

"But the ball?"

"I went down to the Sands. I looked for him too, in case—you know, his body washed up. I went down every day for days and I found the ball. When the tide was out, wedged between the rocks." She is swaying back and forth in her chair, but now looks at him directly. "Don't you see? He must have been coming to me. I told him to leave his house and come to me."

The Minister feels as though he's been holding his breath. His hands are still trembling as he puts the ball on the desk. "Agnes . . . listen to me. Moses always had that ball with him—he took it everywhere. Dorothy commented on it, and I saw it myself. He loved it. None of this means he was coming to you. Your home—it's in the opposite direction. The Steps are just by Dorothy's. Whatever made him leave his home—it wasn't you. Are you listening to what I'm saying?"

Agnes drags the backs of her hands across her wet cheeks. "He always had the ball with him?"

"Yes. This is all just a terrible coincidence. Is this what you've thought—all this time? That it's your fault?" He sighs. "I wish you'd come to me sooner." He frowns. "But why did you keep it?"

"I was going to leave Scott, you know. That day, I decided it, that very day. I decided I'd go and live back home. But after what happened"—she shrugs—"I suppose I felt I deserved my unhappiness. The ball was a reminder of that—so I wouldn't forget what I'd done." She holds it in her hands again. "Minister, do you think I'm mad?"

"No, Agnes. I do not think you're mad. But I don't think you are responsible for what happened to Moses either." He

301

shakes his head. "I'm glad you have come to me and unburdened yourself. You have carried this for too long," and as he wraps his coat around her, she cries softly, and the Minister thinks of Jenny, of all the years of her wanting a baby and a baby never coming, of how she hated him, hated herself for it, how she would pummel him with her fists when her monthly blood came again and again, how she would wonder what she'd done to be punished like this. And he pictures her now, with their child, their late gift of a child that he keeps coming to the Kirk to avoid, and he realizes all he wants is to be with them at home.

He takes the ball from her hands. "It's time to leave this behind you now, Agnes. You are one of God's children. You always have been. Let us pray together. And then we will think about the future."

Joseph

Joseph has pulled out the old oakum he'd used to keep the boat watertight and has replaced the soft planks of the keel. Strange the way the sea gives them life—that it's the blood that runs through them all—yet they must defend themselves from its threat, its unpredictable danger.

It is not just the love of a woman that has escaped him. After the night the lad went missing, Joseph had shunned the company of men too, knowing there were those who cast doubt on him, as though him arguing with Dorothy was somehow connected to what happened later. He knows what the village is like for rumors and lies, and he'd seen their faces himself, when he came back from the Rocks, that small boot in his hand. He had his crew, of course—you can't go out to the fishing grounds on your own—and at sea he's always commanded respect. But he thinks of the nights he has cooked his own supper, not joined the others at the alehouse, and on the rare occasions he has, they still raise their glasses to him when he leaves to go home and shout, "Night, Joe," but mutter after, he's sure of it, about what they think really happened that night. It is as though the shadow of the child walks with him, is his own shadow—is, in fact, a part of himself.

It was too much for him, finding that boot, knowing what

he finally then knew. He'd always been a man of few words, but words people listened to, a man people respected. Those few words had dried up to almost none. And he knew they all wondered why he and Dorothy had fought the night before, down on the Sands. Everyone had seen the lad there too, often enough, bothering him.

Though it was never a bother. Joseph closes his eyes and there he is, the child with the soft way about him.

Joseph had liked his quiet company when he came. The lad would sit on the sand, watching while he mended a net or washed out his lobster boxes and barrels. Once Joseph had gutted and cooked a mackerel in front of him, right there on the shore, on his brazier, the skin sizzling black and crisp, the flesh dripping oil on the leaping flames, the hungry shriek of the gulls above. Joseph had speared a little on his knife and offered it to the child, who had taken it and then, copying him, blown on it, tossing it quickly from hand to hand, mouthed an excited "O," popping it on his tongue with a gasp. Afterward, he had given Joseph one of his rare smiles and shuffled in closer for more.

It has always haunted him, the lanterns bobbing over the beach in the wild dark, the stumble across the Rocks where he'd been led by some instinct when the alarm had been raised. It was the moment—simple, horrifying—when the beam, swinging past and then back again, swept over the small boot, jammed in a cleft in the rock not even a hand's width wide.

My crab! My crab!

Careful, lad. The sea is a dangerous thing.

"No, no," he'd moaned, the waves soaking him, hurling themselves into the fissure as he'd leaned in closer. He'd called no one—later he'd wished he had—but had shouted Moses's name over and again, pointlessly, into the storm, the gale whipping away his words, the sea enraged.

What hope had the child out there?

His son.

He had pulled and pulled at the little boot, on his knees, salt water blinding him, falling backward once it was free. The wind had wailed as he'd climbed back down to the Sands and stood, hands outstretched, calling out into the mayhem for help. He can't remember now what he'd said, nor how anyone had heard him in that mad darkness, but the news had spread and lights had gathered round him, blurred in the rain.

It had been the silence of the villagers that had spoken most loudly to him.

At last, Agnes's husband had spoken. "And where was that, you say, Joseph?"

He'd gestured at the Rocks, and their silence had closed around him again. Dorothy had pushed through till she was standing in front of him—eyes wide in the livid, distorting light of the lamps that glanced over her face—and the look of longing, of desperate need for him to have found their child had stunned him speechless, tears running with the rain on his face, and he'd wanted to go to her, to make it better for her, for them both, but he couldn't, so he'd laid the boot in her hand and, turning, had clambered back up the Steps, the sun still not even a hope on the edge of the world.

Dorothy

Dorothy can't move at first. Then she crosses the room and tucks the blanket around him. She can't speak either, so she goes out and closes the door and goes into her room and sits on the bed, upright and rigid.

She squeezes her eyes shut, gently rocking back and forth; the Rocks, the storm, the woman, just like her, frantic on the shoreline. And the terrible night, the one she has been running away from ever since, the one she has refused to remember, finally comes back to her, in this moment when she is blown wide open.

She'd known as soon as she'd woken up, the way you know when you knock at a door that no one is home.

Moses wasn't there.

The storm was howling, the house a ship torn loose of its mooring, the wind buffeting every window, every door. She doesn't know how she knew, but her frantic glance into his room had confirmed it.

Not tonight, not tonight. Not in this.

And she'd run through the two rooms downstairs, eyes widening in horror. His boots were gone . . . then out through the door. Outside, the air was screaming and slammed her back against the house, snatching her voice and hurling it away from her. Lightning lit up a violent seascape, towering

306

waves, the sky livid, sickening. She'd stumbled and fought the wind, finding herself at Joseph's door, or had he found her shouting her child's name into the chaos of the storm? She'd struggled to free herself of him as she tried to get down to the Sands.

"You can't, Dorothy, you can't. Not on your own," and she thinks now that he'd dragged her with him while he hammered at the nearest cottage till. She doesn't know how long had passed, lanterns were swinging and blurring in the wind and sleet, as the village had come out to help, calling, "Moses, Moses!" into the dark. The night was a blur of freezing rain and her child's name and black wind till Joseph was calling, "Here, here," and she'd swung round. With her heart she'd seen him holding her child, clutching him to his chest, Moses's hair dark silver from the sea, body limp, skin slick with water, beads of it in his hair, clothes dark and sodden and cold but alive, alive, alive . . . but when she'd opened her eyes, Joseph was stretching out his hands to her, holding only Moses's small brown boot and the rain.

Much later, she thinks someone had put a coat over her. In all that time, she'd only been wearing her nightgown. Someone had helped her up the steps and into her home, forced whisky between her clenched teeth, tried to get her warm.

Memories drift back like dreams dissolving when she tries to fix them.

She was cold for weeks; she'd left the door unbolted every night so Moses could get in if she was sleeping, though she tried never to sleep, but sat in the chair waiting for him, keeping herself awake by knitting clothes to keep him warm. Every morning she'd made porridge for him because he would be hungry when he got home. She'd kept his room ready, washed his bed linen, clung to the gansey she'd made for him that he should have worn, wouldn't let go of his boot because he'd need his boot. How would he manage without it? He was too small to be without his mother. And she did not know how she could live a single day without him in it without dying herself, until the day she'd realized she was losing bits of him—his smell, the memory of his voice, his young boy's face, his hands, the touch of them—and she would open his drawers and hold his clothes to her face, she would dream she was running from room to room searching for him, until her fear of forgetting, over time, as more nights and weeks and years separated them and she lost more and more pieces of him, slowly became a fear of remembering.

But this isn't all—there is something else, something snagging on her memory, and she moans softly because she knows what it is now, and here in this moment of truth, there is nothing left but to face it.

Through the door. Through the door. She pictures herself again. The panic, the rush down the stairs, through the rooms, grabbing hold of the handle and the wind blowing it open. She relives it, over and over, but it's always the same. The thing she has always secretly known and been unable to face.

She hadn't bolted the door. It was unlocked.

She hadn't bolted the door.

She hadn't kept her child safe.

It was her fault.

Dorothy stands up at last. She goes into the other room, where the boy turns his face to her, puffy with sleep. She touches his hair. The firelight is playing on his face; he is haloed by it. Some huge feeling threatens to overwhelm her, but she swallows it down.

She goes to her room and puts on a warm dress and thick

woolen stockings, gloves, and boots, and wraps her shawl around her shoulders. Back in his room, she gently lifts him, tucking the blanket around him. She carries him downstairs and through the door, letting it close behind her, and walks away without looking back.

The moon is full and bright, the snow crisp and icy. She walks up Copse Cross Street. It's empty and there are no lights in the windows, not at this hour. The sky is huge, and Dorothy experiences the disorientating sensation of being tiny, toiling up a white hill between tiny houses and shops, while the vastness of the universe turns above her. She stops to gaze up at the thousands of stars pricking the velvet night, and suddenly they blur, like shooting stars streaking across the sky. She blinks and carries on walking.

When they are outside Brown's Grocers and Confectioners, she stops. She takes a deep breath and knocks on the door. The windows are dark, top and bottom. At the top of the street, the lamplighter is lighting the streetlamp. She knocks again. Silence. But Dorothy waits and at last she hears a scuffle, a muffled curse, and then a tiny orange flame appears at the back of the shop. It grows. And there is Mrs. Brown, in a voluminous nightgown, long johns, and boots. She peers through the window, sees Dorothy and the boy, and unbolts and unlocks the door.

She stares at them both, first the boy, then Dorothy. She stands back. "You better come in."

Once inside, Mrs. Brown holds the lamp up to Dorothy's face. Dorothy doesn't know what she sees there, but she nods, as though satisfying herself of something, and says, "Come through."

She leads them to the stockroom where Mrs. Brown must have been busy not long before because there is still a faint glow of warmth from the embers of the fire. Carefully, she takes the sleeping boy from her. "Put a log on, Dorothy. I'll be back."

Dorothy feels no fear for the child, not with Mrs. Brown, and she puts the log on, lets the fire draw till there are lively flames, then sits quietly on one of the wooden chairs to wait.

After a little while Mrs. Brown comes back. She has two glasses held between the fore- and middle fingers of one hand. She gives one to Dorothy, fetches the whisky from behind the bags of flour, and scrapes a chair up next to the fire.

"Where is he?"

"He's sleeping upstairs with Rab and an extra blanket. No need to be worrying about him." She winces slightly as she leans forward and splashes some whisky into Dorothy's glass. "So why are you here, Dorothy?" She tips the whisky into her mouth before refilling the glass and putting the bottle on the floor.

"It was me. It was my fault."

"What was?"

"All of it. Moses. I didn't bolt the door. I had an extra bolt fitted when he was about four because"—she puts her head in her hands—"it wasn't the first time he'd tried to get out. And that night—the night of the storm—I left it undone. I never forget things like that, never."

"Have a sip of the whisky, Dorothy." She gently nudges the bottom of the glass. "Come on." She takes another swig of her own. "I know."

Dorothy stares at her. "What do you mean?"

"You told me yourself."

"I don't understand, when?"

"I'll never forget you down on those Sands, in only your nightdress, looking for your child. I put my own coat around you."

"That was you?"

310

"I thought you'd die of the cold. I thought *I* might." She nearly smiles. "Stumbling around your house in the dark looking for blankets to get you warm. You were hysterical at first, outside of yourself. You told me then." Mrs. Brown looks down at the whisky glass in her hands, quickly blinks. "You just kept saying it, over and over, about the bolt. The shock set in after that."

"But why didn't I remember for so long?"

"There are some things we just don't want to remember. They're too big." She reaches forward and puts her hand on Dorothy's. "What happened wasn't your fault, Dorothy. It was a tragedy." She shakes her head. "A pointless, terrible tragedy."

"But—"

"We're none of us different from each other, not really. All trying to do our best, none of us managing it, not really." She looks at her more pointedly. "You'd know that, if you talked to anyone, you know."

Dorothy is still sitting upright. "Do you believe that? Really believe that? That it wasn't my fault?"

"I know it. Doesn't mean you won't blame yourself. That's what we all do. I never told anyone what you'd said, but even if I had . . . no one bolts their doors round here. No one would have thought . . . And children—well, they're full of mischief, and most of the time they don't come to harm for it. But sometimes . . . " She doesn't finish the sentence.

Dorothy takes another sip, and they fall quiet, the crackle of the fire the only sound. When she speaks, her voice is quiet. "I used to let him go down on the Sands. He got out once and Joseph found him and brought him back, and after that, it happened a few times, and I used to pretend I didn't know. I knew he was safe. I'd watch from upstairs. He seemed happy." She clears her throat. "Happy with Joseph."

Mrs. Brown raises her eyebrows. "He was happy with you too."

"I don't think he was." Dorothy catches her breath. "That's the thing. I don't think he was," and she covers her face. She stays like that a while, her shoulders softly shaking. When she's done, she wipes her face on her sleeve and lifts the glass to sniff the heady liquid. She takes a swig, not a sip, a proper swig of the whisky, and she shuts her eyes briefly, feeling it burn on her tongue and then her throat, tracking its fiery trail all the way down into her stomach where the warmth spreads through her body.

Mrs. Brown's hand is gentle on her knee. "It takes everyone like that, as far as I can see. Mothers and guilt. I've seen enough of them in the shop over the years. I don't think you were any different, not really."

Dorothy is quiet while she thinks about this, about how she's never known what it's like for anybody else. "You understood what he was saying then, in the shop, the other day, the boy?"

Mrs. Brown nods. "I don't know much Norwegian, but enough to recognize it. He wanted the cakes." She smiles, then her face is serious again. "Did you not guess? What did you think?"

"I—I don't know what I thought. He only started to say things I didn't understand a few days ago. Before that he was saying a few words, ones I thought I recognized." Dorothy opens her mouth to tell her what the words were, then closes it again. "I've done a bad thing."

Mrs. Brown's expression doesn't change "Well, we've all done those."

Dorothy takes another sip. "I stole a telegram. A telegram for the Minister."

This time, Mrs. Brown's eyes widen. "I didn't think you had it in you. What did you do that for?"

So Dorothy tells her, but she doesn't just tell her about the telegram, because she needs to begin at the beginning, and she wonders where the beginning is because tonight it feels as though all her life has been leading to this room with this woman and a telegram in a drawer calling the child home. She tells her the story of Moses, of his quiet way, and how she failed him because she can't remember him being happy, and she never really understood what she was doing anyway, and even before that, of when she first came to Skerry so full of hope. She says nothing about Joseph, about how much she had loved him, about their one beautiful summer, and later, their night on the Sands, because it is not only her story to tell. She tells her about the dreadful night Moses left her— all of it, the unbolted door again too—and then she tells her about the long frozen winter that came after, in which she didn't feel anything at all, until she thought the boy upstairs might be her very own child, given back to her by some miracle. Mrs. Brown lets her talk, sometimes pouring another splash of whisky into their glasses, and the fire it has lit in Dorothy's belly runs through her blood and keeps her talking.

When she finally stops, her face is wet.

She didn't know she'd been crying.

They sit in silence for some time, while Dorothy composes herself and her breathing steadies.

It is Mrs. Brown who breaks the silence again. "Losing a child is a dreadful thing. The worst grief. Someone I know . . ." She pauses and clears her throat. "Someone I know had a child, a boy too, as it happens, who died when he was very small. Breathing in his crib one moment, then the next—"

She breaks off. "I've often wondered what she did for that to happen."

Dorothy frowns. "No, that's not the right way to think of it at all. My own mother had a little boy after me. He died like that when he was only a few months old. It was nothing she did; it wasn't her fault."

"How can you know? What makes you so sure?"

"The doctor. A good physician. He said doctors used to blame the mothers a long time ago—you know, neglect, drunkenness, that sort of thing. But not anymore. They know now it just happens to some babies; it's no one's fault. I hope you didn't tell your friend it was."

Mrs. Brown takes a long swig of her whisky and closes her eyes. "She wasn't a friend exactly." She opens them again. "And the doctor was sure of that?"

"Yes, he said . . . " and Dorothy pauses, as though she's just realized something. "I think your friend probably loved her little boy very much and did everything she could to look after him and keep him safe. You should tell her to forgive herself. Actually, you should tell her there's nothing to forgive."

Mrs. Brown's eyes are overbright in the firelight.

"Yes, yes. I'll be sure to do that. Thank you." Mrs. Brown holds up the bottle of whisky to look at what's left and takes a moment before speaking. "Look at us, drinking and talking the night away. I told the Minister, by the way. About the boy—where he's from. You understand why, don't you?"

Dorothy nods. She does, but doesn't want to think about it, not in this moment by the fire, her limbs soft with the whisky-warmth and her thoughts soft too, the fire blooming with the last log Mrs. Brown is putting on in this room where the women do the knitting, the planning, the gossiping. The stockroom with all the things in it the village needs. She's dimly aware of Mrs. Brown wrapping a blanket around her but doesn't hear her quiet tread on the stair.

For the second time in her life, Dorothy falls asleep in her clothes. When she wakes, the fire is dead and her head hurts. The blanket has slipped and there's a nearly empty bottle of whisky by the leg of the chair Mrs. Brown had been sitting on. It is just before dawn, by the look of the small square of sky she can see through the window.

She heaves herself up and knocks the chair over. It sounds loud in the silence. She hears footsteps on the floor above, and a little while later Mrs. Brown appears with a cup of tea. The boy appears behind, carrying Rab and smiling. He comes and stands next to Dorothy, leaning in very slightly.

When it's time to leave, Dorothy says thank you, and Mrs. Brown says, "Thank you too," and, "Good morning, Dorothy."

Just as the door is about to close behind them, Mrs. Brown says, "You know what you've got to do, don't you?" and she and the child step outside into the new morning. But before they go to the Manse, Dorothy wants to take him to the Tops to watch dawn unfurl across the sky. There is no one around yet, and together they walk up the hill of the still-sleepy town. She squeezes his gloved hand and he squeezes hers back.

And there is something in this moment of silence, coils of smoke starting to rise from chimneys, lights starting to glimmer in the windows of the little fishing village clinging to the rocks, that is holy.

The Manse

When they get to the Manse, it's bustling with excitement. Martha opens the door, and just behind her, the Minister is pulling on his coat.

Martha turns to him. "They're here already," and the Minister looks up.

Though his face is drawn with tiredness, he beams. "Dorothy, come through, come through. Martha, take the child into the kitchen and find something nice for him to have."

"Come with me and let's see what we can find in the kitchen," and she reaches out her hand, and she is so engaging that Johan naturally takes it and allows himself to be led.

Dorothy follows the Minister into a room where a fire spits and cracks and a few faded armchairs are gathered round it. She practices in her mind what she is going to say. She takes a deep breath.

"There's something I need to tell you, something I'm ashamed of, actually—"

"Don't worry about that now. We can discuss all that later in the Kirk. I have news—so much has happened. As I'm sure you know, Mrs. Brown let me know about the boy speaking Norwegian, and then we had a big mix-up because I let the appropriate authorities know, but Tom Carnegie didn't deliver their reply."

"That's what I'm trying to tell you—"

"In fact, I didn't realize there had been one till I bumped into the postmaster."

Dorothy holds up the telegram. "That's because I have it. Look."

"And then—" Finally the Minister notices what Dorothy is trying to show him. "Oh, let me see?" He peers at it and frowns in confusion. "Yes, this is the one the postmaster told me about. Did Tom give it to you, then? He said he lost it. Broke the bicycle too."

"This is all my fault. I was with him when he fell off the bicycle—I was in the way. I promised I'd bring it to you, but—"

"Well, never mind all that now. We've found the family. A young mother and father in Norway, from a little fishing village a bit like Skerry, would you believe? So there's no harm done because the news is, the Norwegian authorities are sending a steam trawler with his parents on. It'll be here in three days. If this is our child, then he can go home. We can finally get him home. Is it him? Is it Johan?"

Dorothy can't speak. She nods her head.

Three days.

Only three days left.

The Shop

Later, they walk up the hill together. Dorothy holds herself straight, as always, Johan reaching out his hand to hold hers. She's used to people staring in curiosity, but today she notices that they nod their heads in her direction and she nods back, feeling a flicker of pride as she glances at the boy in his clothes, so smart and warm.

When she opens the door to the shop, the warmth rushes out with the sound of the usual chatter, and she steps into it, pulling Johan behind her and shutting the door to the jangle of the bell and the silence that follows. The women are there and Mrs. Brown herself. After a moment, the inquisitive eyes are lowered but not Mrs. Brown's. She stares at the boy, and she stares at Dorothy's face. Dorothy wonders if she can see that her eyes are red, her face puffy from crying. Mrs. Brown breaks her gaze and picks up her pencil, uses it to pin her hair, and, lowering herself to his level, she smiles at Johan.

"Hello," she says, and Dorothy thinks an unaccustomed thought—that it is a kind thing Mrs. Brown is doing, and how lovely it would be if someone looked at her like that, like they liked her, and so when Mrs. Brown looks up and says, "Hello, Dorothy," in exactly that way, Dorothy suddenly finds she can't speak at all.

There is a painful silence where she can neither command

her breath nor her mouth till she clears her throat and says, "Good afternoon, Mrs. Brown." She turns so she includes Ailsa and Norah in what she has to say next. "I have news. Good news." She takes a moment to gather herself. "The boy—" She places her hand lightly on his head. "Johan's family have been found. He goes home in three days." She blinks quickly. "I would like to buy some sweeties for him, please, enough to have now and to take home with him. For his family," and she gestures at the shining glass jars on the shelves behind Mrs. Brown, full of sweets she doesn't know the names of, apart from the candy canes—and for sure she won't be buying those, because some things can be made better, and some you just have to leave in the past.

Dorothy and Jane

And there are other things she must face in this moment of truth in her life.

She takes Johan to the Manse and asks if he can spend the rest of the day there. She has earned the right to ask that, after everything. She leaves him in the kitchen, where Martha has made a dough, and Johan is at the table turning it into buns while they share some of his sweets.

The whitewash on the outside of Jane's cottage is dirty, and in places the stone shows through. They have avoided each other over the years. The last time Dorothy had tried to speak to Jane properly had been when she'd received no reply to her letter to William after Moses died. She can hardly remember what was said between them in that time of terrible, frozen grief, but Jane had come to the Kirk alone to mark his death, and Dorothy couldn't blame William for not wanting to come to the funeral of another man's child. She takes a deep breath and knocks on the door, heart banging. There's a footstep inside, and then the door opens. If she was taken aback at the condition of the outside of the cottage, she is even more so by the sight of Jane herself.

Close up, even the lines of her face seem to have a sort of

fine dust in them; her hair straggles over her face, and for a moment the reason for her visit escapes Dorothy.

"Jane, are you quite well?"

Jane's gaze is steady. "What do you want?"

Dorothy remembers herself. "I wondered if we could talk?"

Jane's gaze hardens, her eyebrows lift. "I cannot imagine what we have to talk about."

"It's—it's about William," and to Dorothy's surprise, Jane steps out of the doorway and glances up and down the narrow lane, before stepping back again.

"You better come in."

It feels like going back in time to enter Jane's home. Everything is the same, except it has all faded and dulled with time, as though a thin layer of dust coats everything. There is the table where she first ate with Jane and William, and later saw William eat through the window; there is the cupboard with the clock and the jug. Nothing shines anymore. It is still a house of ghosts. A pang of compassion catches Dorothy off guard.

"Don't come here and pity me, Dorothy."

"I wasn't—I—" Except she was. She softens her voice. "I must speak with William. I need an address. I want to see him and, if not, the very least I must do is write to him."

Jane stares at Dorothy, and then her eyes narrow and her face twists.

"His address? You want his address? It's too late for that, Dorothy."

"You don't understand. There are things I should have told him a long time ago. Things he deserved to know."

"There's nothing you can say to him to make anything right, not now."

Dorothy feels hot. It is not for Jane to decide what should happen. It is Dorothy who is married to him, though Jane's hostility to that fact has long been noted.

She keeps her voice steady, her syllables icy clear. "I am his wife."

Jane looks directly at her. "No. That is where you are wrong. You are not his wife."

Dorothy frowns, puzzled. "What are you talking about? Of course I am."

"You are his widow," and Jane's face folds in on itself, and her hands fly up to cover her grief.

Dorothy pulls out a chair and sinks into it. "I don't understand."

Jane stays standing. Her gaze is stunned, as though it is she who has only just been told this terrible fact. "He—he took his own life."

Dorothy feels her gorge rise and rushes out of the room to the door that leads to the yard, now ruined and derelict, and she is sick, bent over, retching. She straightens herself and drags herself back into the room, forces herself to face whatever it is Jane has to tell her.

Jane is sitting now, her head in her hands. Dorothy sits again too.

"When?" is all she can manage. She frowns at first, but then her expression changes. "That night—the night you took Moses!" She can see from Jane's face that she's right. Dorothy's voice is bewildered. "But that was so long ago." Dorothy wants to ask why, but she can't bring herself to, because she knows already. William crying by Moses's bed comes back to her, with the horror of her own guilt. "I don't understand—why didn't you tell me?"

"I should never have done what I did—try to take the child—but I'd only just had the letter. And tell you he'd killed himself? On top of everything else? No." Jane's voice is flat now, all anger gone. She is like a woman who has been emptied out, utterly defeated. She can't even seem to summon her ancient dislike of Dorothy.

"Where is he?"

Jane's eyes shine with tears. "Somewhere alone and cold, that's where. Not even in the Kirkyard here, with his family. My brother, my poor brother." Her shoulders shake with long-held grief.

"I'm sorry, I'm so sorry. Please forgive me." She puts out her hand, touches Jane's arm, but Jane pushes it away.

"I tried to stop him. I tried to stop the both of you. I knew what would happen."

The idea that she has always been the sort of woman to commit adultery, to give birth to another man's child, is new to Dorothy. She hangs her head in shame.

"You should never have married him. We all knew who you really loved. It was the talk of the village. You married my William because he was kind, because he was safe. It was bad enough for him, for me, knowing what he was, without you marrying him for the wrong reasons. I've never been able to forgive that." She looks into Dorothy's eyes. "Although that's one thing I'll say for you. At least you never said," and her tears come again.

"Wait." Dorothy puts her hand on Jane's arm. "What are you talking about? What do you mean, 'what he was'?"

Jane shakes her head. "He was a good man, my brother. It wasn't his fault."

"What wasn't?"

Jane frowns. "But I thought you knew?" Her voice breaks. "Oh God, don't you see? Do I have to spell it out? He didn't like women."

Dorothy is silent with disbelief, but then those early days

come back to her, the painful nights of trying, how sorry William always was. She feels faint.

"In his own way, he loved you. I wonder, sometimes I wonder if—" And her voice breaks. "Maybe he married you to get away from me."

Dorothy looks around the home. She thinks of Jane and what William must have been to her, the only one left after all the others had gone. She remembers her desperate attempts to keep him with her. *Yes,* she thinks, *maybe he did,* but she doesn't say it because the enormity of the truth is only just dawning.

"And he loved his child." Jane can't stop talking now, as though all the years of silence can finally be expressed. "He wouldn't have ever wanted him to know what he really was. He felt he wasn't enough for you and Moses. He was so ashamed but"—she covers her face again—"he would have stayed if I hadn't said what I did to him."

"What do you mean?"

"That night we argued. You must have heard us—when I came to stay after the child was born. I told him." She shuts her eyes. "I told him he would never be man enough for you, or be a good father." She is sobbing now. "God forgive me, what have I done?"

Dorothy remembers lying in bed, trying to hear what they were saying. After everything, he never knew about Joseph. Jane never knew. It wasn't the knowledge that Moses wasn't his that drove William away. Of all the reasons for the failure of the marriage, William's own suffering, his own attempt to hide his true self, had never occurred to her. Her own shame blinded her to his.

"So he left because he thought he wasn't good enough. For me, for Moses." Dorothy puts her head in her hands and cries softly. William, with his tender kindness, his gentle love. It's hard to remember him now, with the way time distorts memory, but she recalls how sad he became. She can't bear to think of the battle he must have fought with himself, alone in the dark, and lost.

It is some time before she looks at Jane again. "No, Jane. He loved you too. It will have been himself he couldn't forgive, though there was nothing to forgive himself for. If only I had known. I don't know what I could have done, but it would have been better than . . . this. He was a good man, a good father."

Jane looks at her, eyes red, hands shaking. "You can say that? Even now, knowing what I have told you?"

Dorothy reaches out and covers Jane's hand with her own, and this time Jane doesn't push her away. "Of course. I loved him too, in my own way. Very much." A thought occurs to her. "But if it was so long ago, where has the money been coming from?" Dorothy looks at Jane in growing horror. "No, Jane, please say not you."

"Yes. Me. I paid it. All my savings gone. What little our parents left us, gone."

Dorothy feels winded. "But why? Why give it to me?"

"Why?" Jane almost laughs. "Dear God, hadn't William suffered enough? I didn't want anyone to know what had happened. And it wasn't just me who paid. William sent me quite a lot of money once. I didn't understand it at the time. He just said I'd know what to do with it when the time came. Afterward, I realized he must have planned it all, thinking they'd confiscate everything of his because . . . because of the manner of his death. I think he sent it to keep you and the boy safe, so I just kept giving it to you, as though he was still alive, till it ran out."

"Doesn't even the Minister know?"

Jane looks horrified. "Have you heard nothing? I can't tell

325

him this." A look of fear crosses her face. "You must not tell him, Dorothy."

"I have no intention of saying anything. It would help no one, coming from me. But it might help you, Jane." She gets up and goes to the stove. She fills the kettle up.

"What are you doing?"

"We're going to drink tea together." She puts the kettle on the hob, searches for the leaves. "I will find a way to pay you every penny back, with what I have put by and my work at the school, which will begin again when the child goes home. I promise. And if we are to be the only two people to know who he was and what happened, we have to be able to talk about him," and she goes back to the table with the pot, two cups, and a bottle of milk and sits down, and her own tears come.

Much later, when she leaves, she thinks of secrets and lies and how a time comes when we have to lay the burden down. Dorothy takes a deep breath.

There is one more person she must visit.

Dorothy and Joseph

She stands in front of his door for a long time—this man she hardly knows yet who somehow has shaped her whole life. She raises her hand to knock several times and then lets her arm drop again. She wants, after everything, to make peace with him. To finally lay the past to rest. She tightens her shawl against the cold, feels the weight of all the years, of all the things unsaid. She doesn't know where she'll begin.

Joseph opens the door before she summons the courage. Seeing him so near silences her. His eyes, once so warm in their gaze, are unreadable. "Why are you here? Is it the child?"

She can't find the words, here on his doorstep, but knows they must be said, so before waiting to be invited in, she steps over the threshold.

It is neat and tidy, with nothing to soften the masculine lines of the room, its functionality, other than the half-made toys on the table that catch her eye, next to some odds and ends: twine, large needles, a marlinspike. Almost nothing has changed in all these years. No woman, no child, only his loneliness filling the cottage, swelling into corners.

"I've come to tell you that the child is going home. In two days." And then the words she has really come to say. "I'm sorry, Joseph. I'm sorry for everything."

It is as though this is a conversation begun an age ago, the

327

single shining thread of it left unbroken between them across the span of years.

He says nothing for a long time, his body tense, his gaze unflinching. "It is too late for that."

She is determined not to cry. She opens her mouth to speak, but he hasn't finished. What he says has been a long time in the making. "How could you keep it from me? How could you not tell me? My child," and now his composure breaks down, his voice rises. "My child. I was a father for so short a time. Do you know what that has done to me? And to have found—"

Dorothy's voice rises to meet his. "Do you not know what it did to me too? I used to let him go to you; I don't know why. Maybe a part of me wanted you to realize, to guess what I couldn't bring myself to tell you. I'd watch from the window. It was as though he knew, somehow. He was always drawn to you." *Like I was, like a bird knows where to fly in winter.* She stretches out her arm, then drops it again.

"But why didn't you ever say?" He looks utterly bewildered, and Dorothy remembers herself then.

"Why? We committed adultery, Joseph."

"We fell in love."

The word silences her. And suddenly, unexpectedly, she wants to say, *Show me a way back to you*, but instead she says, "But it was too late. You and Agnes—everyone knew. Everyone but me."

"Agnes? Dear God, is that what you thought? There was no one for me but you, not ever. You let yourself be scared away, Dorothy. You couldn't trust yourself. You married a man who could never really know you, a man you didn't love—to what? Spite me? Because he could never have any power over you?"

It is her turn to cover her face. "Don't speak of William. What we did to him was wrong. I betrayed him—"

"You betrayed *me*!" He is shouting now, and she has never heard him shout before. "You betrayed our child."

The words *our child* hang between them in the air. They are the saddest words ever spoken.

Dorothy pulls out a chair, sinks into it. Her elbows are on the table, her head in her hands. "I was ashamed," she says.

"Your shame be damned. What was the point of it, your worthy shame? William left you anyway—I would have looked after you both. God, it was the only thing I ever really wanted."

He is still standing, and shaking his head now in disbelief. They stay in these positions, each caught in their own misery. At last, Joseph takes a deep breath and goes to the door, pulling it open.

"Get out, Dorothy Gray. I've done my weeping over you, though I will never be rid of my grief for the child I knew was mine for all of a minute before he died. And I'll never forgive you for it. Get out."

Dorothy drags herself to her feet. Every step is an effort. He doesn't look at her; he doesn't move. As she steps outside, she turns once and looks him in the eye.

"How did you not know? Tell me—no, don't." She holds up a hand. "Ask yourself, Joseph—how did you not know?"

She sees his mouth open in shock in the seconds before she pulls the door shut behind her.

That night, Joseph can't sleep. He stays by his fire, stokes and feeds it. The blaze could burn his house down. Her question haunts him. How didn't he realize? He has never been a man of the world, but he knows how bodies work. All the times the child had come to him, had it really never crossed his mind? Had his pride really blinded him that much? Has he, in fact, spent so much time blaming her, setting down resentment like the layers that form the bedrock of the village itself, that he has never looked to himself, never gazed at what he might, or might not, have done? He starts to think of Dorothy and of all the years she has managed alone, and as dawn comes, and the fire dies down, he thinks that maybe he is starting to understand.

Agnes and Jeanie

"What's all that for?" Jeanie peers at the bags and heaps of clothing Agnes has piled up on the table. "I hope you're not leaving all that there for me to sort out."

"No, Mam, I'm not." Agnes straightens the blanket over Jeanie's knees, positions the cushion behind her head. "I've something to tell you."

"Is it bad news?"

"No, I don't think so, but it's important news." She pulls up the other chair so she is sitting opposite. "Are you listening, Mam?" She leans forward and places her hands on Jeanie's knees.

Jeanie turns her head from gazing out the window and looks at Agnes. "Has something happened to Matthew?"

"No, Dad died, remember?"

Jeanie looks confused, then her face clears. "I remember now. The funeral. There weren't many came." She is preparing to be indignant about it all over again.

"That's right, but it's not about that. This is something else." Agnes takes a deep breath. "I've left Scott."

It takes a moment for Jeanie's face to show she's understood. Then her eyes widen. "Left him? Left him, Agnes? What have you done that for? What will people say?"

"I don't care what people say. And you know why. I've

been knocked against every wall in that house. I've seen every inch of the floor flat on my face. Well, that's it. I'm done."

Jeanie fixes her with a look. "I never left your father."

"Well, maybe you should have done. But that was your story. This is mine."

"What will you do?"

"I thought I'd move in here with you. Look after you. We'd rub along together fine, I think."

"With me?" Jeanie tries to hide the smile that brightens her face. "What about children? Don't you want kiddies?"

"I think I'm getting too old for them now, Mam." She stands up and adjusts the curtains so her mother can see the Sands and the waves and, farther out, the boats—and also to give herself a moment. "And there's something else. I've been talking to the Minister. He thinks he can get me a job, just a few days a week, at the orphanage in Bonnyburn. You know, instead of the alehouse. And I'm going to help more up at the almshouses too." She takes a deep breath. "Now, I've made soup. I'll go heat it through and bring a bowl on a tray."

At the stove, Agnes finds she's humming. There'll be no tension here, no black moods to fear or avoid or try to get out from under. God forgive her, but she feels as though she's come out of a fog and into sunlight. Back at the window, she settles the tray on Jeanie's knees. Tears run along the wrinkles of Jeanie's cheeks.

"No need to cry. I'm not sad. I'm glad I can be here now."

Suddenly Jeanie grabs her arm, and the tray wobbles dangerously. "That bitch will ruin everything."

Agnes nearly laughs in astonishment. "Who? What are you talking about?"

"That bitch in the Schoolhouse with a broom up her arse.

You've seen him, haven't you? Always up there, making eyes at her."

Agnes sighs. Not this again. "Don't worry about that now—"

"I'm telling you, Agnes, he will slip from your grasp, like a fish off a hook."

"All that's done with. It was a long time ago. He never married her, remember?" And she pictures a gaggle of girls outside the grocer's and how she'd pretended Joseph was more to her than he was. She should never have said it. Dorothy's face had fallen, which was just what Agnes had wanted at the time. But none of it was Dorothy's fault, not really. It was only what Agnes had wished was true—and who could blame her for wishing that?

"She married William, remember? Now come on, eat your soup."

Jeanie screws up her face in concentration. "I remember William. Nice lad." Her shoulders sag. She grips Agnes's arm again. "I only wanted you to have a better man than your father. Your Scott's a bastard."

"Mam—"

It's true about Joseph, though. He was a better man than her father. Than Scott. It was the glimpses of his kindness that drew her to him. When you have a father who beats seven bells out of you and your mam, kindness is what matters. And he had been what he said he was—a big brother to her. But there it is.

"It's over. All of this, it's over." She thinks of the Minister's words to her in the Kirk. "Time to leave it behind, Mam." Jeanie nods obediently. "Now, give me the spoon. Let me help," and she smooths her mother's hair, tucks a stray lock behind her ear, and places a kiss on her forehead.

The Last Morning

Dorothy is up before him on the last morning. Dawn glimmers on the horizon, though the North Star is still shining. She cleans the grates, puts the oatmeal on to warm, and lights the fire, ready for the child.

She laid out his clothes the night before and packed her leather case with some of the jumpers she has knitted, the trousers Mrs. Brown had brought down and the little bags of sweets from the shop. When he comes down the stairs, she is standing at the bottom, and her heart catches, for he doesn't look as much like Moses as she had first thought: his hair is maybe a little darker and his body stockier.

First, they take the splint off the plover's wing. The bird tucks it neatly against its body like the other one. It's mended, and they smile at each other with satisfaction. After breakfast, she shows him his case and what's inside, and all the while he is gabbling. Being given back his name has reminded him of who he is, and he can't stop talking—to Arthur, to the plover, to her.

She picks up the wooden bird that Joseph had made with love for another child in his heart and suggests he put it in the case, but he wants to hold it in his gloved hand. Picking up the case, they go to the door, and she opens it, and they step outside.

The sky in the east is a delicate pink now, and ice crystals sparkle on the path and verges. Together, it is like the world is glowing. Away in the distance, Dorothy thinks she sees a ship, and she points to it and says, "Home," and the boy's face is worth all the pain of him leaving her.

The snow is softer. Johan laughs, picks some up in his gloved hands and says something in his own tongue, but she makes out one of the words clearly, "*Smelte.*" He says it several times, and she nods, "Yes, yes." He's right. At long last, the ice is melting, and Dorothy's eye is drawn to an unexpected splash of white—a single snowdrop, shivering on its stem in the wind coming in off the sea, the first sign of spring.

Halfway to the Steps, Dorothy puts her hand on his arm. "Wait here, I'll be just a minute," and she runs back in and up the stairs. She reappears with Arthur. "Here," she says. She holds Arthur to her heart, and then, with her eyes shut, kisses his head before giving him to the boy. "For you."

They are the first down on the Sands, as Dorothy had hoped, and the plovers are feeding at the water's edge. The wind is strong, but its bite is not so fierce. The plovers are doing their quick, darting dance and digging their beaks into the sand to find lugworms. Dorothy and the child crouch down and lift the cloth from the basket. The boy gently cups the bird in his hands and lifts it onto the ground. Dorothy thought it might be uncertain or disoriented, but it hops toward the others, its kith and kin, and in a moment is a part of them once more, one almost indistinguishable from the other. They stand up and the boy reaches for her hand and looks at her, his face lit up with joy at its recovery.

How much she has learned from the simple, uncomplicated love of a child, about letting go.

The sky is blazing now with pinks and blues as the sun rises; their breath smokes on the air. They go to the Rocks and prize off some of the mussels and throw the meat, to watch the birds waddle and hop. When the seagulls come, they stop and run, laughing, from the blizzard of their wings. The air sparkles and Dorothy breathes in its early morning freshness.

Mr. MacDonald has arrived now and touches his cap. "I'll get the boat ready now, Mrs. Gray," he calls and goes down to the shoreline and starts to take the cover off his rowing boat.

The ship is closer now. Its funnels send clouds of smoke from the engine pumping out into the morning. The Minister is coming down the Steps too, his arm raised in greeting.

There is another movement at the top, on the path, and for a moment everything is suspended: the shining dawn, the waving vetch, the scatter of snowdrops. It is Joseph, in his cap and coat, and Dorothy can only watch as he gets closer. When their eyes catch, he makes one brief incline of his head, which seems to acknowledge more than just her presence.

"Lovely morning," says the Minister, rubbing his gloved hands, and Dorothy turns back to the sea and takes hold of the child's hand in two of her own. He leans into her as they watch the ship stop in its course to wait, and Mr. MacDonald makes ready the boat to row him out.

Mr. MacDonald raises a hand and shouts; Dorothy can't hear what he says, but she knows what it means. She bends to pick up his case, but Joseph is already there to carry it, and together the three of them walk down to the shore. Dorothy turns and is surprised because even the Minister seems to know, on this occasion, to hold back.

And now it is time to say goodbye; she crouches down to hug the child, who hugs her back, but he is distracted, turning his neck, straining to see the ship which will take him home. Dorothy imagines his mother and father, leaning over the rail of the ship, maybe even glimpsing her and Joseph and the child on the Sands. She feels their desperate yearning, their joy knowing their child will soon be with them, that he is alive. Joseph hands the case to Mr. MacDonald, who places it in the boat, and Johan hands him the wooden plover, all the time stretching to keep the ship in his sights. Joseph says his name, and Johan sees his outstretched hand and remembers himself, straightening and holding his hand out too, to show how grown-up he is. But just as Mr. MacDonald is about to push the boat out into the shallow waves of the shoreline that are already licking the bow, Johan runs to Dorothy, all attempts to be grown up gone, and she only just catches him in time as he throws his arms around her waist and buries his head in her dress. She feels the gentle shake of his shoulders. Kneeling down, she holds him away from her and cradles his face in her palms and kisses his head.

"Thank you," she says, and everything blurs as she holds him to her again. When she stands up, the boy goes to Joseph and puts his arms around him too. Joseph lifts him up, and the child rests his head on Joseph's shoulder. He carries him like that to the little fishing boat and lifts him in.

Everything happens very quickly now. The two men push the boat into the water, then Mr. MacDonald jumps in and picks up the oars. The boy faces the waiting ship and then, turning back, grips the sides of the stern, and watches and waves until Dorothy can no longer distinguish the features of his face—he is a child with silver hair glinting in the sun and soon just a dazzle of light on the water, the boat a ripple of the waves.

They stand for a long time, saying nothing. Dorothy realizes that, somehow, their hands have drifted together, fingers interlocked. Quickly she pulls hers away and, not looking at each other, they turn at last from the water's edge.

The Minister is waiting, and just as Joseph seems about to say something, he calls. "Joseph, I wonder if I might ask your help with something? You won't mind us, will you, Dorothy? I expect you'll be keen to get things straight at home," so Dorothy never finds out what it is Joseph was going to say, but instead follows them at a distance, across the Sands and up the Steps and back to her own empty cottage.

When she shuts the door behind her, the house feels cold; the fire is out, nothing is cooking in the kitchen, now there is no one to cook for. Dorothy doesn't go into the other room or upstairs but sits at the table, feeling nothing.

The sun flashes on the copper pan that Martha brought down that very first day the child came. Dorothy jumps up and takes it down from the hook, surprised she still has it. In a moment she is wearing her coat and outside again, anything to avoid being in the house that had briefly been a home.

After she has returned the pan to Martha—"No, I won't come in, thank you, Martha, I only wanted to drop this off"—she walks slowly down Copse Cross Street past the Village Hall, past the Kirk, past the Schoolhouse and her old home in the schoolteacher's cottage, past Brown's Grocers and Confectioners, all the places where the small dramas of her life have played out, and she has a vision of a young woman on a spring day a long time ago, arriving in Skerry, only half listening to the Minister carrying her case, gazing out at the sun-blaze on the sea she was seeing for the first time. And here she is now, almost an old woman, trudging through snow to an empty house. Soon she is back on the path leading to her own cottage. She hesitates before going in, and when she has, she closes the door behind her and leans her back against it.

So that was my life, she thinks.

338

Dorothy

Dorothy sits at the kitchen table in the cold and dark. What is there to do now that would be worth her while? After a long time she sighs and scolds herself. She makes herself light the lamps and the fire, then ties her apron around her waist and takes a deep breath. It is time, as the Minister said, to get things straight. In the other room, the tin soldiers and the top lie on the floor. She makes a hollow of her apron and puts them in it, to take upstairs and tidy away into the chest with the other things, but in Moses's room she catches her foot on the edge of the rug and stumbles. Although she reaches for the bedpost to steady herself, the top falls to the floor and the soldiers scatter, one dropping behind the chest.

She sighs and sinks to her knees. Pulling the trunk away from the wall, she leans over, feeling behind it. She touches cold tin, and reaching farther to retrieve it, her fingertips brush something else. Curious, she pulls the trunk right out. There, half trapped beneath it, are two things. A yellowed pack of cards and a book.

Puzzled, she places them on her lap.

It's strange because she doesn't remember them at all. She leaves the room topsy-turvy and takes them downstairs. She doesn't sit in her chair but pokes the fire into a bit more life, adds a couple of logs, and sits in front of it, on the floor, and looks at the cover of the book.

It is *Nonsense Songs and Stories* by Edward Lear. She has no recollection of owning a copy. The cover plate inside has grease spots on it.

She opens the pages and starts to read.

The Owl and the Pussy-cat went to sea
In a beautiful pea-green boat

—and she has a sudden vision of sitting just where she is now, next to a blazing fire. It's as though she can hear her own voice reading the words.

They took some honey, and plenty of money,
Wrapped up in a five-pound note.

A soft voice takes over, a small boy's voice.

The Owl looked up to the stars above,
And sang to a small guitar

—then both voices together.

O lovely Pussy! O Pussy, my love,
What a beautiful Pussy you are,
You are,
You are!
What a beautiful Pussy you are!

She freezes; as though coming from a long way away, she hears laughter as the voices chime on the rhyming words, then it's gone again like a bird call on the wind. She carries on reading. She is entirely immersed as the forgotten words sound clear in her mind once more. When she gets to the end of the poem—

And hand in hand, on the edge of the sand,
They danced by the light of the moon,
The moon,
The moon,

They danced by the light of the moon.

—she lays the book on her lap and stares into the fire. She is very still. Then she turns and picks up the cards. Even taking the age of them into account, they were well used; she slips them out of the yellowed packet. She brings them to her face and smells them, eyes shut, and like a dream, images flick past her eyes.

Once she saw a zoetrope in Edinburgh, peering through the slots to watch a seagull at rest raise its wings and take flight, and it is like that, only the images are of her and Moses and tell a story of a mother and child—

sitting by the fire
reading stories and poems
making biscuits together

—and now they've started, they come thick and fast as the zoetrope spins faster—

playing Snap and Beggar My Neighbour
his quiet way of looking at her and smiling
of taking her hand, of leaning into her
of reciting the bits of stories he'd learned off by heart, he'd heard them so many times,
of Moses rocking with laughter when he either lost or won at card games

—and she doesn't know it, but her mouth is open and her hand is on her chest.

She goes back to the book, to the greasy thumbprints, the pencil drawings in the margins, and she flicks through the pages till she comes to the final blank page. On it, Moses has drawn a picture. It is of a child and a grown-up. They have big heads and stick bodies. Their arms come out of their heads where their ears should be. One is clearly a young boy in triangle-shaped shorts and the other is a woman with a bun on her head and a long frock on her stick body. Their smiles are wide and their stick arms reach out to the other where they meet in a knot of fingers.

They are holding hands.

They are happy.

Then

Moses and the Children of the Waves

He listens for Mam sleeping. A gentle snore. A sigh. The wind sighs too. Turning the blanket back, he kneels up on the bed, opens the curtain. The night sky flashes white, and for a second he sees them, tumbling, playing.

The children.

His mouth drops open and he laughs, then clamps his hand to his lips, eyes wide.

The sea is black again.

Alone, Moses waits.

When it comes again, he sees them more clearly, silver curls like his, faces full of laughter. They turn and twist in the foam, their arms outstretched.

Come play—

Come play? His heart leaps but then he is suddenly frightened. What will Mamma say?

In the darkness, he listens.

Snore.

Sigh.

He thinks of his red ball and puts his hands to the glass, presses his nose against its chill.

Do you want to play with my red ball?

Yessss, they call in their silver voices. *Come play with us,* say the children of the waves.

Moses isn't sure, but there is something about their voices, so clear, so full of joy, and he is happy they want to play with

343

him, so he scrambles off the bed, squirms on his belly under it, and feels for his red rubber ball.

He goes to run out of the room but then remembers it will be cold. *Socks and boots, Moses, or you'll catch a chill.* He opens the drawer quietly, pulls out his socks and sits on the edge of the bed to put them on.

Come play, Moses, sing the voices.

And he turns, pulls open the curtains. When the flash comes, he holds the ball up, and they laugh, the children of the waves. They are bigger now, riding the stormy crests.

He creeps downstairs, puts on his small leather boots and goes into the kitchen to fetch a stool. Even on tiptoe on the stool, he can only just reach it, and carefully, quietly, he lifts the upper bolt of the door, then climbs down. And because his mam likes things to be tidy, he takes the stool back into the kitchen and tucks it under the table in its place. When he goes back and unlatches the lower bolt, the wind nearly snatches the door from him, but he leans his back against it, mouth open in the force of the gust that takes his breath.

The wind is not sighing, it is howling, but Moses pushes his red ball deep into his pocket, pulls his coat tight around him and heads down into the wind, makes his way along the path to the stone steps.

He knows where to put his feet, knows every pit and rock of the path, even as the freezing rain pours down the back of his neck, even as the wind tries to keep him away from Skerry Sands.

Here, Moses, here—

He feels a little flutter of fear. Should he be doing this? The Steps are slick with rain and moss, and the sea roars, but still he can hear the voices so full of fun and mischief, the moon silvering the sands as it glances between thundering clouds, silvering the waves with their frothy bubbles, where the sea children dance and play.

I'm coming, he says and they laugh with delight.

They are over by the Rocks to the left of the beach—*Here, here*—and he toils against the wind that still wants to save him. He is very cold now. His face hurts and he can't smile; he can't feel his feet, even though he is wearing his socks and boots. He grips the rocks with hands that are almost numb, and the sleet is blinding him, but at last he is near the edge where they are. Their song has changed.

Come away, they sing.

Moses's eyes are slits, and he sees the children in the wild water at their wild fun and realizes then that he shouldn't be out here at night in a storm like this. He turns his head and can just see the watery light in Mam's window up on the cliff, a flickering golden star.

I need my mam, he says.

Come away—

He plunges his hand in his pocket, pulls out the ball.

You can have my ball, he says and reaches his arm back to throw it; he's a good thrower, but as he moves his arm forward, his foot slips.

And he tries to pull it back, but his weight is already shifting and the children are reaching for him. They are throwing the ball between them, hands mingling, so he tries to wedge his foot in the cleft of the rock, because he remembers the sea is a dangerous thing, and if he goes with them he isn't ever coming back, and he doesn't want his mam to cry, he doesn't want to break her heart, but the children already have him and they are tossing him and his ball on the waves.

Moses, Moses—

And Moses can't feel anything now. He takes a great deep

345

breath and thinks of his mam—he thinks of porridge, and the smell of bread, and the hiss of the kettle on the hob, he thinks of her saying grace in the halo of light that comes in through the window overlooking the sea, and he starts to feel safe and warm . . .

And as the thunder cracks, and the lightning flashes above, the children of the waves take him and carry him away.

Now

The Shop

The next day, she gets up before dawn. She feels awake in a way she hasn't for a very long time. She takes a lamp into Moses's room and tidies up. It is as though, now her heart is open, everything in the room has a different and greater meaning—the tin soldiers, the top and whip, the quilt she made when she was carrying him. She puts everything in its place and wonders why all she had been able to remember were the times she wasn't good enough. *Why is it*, she asks herself, *that we only ever remember the things we did wrong?*

She still isn't tired when the sky takes on light, bringing with it the snowmelt and a few more snowdrops on the edge of the cliff. She cleans the grates and lights the fires and stays in her nightgown. All day she tidies and cooks. Properly, even though it is just for herself. She makes dough and a fisherman's pie and prepares the ingredients for a broth. Much later, she washes and dresses in a warm frock and shawl to go into the village. There is something she must do at the shop. She almost smiles when she thinks how she'd slept in the storeroom after drinking too much whisky. How ashamed her mother would have been, how disapproving, to know that she, Dorothy Gray née Aitken, had been sleeping drunk in her clothes at the back of a grocer's shop.

Yet Dorothy finds that somehow she herself isn't ashamed at all.

Copse Cross Street isn't busy now the shops are closing

and night is falling. It is a delicate late-winter sunset of soft grays and pinks. The bell jangles when Dorothy opens the door. Mrs. Brown is wrapping the last of Norah's parcels in brown paper, totting up the cost in her notepad. She nods at Dorothy without stopping in her task. Dorothy goes straight to the counter, catching the end of their conversation.

"You know how it is. You spend most of your life hating them, wishing they weren't your husband, then something like this happens . . . " Norah clears her throat before continuing. "And you realize that for better or worse, they're yours, that maybe you don't hate them as much as you thought."

Mrs. Brown pins her loose hair with her pencil behind her ear. "That'll be one shilling and sixpence, please," and Norah fumbles in her purse, drops a couple of coins to the floor.

"Let me," says Dorothy, and bends down to pick them up. She hands them to Norah and notices the worry lines on her brow and around her mouth. "Your husband, how is he? I heard he was unwell?"

A surprised silence follows this.

"Why, thank you, Dorothy. He's not himself, it's true, but on the mend, now, thank you for asking." Norah gives Mrs. Brown a sidelong look, and Mrs. Brown raises her eyebrows just a little in reply.

The bell jangles again, and now it is just the two of them.

"The lad has gone, then?"

Dorothy takes a deep breath. "Yes," she says. "That is what I came to tell you." Her voice is a little wooden at first but grows stronger. "He was a beautiful boy."

Mrs. Brown looks her in the eye in a way she never has before. "Yes, he was so, Dorothy. A most beautiful boy." Dorothy is determined not to cry and almost manages it, as she tightens her shawl about her shoulders. "Thank you, Mrs. Brown, and a good evening to you."

"One more thing," Mrs. Brown says as Dorothy turns to leave. "I hope you'll be coming again soon to the knitting evenings. A few of the women are keen to host it, on a sort of rota, you know. Jane and Agnes too, I heard."

There is a moment's pause in which Dorothy's heart beats faster. "Yes, I would like that, thank you. And to do my bit, too, of course," and they nod and smile and the little bell jangles as Dorothy leaves the shop and closes the door.

She is about to head for home, but something makes her turn and look back through the window. Mrs. Brown is starting to tidy everything away, wiping clean her scales and the counter, reaching for the broom to sweep the shop. Mrs. Brown, who knows everything about everyone, preparing their orders barely before the door has shut behind them, so used is she to everyone's habits. *It's a funny thing*, thinks Dorothy, *that I know nothing about her at all*, and she wonders, as she turns to face the sunset, deepening into shades of red and fiery orange, what her story is.

One day, she thinks, *when the time is right, I'll ask her.*

Closing Time

It's almost time to shut the shop, and Mrs. Brown goes to the window to check no new customer is coming. She looks up the road, toward the Kirk and the Schoolhouse silhouetted against the blazing sky, and down the road where Dorothy is walking home through the melting snow with her basket. Another figure catches her eye. Joseph is walking up the hill on the other side of the street. Mrs. Brown leans on her broom and watches. Dorothy stops. Mrs. Brown's face almost touches the window. She sees Dorothy raise her hand to Joseph, and now Joseph stops too. Mrs. Brown holds her breath and waits. Slowly, Joseph raises his hand back in greeting. They stand and look at each other for just a little longer than you might expect, and then they turn away, Joseph continuing up Copse Cross Street and Dorothy down toward home.

And Mrs. Brown remembers a night, nearly a lifetime ago, when she saw a woman in her nightgown at the top of the Steps and a fisherman down on the Sands in the middle of the night. She had stayed hidden in the shadows, brought there by her own thoughts and griefs, but had said to herself at the time that no good would come of it, and so it hadn't, but she has to admit to herself that even she, Mrs. Brown, isn't always right.

After all, she thinks, *God works in mysterious ways.*

And she turns the closed sign to the window.

Epilogue

When she gets home, Dorothy lights a lamp, puts the kettle on the hob, and sits down at her table. The evening has settled around the house. Through the window, the sky has faded over the sea in gentle, darkening blues, and the first stars are appearing. Amongst them, the North Star is the brightest. On the stove top, the kettle is warming and the bread she made earlier is in the oven.

When she hears bootsteps on the lane, she wonders who is on their way down to the Sands at this time. The steps stop, and the strangest feeling comes over her; she feels it on the skin of her arms, at the back of her neck, in the expectation of her held breath. A few moments later, they start up again, this time crunching the snow to her very own door, and she finds herself rising from the chair and waiting for the knock that comes at last, slow and steady as it ever was.

Acknowledgments

It would seem that raising a child is not the only thing that it takes a whole village to do, and I have many people to thank for bringing *The Fisherman's Gift* into the world. First and foremost, I want to thank my exceptional agent, Hellie Ogden. If you hadn't made the decision to represent me on a partial manuscript, I'm not sure I would have finished this book at all. Your belief in this story and in me as a writer has been life-changing. You have quite simply made a dream come true. I would also like to thank the lovely Ma'suma Amiri for her support and encouragement, as well as the marvelous Dorian Karchmar and Sophia Bark. Also, thank you to James Munro and Cody Siler for managing international rights and indeed all at William Morris Endeavour both here and in New York.

I feel so privileged to be working with the brilliant editors Liz Foley at Harvill Secker and Carina Guiterman at Simon & Schuster. It is a thrill and an honor to learn so much from your illuminating editorial advice and direction. I am so grateful for the passion you both have for Dorothy and her story.

I would also like to thank the superb Harvill Secker team: Christopher Sturtivant, Leah Boulton, Shân Morley Jones, Jane Howard, Kris Potter, Konrad Kirkham, Lucy Upton,

Sophie Painter and Aidan O'Neill. Equally, at Simon & Schuster, I would like to thank the fantastic Sophia Benz, Morgan Hart, Shannon Hennessey, and Emily Farebrother.

Thank you to Emma Haynes, Sarah Sarre, and everyone at the Blue Pencil Agency for your early belief, and likewise to Monica Chakraverty at Cornerstones.

Without a doubt, I would not have persevered with writing and its ups and downs, challenges and joys, without the friendship and solidarity of the very best writing group in the world, the Virtual Writing Group. Your support, friendship, and ridiculous gifs have kept me going through good times and bad.

A few honorable mentions: Fíona Scarlett and Jenny Ireland—thank you so much for believing in, championing, and reading this story from the opening words to the final full stop. When I didn't believe, you did, despite some decidedly irreverent comments along the way. Your support has been unflagging. Wiz Wharton—your early insight and conviction that this was The One enabled me to believe too, and to persevere. I will always be grateful to you for this—thank you. Neema Shah, thank you for your gentle support throughout; Dan Aubrey and Danielle Devlin, thank you for your not-so-gentle support, dragging me through multiple edits in exhausted late-night writing sprints; Dr. Stephanie Carty, I love our magical character-conjuring sessions and look forward to many more; Anita Frank, thank you for your (in)famous forensic and brutally honest readings. And last, but by no means least, thank you to my sister Rebecca Netley, with whom I share so much, in both writing and life. I feel privileged to share this journey with you all.

Behind the scenes for most disabled and chronically ill people, there is a team of support. So thank you to my carers—Tash, Kate, Pauline, Carol, Hannah, and Dee—for making life comfortable and safe and so much more fun. Thank you also to my exceptional GP, Dr. Simon Lennane.

As I finally leave teaching, I want to thank the wonderful English Department at John Kyrle High School for the long years of solidarity and friendship, and Darcy, Julian, and Kris, who have made the difficult decision to leave, and the daunting process involved, so painless for me as I enter a new way of living and working.

Thank you to all those friends who have haunted me with the question every writer dreads—*How is the book coming along?*—and then pretended to be interested in the answer: Hazel, Lou and Sal, Brigid and Cara, Nicky, Martin, Julie, Kim, Gail and Tracy.

Thank you also to Mark Kirwin, who once told me that all writing is practicing and thus unleashed a lifetime of stuck words. I am grateful for these words of wisdom and so many more.

And then to my family: thank you, my beloved sisters, Rebecca and Louise, and my precious cousins, Katie and Sarah. Also thank you, Granny Whish—you are no longer here but are always with me. I know how excited and proud you'd be. Thank you to my beautiful children, Oliver, Calum, and Emily—you give my life meaning and purpose and so much joy. Thank you to my wonderful step-children, Kyro and Isaac—you have enriched my life more than you know.

And finally, thank you to Stewart, who makes everything possible. I am so grateful to have you as my traveling companion. I love you all with all my heart.

About the Author

Julia R. Kelly is a mother, writer, and teacher. She has been longlisted for the *Mslexia* Novel Prize, the Exeter Novel Prize, Penguin WriteNow, and the Bath Novel Award. In 2021, she won the Blue Pencil Agency First Novel Award. Having grown up in a house without television, Julia read anything she could lay her hands on from an early age, and as an English teacher, has tried to pass on her love of stories to the next generation of readers and writers. Since becoming a wheelchair user, Julia appreciates even more the journeys the written word can take us on. She lives in Herefordshire with her partner and dog, and between them they have raised five wonderful children. *The Fisherman's Gift* is her debut novel.